HER COWBOY BILLIONAIRE BIRTHDAY WISH

CHRISTMAS IN CORAL CANYON, A HAMMOND BROTHERS NOVEL, BOOK 1

LIZ ISAACSON

ISBN-13: 978-1-63876-166-2

CHAPTER 1

The life and energy of Whiskey Mountain Lodge pulsed through Annie Pruitt as she climbed the steps from the basement to the kitchen. The door at the top of the steps had been slid closed, but as the family gathered in the kitchen burst into laughter, no barrier could contain the sound.

Annie smiled, because she loved the Whittaker family, and all those that had come to be included in that family. Herself and her girls included.

She paused on the top stair, her fingers scrambling for the divot to latch onto so she could slide open the door. It moved easily, because everything at Whiskey Mountain Lodge now ran like a well-oiled machine. Not that it hadn't before, but Graham and Beau had worked together over the course of eight months to bring the lodge out of retirement and back into a full luxury vacation destination in the beautiful Teton Mountains.

They'd hired four more people to work at the lodge, increased Annie's hours to full-time, and made every room available for nightly stays, even the master suite. Beau and Lily had moved down the canyon to the town of Coral Canyon, and the brothers had built a cabin on the hill in the backyard for the manager who now ran this place.

Annie liked Patsy Foxhill a lot, and she ran a very tight ship for someone so petite and a decade younger than Annie.

"There she is," Graham practically yelled as Annie entered the kitchen. "Celia was just suggesting we come down and get you." He grinned at her, his eyes bright and glinting.

Annie shook her head. "You said dinner was at six. It's quarter till." She glanced around at everyone gathered at the table. Tonight was the first night they'd all gathered to the lodge for their annual family Christmas celebration.

Over the course of the next six days, they'd transform the lodge into Holiday Central, with a tree-cutting expedition planned for the day after tomorrow.

For starting tonight and continuing through at least the next twenty-four hours, Mother Nature would be dumping snow. At least according to the forecast and the National Weather Service. In fact, the family wasn't supposed to gather to the lodge until tomorrow night, but they'd come early to avoid the weather.

All of the guests had left that morning, and Annie was supposed to have two days to clean the lodge from top to bottom before the Whittakers and Everetts arrived. She'd had four hours.

As Eli and Meg arrived, then Andrew and Becca, then Beau and Lily, they'd simply put their bags in the rooms where they'd be staying, and Annie had stripped beds and scrubbed tubs around the luggage.

Lily's sisters and parents had become an integral part of the Christmas traditions at the lodge too, and Vi and Todd and Rose and Liam had arrived that day as well. Fran and Jack Everett had come after Annie had finished the upstairs rooms, as had Amanda and Finn, her new husband, and Celia and Zach.

Annie's thoughts lingered on Amanda and Celia the most these days. She'd watched them find their second chance at happily-ever-after, and she wanted it for herself. She'd been out with a couple of men in the past couple of years as the lodge went through the changes, but neither of them had panned out.

She found herself stuck in the middle of her life, taking each day one at a time the way she'd learned to do after her husband's death, alone. She didn't want to be alone forever, and she certainly didn't want to be a burden to anyone.

"Where's Bree?" she asked. "Everyone's not even here yet."

"Happy birthday," Amanda said, appearing in front of her and hugging her.

Annie giggled as she hugged the woman a couple of decades older than her. "Thank you."

"I know it was a couple of weeks ago," she continued. "But Finn and I haven't been down to the lodge in that long." She extended an envelope toward Annie, who looked at it with love and appreciation for Amanda and Finn streaming through her.

"You didn't have to get me anything." She glanced to the table, where several others still loitered. A couple of kids ran into the kitchen, excitedly asking Celia for just a pinch of the chocolate bread she'd made that day. She shooed them out, and Annie still hadn't taken the envelope from Amanda.

"We got you something too," Graham said, setting a bright red package on the counter that separated the large kitchen from the dining area, where most people sat to visit. More gifts appeared, and Annie pressed her hand against her heart. Tears threatened to spill down her face, but she held them back.

Maybe she was simply closer to fifty than forty now, and her emotions couldn't be controlled as easily, because one tear managed to slip out of the corner of her eye. She swiped at it, and said, "You guys. You didn't have to."

"But we wanted to," Eli said, standing up as he picked up the slim, blue package someone with less clumsy hands than his cowboy fingers had wrapped. He nearly shoved the gift at her, and Annie finally took it and the envelope.

"Well, I appreciate it," she said.

"You don't turn forty-six every day," Amanda said. "It's a good year. One of my best." She smiled, and it sat beautifully on her face. Annie would've never guessed she had turned seventy years old that year, and she could only hope she looked as good as Amanda in twenty-four more years.

The thought made her stomach clench. Twenty-four more years. Would she have to spend all of those days with a sponge in her hand, her two cats the only living things waiting for her at home?

She reminded herself that both Emily and Eden still lived at home, though they were adults, as she looked down at the envelope. Before she could open it or the gift, a child screamed from somewhere in the house, and someone came through the back door, yelling the words, "The storm is starting already."

Bree poked her head around the corner as she removed her hat, which bore enough snow to shake to the floor and gather into a fist-sized ball. Annie frowned at it, because she knew she'd be the one to clean it up.

"It's coming down out there," she said. "We barely made it up the path."

"Good thing we're all staying here tonight," Celia said, and Bree ducked back around the corner to hang her winter gear in the mudroom off the back entrance. The chatter picked up again; Rose left to discover the source of the screaming, assuming it to be one of her triplets. She and Liam had two boys and a girl that had just entered their terrible two's, and they all possessed a healthy set of lungs.

Bree and Elise entered the fray of people, and Annie felt less alone. They didn't have boyfriends or husbands either, and she suddenly wasn't the only one.

"Everything's ready," Sophia said, putting a large pot on the counter. She'd been hired as the full-time cook at the lodge, which offered breakfast and dinner to its guests. Celia worked weekends now, when they only offered dinner on Saturdays and lunch on Sundays, choosing to spend the rest of her time in Dog Valley, on Zach's farm with him.

Annie wondered what that life would be like. Working a few

hours a day, and living in a beautiful, modern home with the man she loved. Her chest tightened again, and she gathered the gifts from everyone, keeping her smile cemented in place.

Annie had learned long ago to smile, to find the silver lining in any situation, to make the best of what she'd been given.

But would it be so hard to give me someone to grow old with? she wondered, directing her question up. Up through the ceiling. Up through the storm. Up, up, up and hopefully, all the way to the Lord's ears.

"Thank you," she said to everyone, nodding and smiling. "Thank you so much." She hurried into the family room and put the gifts in a pile on the armchair there, reaching for the two teens sitting on the couch. "Come on, guys. It's time for dinner."

Bailey and Stockton were the oldest of the Whittaker children, with mostly kids under the age of five to play with. So they tended to stick together, talking about their friends or looking at things on their phones.

They got up and Bailey wrapped her arms around Annie. "Oh," she said, patting the girl's head. "What's that for?"

"Happy birthday," she said, smiling up at her. Bailey had always been a sober child, and she'd matured into a fourteen-year-old with the same calm demeanor as her mother.

"Thank you," she said.

"Stockton and I helped Sophia and Celia with the cake," she said. "I think you're going to like it."

"I'm sure I will," Annie said, further relaxing. "In fact, do you think we could have cake first?'

Stockton said, "I'm going to go ask Celia," and ran ahead of them.

"I don't think we can have cake first," Bailey said.

"Why not?" Annie asked. "I hate waiting until after dinner to eat dessert. I'm always too full then."

"Good point," Bailey said, and Annie giggled again.

They stepped through the doorway, a wall in front of them

forcing them left or right. To the left and through that doorway was the main kitchen. To the right was the dining area, and Annie stepped that way, very aware that for the number of people in the house, it was entirely too quiet.

And she knew from experience that silence meant nothing good. In fact, when children were quiet, that spelled trouble. Emily and Eden had drawn all over one of Annie's walls during one of their silent bouts.

So something was definitely happening in the dining room. Annie rounded the corner behind Bailey, trying to see into the kitchen and left and right and back to everything in the dining room at the same time.

A loud blast of singing hit her, and she couldn't help grinning as everyone who'd gathered for their second annual family Christmas party started wishing her a happy birthday. Those darn tears came again, and Annie didn't even try to swipe them away this time.

Celia lit the candles on a massive chocolate cake that had been set on the edge of the table, and Annie led them with both hands as the song wrapped up.

She stepped forward to blow out the candles, and someone called, "Make a wish!"

Annie closed her eyes, wondering what a forty-six-year-old widow should wish for.

I wish…I wish…I wish for a cowboy billionaire of my own to fall madly in love with.

She giggled at the ridiculous thought, opened her eyes, and blew out the candles. Thankfully, Celia had not put on forty-six, but just a four and a six, and she only had to get out two flames.

"Thank you, everyone," she said when the last bits of applause stopped.

Celia gestured to the kitchen, where Sophia came out with a stack of plates and Stockton followed with forks. "And because I've known Annie since she moved to town, I know she likes her sweets first. So we'll be having cake first."

Annie grinned at Stockton, who wore a look on his face like Christmas had come six days early. "Did you ask?"

"She already had the cake out," the boy said. "Honest."

"Hello?"

Annie turned toward the unfamiliar male voice as others started to look past her and the cake.

A tall man stood there, wearing cowboy boots, jeans, the biggest, puffiest coat Annie ever did see, and a deliciously white cowboy hat without a speck of snow on it.

"I knocked," he said. "But you must not have heard me." He put a smile on his face, and Annie darn near swooned on the spot. He had a handsome smile, perfectly framed by a dark beard with more salt than pepper. She sure did like that silver hair on a man, and her heart shot out several extra beats.

"I can see I'm interrupting," he said. "I was just...hoping you'd have an open room tonight. See, my brother stayed here once with his son, and he said it was a great place, and—"

"I'm sure we have a room," Lily said, one of the closest ones to Celia and this new man crashing the party. "And you can stay for cake and dinner too."

"I can pay," he said.

"Oh, the lodge is booked," Patsy said, glancing at Lily and then Graham, who'd also come forward. "But I think we can manage to have you for one night." She gave him a tight smile, but Annie honestly couldn't look away from him. She needed to know his name, and where he was from, and how long he was going to be in town.

One night rang in her ears, and she started desperately praying that God would send more snow. So much snow that none of them would even be able to leave the lodge for days.

"Okay," the man said, peeling off that huge coat. "I'm much obliged." He stuck out his hand for Patsy to shake. "You seem like you're in charge. I'm Colton Hammond."

Colton Hammond. It was the type of name Annie could float away on as she tried to drift to sleep, and she caught herself sighing before she jolted to attention and turned back to the cake. Chocolate. Yes, all she needed was chocolate to get herself back into the right mindset.

A lot of chocolate.

CHAPTER 2

Colton Hammond faced the group of people, picking out the ones who belonged together. There were couples here, and single women. A few women with very similar hair. Generations of people, with grandmothers, mothers, and children. Cowboys who looked a whole lot alike. Colton knew all about families like that, as he had four brothers, which included a set of twins.

He didn't much care who was with who and how they all connected. He needed a place to stay, and Gray had texted him the name of this lodge as Colton put the town of Ivory Peaks, and then the entire state of Colorado, in his rear-view mirror.

And it would be just fine with him if he never went back.

A couple of people turned and looked at him, and he moved further into the expansive area at the back of this building. No wonder they hadn't heard him knock. The noise level here was enough to make Colton think that perhaps the back seat of his truck would make a nice bed after all.

Only the temperatures and the threat of being buried under several feet of snow kept him standing in that kitchen. He reached up and adjusted his white cowboy hat, at least feeling like he belonged here, with all these other men wearing practically the same thing as him.

"Cake," a woman said, handing him a plate with a thick slab of chocolate cake on it.

"Thank you, ma'am," he said, but she'd already moved on. The blonde who'd spoken earlier edged over, and Colton got the hint that he could take a spot at the table next to her. Another woman sat right in front of the cake, and he glanced at her.

"Is it your birthday?" he asked.

"Kind of," she said.

Colton reached for a fork, taking one from the pile several inches in front of him. "How do you *kind of* have a birthday?"

She smiled, and Colton sure liked the way her face lit up. She had a spattering of freckles across her nose and cheeks that spoke to Colton. But he would not be getting trapped by a pretty face with freckles.

Been there, done that.

"My birthday was a couple of weeks ago," she said. "But we decided to celebrate it at the lodge this year." She gave him that smile again, and he noticed her straight, white teeth this time, framed by those pretty pink lips.

His face heated and he focused on his cake. His heartbeat screamed through his bloodstream, and Colton tried to mentally reassure himself that he didn't need to run. This woman wasn't a threat to him. She wasn't.

"What's your name?" he asked.

"Annie," she said.

"Like, the sun will come out…tomorrow?"

She blinked at him, and Colton realized how he'd sounded. "I mean, it's a nice name."

"Thanks." She took another bite of cake, and Colton took his first. His taste buds told him to take another bite. Then another.

"This is the best chocolate cake I've ever had," he said. And he'd eaten at dozens of high-end restaurants in his life.

"Celia's doing," Annie said, pointing with her fork. "She's

the one who gave you the cake. She's been the chef up here for years."

Colton found her talking to a cowboy in the kitchen and enjoying her own cake.

"Sophia is a chef here too," Annie continued. "She works full time during the week. Celia's just here on the weekends."

"And you're all up here right now," he said.

"Yes." Annie tucked her shoulder-length hair behind her ear, shooting a glance at him before looking away again. "The Whittakers own the lodge, right?" She nodded to the man who'd emerged from the back of the crowd. "Graham bought it several years ago. He hired me to clean, Celia to cook, and Bree to do décor and grounds. Each of the four brothers lived in the lodge at some point, but they've all got other houses now. They turned the lodge back into a mountain resort about eighteen months ago."

Colton liked listening to her voice, though he didn't much care about the family history lesson. He nodded though, wondering if he could simply serve himself another piece of cake once he'd finished this one.

"Anyway," Annie said. "They hired a bunch more people, rent out all thirteen rooms—except from December twentieth to January fifth. Or so. That's when they all gather here for their holiday family traditions and to spend time together."

"It's only the nineteenth," Colton said.

"Yeah, we came up a day early, because of the storm." She flashed him another smile, and Colton wondered what it would be like to be able to do that. He hadn't had a reason to smile at will for several weeks now, and it felt like several years instead of just weeks.

"So," a man said, pulling out the chair the blonde woman had vacated at some point. "What brings you to Coral Canyon?"

Colton looked at the guy, his defenses already in place. He hadn't anticipated having to talk to anyone for longer than a few minutes. Just his luck that he'd walk in during a family party.

"Just getting out of town for the holidays," he said coolly. He hadn't fooled the other cowboy for a moment, though.

"Well, I'm Graham Whittaker, and you're welcome to stay as long as you like." He glanced up as someone said his name. "I'll have Patsy find you a room."

"Thanks," Colton said, finishing his last piece of cake.

Graham got up and clapped Colton on the shoulder, which sent a physical vibration through his arm as well as a buzz of annoyance. He was forty-two-years-old, and he didn't need to be talked down to like a thirty-year-old.

He'd started businesses and sold them. He'd gotten an MBA while working at the family company as the executive marketing director. He had a master's degree in biology and biological research from Yale University, and he'd worked on highly developmental scientific projects.

He hated to admit it, but Colton had drunk in the whole lodge in a single look, and he knew exactly what he'd do to get more people staying here. Not to say that the lodge didn't already have every night booked for the next year, but if he worked for them, they would.

"You might be here more than one night," Annie said on his left, and Colton was starting to get whiplash from looking left and right, right and left.

"Yeah, the snow is supposed to be bad," he said. If the weather had been clear, Colton would still be in the truck, aiming himself for the Canadian border. Frustration built in his chest, and he pushed against it. Pushed hard.

"Time to eat." Celia got up on a chair and held up both arms. Everyone settled down, and Colton basked in the relative silence. This place had great energy though, and Colton did like that. At least compared to the farmhouse on the eastern edge of Ivory Peaks, where Colton had escaped after the failed attempt to get married, which had only offered sadness and the ability to completely overwhelm a man in a single moment.

His father had just turned seventy-eight, and he couldn't

keep up with the chores around the farm. His mother hadn't done anything on a farm, ever, and most of her time was spent taking care of Dad's mother, keeping them all fed and wearing clean clothes.

Colton had thought he might be able to lie low there for a month or two. Through the New Year. Then he could return to the high-rise building in downtown Denver where HMC operated their global office.

Then the article detailing his humiliation had been leaked to the media, complete with cellphone photos. Colton wasn't new to dealing with the fallout of bad press. Heck, he'd done it for a living for HMC—Hammond Manufacturing Corporation—for a decade.

But the fact that Priscilla, the woman he'd invested five years of his life into, had left him to stand at the altar by himself had destroyed his confidence. He didn't know how to put together a media package to dispute the photos. He couldn't write a statement to read to the microphones thrust in his face.

Well, he did know how to dispute the photos, and how to write and deliver the official HMC statement.

He didn't *want* to. Not anymore.

So he'd taken a security team to his condo on the north side of the city and snuck into his own house to quickly pack a couple of bags. He'd put them in the back seat of his truck, gassed up while the security guards watched, and tipped his cowboy hat to them.

He'd been driving all day by the time the National Weather Service alert had come on the radio station he'd put on but hadn't really been listening to. And he'd immediately called Gray to help him find somewhere to stay.

"Whiskey Mountain Lodge," his brother had said without a single beat of hesitation.

And now Colton sat at the table while a petite woman controlled a room full of adults and children.

"We have barbecue pork sandwiches," she said, and Colton's

stomach growled. "Plenty of chips and dips. Vegetable tray. Tomato basil soup. Chicken noodle soup. Cheese biscuits. There's plenty of everything, so come eat."

Another man stood up before Celia could get off the chair. He said nothing, but he swiped his cowboy hat off his head and folded his arms. To Colton's great surprise, everyone else in the room did the same, and Colton hurried to remove his hat before anyone saw his shock.

This man—clearly one of Graham's brothers—said, "Dear Lord, we thank Thee for this bounty in front of us today. We're grateful for our daddy, who worked and built a bright future for us. We're thankful for all who work here at the lodge and provide such an amazing family experience for us. Bless them in their individual lives, and help us to remember who we are, where we came from, and who we represent. Oh, and we're grateful for Colton and that he arrived safely. Amen."

"Amen," everyone chorused, and a wave of noise rolled through the room as everyone stood up, gathered their children to them, and started filling plates with food.

Colton got up and got out of the way, his heart touched by the prayer. *We're grateful for Colton.*

He didn't even know that man's name. He now held a little boy in his arms that looked to be two or three. He asked the child if he wanted every item, finally putting him in a highchair in the corner and returning to the line.

"Come get something to eat," a woman said, and Colton turned toward Patsy.

He gave her a smile, but he secretly wanted to escape. His stomach growled at him to stay put, so he did. "Thank you."

"I'm going to put you in room three," she said, extending a white card toward him. "Annie will go down with you. She's right next door in room four." Patsy gave him a professional smile and joined the fray of bodies in the kitchen.

He made it through the line with a smile on his face, talking to anyone who spoke to him. He'd seen a couple of people leave the kitchen, and he followed them, as there was no room at the table.

He found them in the living room, sitting on the couch with their food balanced on TV trays in front of them. "Room for one more?"

A dark-haired woman looked at him and smiled. "Sure," she said. "There are trays beside the fireplace."

Colton grabbed one with his free hand as he passed the fireplace and set up his dinner in front of the loveseat, as three women had taken the spots on the couch.

"I'm Bree," the dark-haired woman said. "I do all the room decorating, as well as events here at the lodge."

He nodded at her, and she turned to the woman next to her. "This is Elise. She does all the grounds keeping."

"So you're part of the family?" he asked.

"No," Elise said, her long, blonde hair swinging as she shook her head.

"Yes," Bree said, correcting her. She shot her a look and then faced Colton. "Yes, we're part of the family. I've worked here for eight years, and yes, when you work for the Whittakers, you become a Whittaker."

Colton switched his gaze to Elise, who clearly hadn't worked for the Whittakers long enough. He could tell she didn't feel like a Whittaker.

He moved his gaze to the last woman on the couch, and she said, "I'm Rose. I'm out here, because I have three two-year-olds, and I need fifteen minutes to eat a full meal." She smiled and started slowly buttering her roll.

"Wow," Colton said, unsure of what else to say. "Three two-year-olds?"

"That's right," she said. "I'm sick of eating my meals one bite at a time over the course of an hour while I chase them."

Colton wondered who was chasing them if Rose sat out here slathering a rich, orange jam on her roll now. But he didn't ask.

Another woman came into the living room, and Annie paused as she assessed the situation.

"There's room by Colton," Bree said, and Annie looked like she might kill the woman later. But when Annie looked at him, she had that gorgeous smile on her face. She got her tray too, and she perched on the love seat as far from him as possible.

Colton knew he didn't smell; he'd showered that morning. She hadn't had a problem talking to him in the kitchen, and his mind went round and round about what he'd done to cause a change in her.

He finished eating while the four women chatted with each other about familiar things to them that made no sense to him. When he pushed his tray back so he could stand up, Annie asked, "Would you like me to take you down to your room right now?"

"I'm sure I can find it," he said. How hard could it be?

"I want to check it anyway," she said. "Since we came up early, I cleaned the rooms in the order they were getting used. It might not be ready for you." She left the remains of her food on her tray and joined him. "This way."

She led him back toward the kitchen, to the right down the hall past it to a pocket door that slid into the wall. She went first, saying, "Slide that closed behind you, would you?" as she started down a flight of steps.

Colton did as she asked, the noise level almost disappearing behind the closed door. By the time he reached the bottom of the steps and turned to go down a few more, he couldn't hear the zoo in the kitchen.

"This is a big common area," Annie said, indicating the two couches in the room. "There's a theater room there. Someone will put up a schedule for the holidays, and there's usually food down here too."

He noticed the kitchen built into two walls of the room, directly across from the theater room. Annie went past the theater room down a wide hall. "These are rooms one, two, three, and four." She held out her hand. "Do you have your key?"

He handed it to her, and she went to the room in the back left corner and flashed the card in front of the sensor to release the lock. With the green light on, she opened the door and pushed her way inside.

"Thanks." She handed the key back to him, and he stood in the doorway instead of squeezing in behind her. The scent of her floral perfume tickled his nose, and his male side once again told him how attractive Annie was.

He shut down the feelings fast, because he was not interested in another relationship. Not now, and not ever.

The sigh Annie let out wasn't lost on Colton, and he took a step into the room then, easily able to peer over her shoulder. "What's wrong?" He saw the unmade bed, as well as the overflowing trash can next to the desk in front of the window.

Annie turned to face him, and they suddenly found themselves face-to-face, only a few inches separating them. "Do you mind...?" She stared at him, and Colton tried to back up, but the door had started to close, and he hit his elbow on the door.

"We could just switch rooms," she said. "I know mine is clean."

"No," Colton said instantly. "I'm not going to make you do that." It did seem like she'd have to clean a room no matter what, and he hadn't meant for that to happen.

"It's your party," he added. "I can empty trash and make a bed if you'll point me to the sheets and garbage bags." Yes, he had a housecleaner for his condo in Denver, but that didn't mean he didn't know how to clean up after himself. Or, apparently, other people.

"If you'll help me," Annie said. "We can get it done in fifteen minutes and both go to bed."

"Deal," Colton said, finally smiling for the first time since the day he was supposed to get married but hadn't. Fifteen more minutes until he could be alone. They couldn't pass fast enough.

CHAPTER 3

Annie left Colton standing in room three and went to the storage closet under the stairs. She pulled out clean sheets, a couple of garbage bags, and her cleaning bucket. She turned, smashing right into the very solid body of Colton Hammond.

He grunted, and she sucked in a breath that sounded somewhat high-pitched.

"Sorry," he said, backing up. She shoved the bucket at him, a reaction done without specific thought. He took it, his eyes locked on hers.

"I'll grab the vacuum cleaner," she said, tucking the garbage bags into the bucket only a couple of feet away. "You can start with the trash."

"All right." He turned and walked away, and Annie tried not to stare. Tried, and failed. He didn't have the same western twang she'd heard Graham or Beau speak with. Eli had been all over the world and didn't have much of a cowboy accent either. Andrew worked as the public relations director for Springside Energy, and every time he spoke, it was with polish and precision.

Finn and Zach definitely carried some cowboy in their voices, as did Todd. Liam worked at the clinic, and he only wore a cowboy hat on weekends, if Rose was to be believed. Annie knew many of the men around Coral Canyon, and their accents made her smile—the same way Colton's did.

He possessed some refinement too, and Annie wondered where that had come from. College? Family business? A job? Did he only wear his cowboy hat on the weekends too?

Annie shook the questions out of her head, reached for the vacuum cleaner, and followed Colton. A full trash bag sat by the door, and Annie found Colton inside the room, stripping the blankets and sheets from the bed.

He tossed them against the wall, while Annie parked the vacuum in front of the closet doors. "I'll take those." She bent to pick up the used comforter and sheets, dumping them beside the trash bag in the hall.

She tried to find something to ask him as he handed her one end of the fitted sheet and went around the queen-sized bed. But for the life of her, all of her chatty genes had gone to sleep. They worked together in silence, making up the bed with fresh sheets and a new comforter. She put the pillowcases on the four pillows while Colton ran a disinfectant wipe over the desk, the nightstand, and the slim television cabinet.

"I'll run the vacuum if you want to go get your bags," she said.

He ducked his head and left the room, and Annie breathed a sigh of relief. She wasn't even sure why. Colton existed on a new level of handsome she hadn't seen in a while, and maybe that just made her nervous.

She'd heard him say he was only going to be in town for one night, but Annie knew the snow would keep him here for at least two, probably three. *Maybe more*, her mind whispered, and her heart leapt.

"No," she said out loud, as she often did when she vacuumed at the lodge. She liked to get things out of her mind, and the best way to do that was to say them out loud. The curtains and bedspreads didn't care what she said, and she'd been able to work through several problems by chatting it up with the vacuum cleaner.

"No," she said again, moving the machine back and forth over the carpet. "You're not interested in having him stay for longer than it takes for the roads to clear. He's closed off—obviously—and he doesn't live here. You do."

She did. And she didn't want to leave.

"So be kind to him. Enjoy the holidays. Maybe you can join one of those dating websites once the New Year starts." Her last several words echoed around in the room, as the vacuum cleaner had come unplugged, and the roar of it had silenced.

Annie turned to plug it back in, freezing at the sight of Colton standing there, a bag in each hand. Their eyes met, and Annie's stomach fell to her toes. Colton definitely had some experience dealing with difficult or tense situations, because he simply put his bags down, bent, and plugged in the vacuum cleaner.

The roar returned, but Annie had lost her train of thought. Colton straightened, and his gaze now barely beamed out from underneath the brim of his cowboy hat. Annie tore her eyes from his dark, dreamy ones and looked at the floor. Vacuuming. Yes. She moved the machine along the line she'd already made, determined to get out of there before she embarrassed herself further.

Colton moved out of her way as she backed her way out of the room, and she finally switched off the cleaner and leaned down to pull the plug. "Good night," she said, because she couldn't just pull the door closed without saying anything.

"Ma'am," he said, touching the brim of that white cowboy hat that only made the dark-and-silver beard that much more appealing. And his manners called to Annie's sensibilities as well. She felt tethered to him, and she didn't know how to sever the connection. They'd spoken for a few minutes, and she'd sat by him on the couch to eat. Her feelings were ridiculous, and Annie commanded herself to regain control of herself.

She reached for the doorknob, and the door closed between them. Relief covered the tense situation, and Annie breathed out harshly. She wound up the cord on the vacuum and reached for the trash bag. It could wait in the closet, just like there would be time to do the laundry tomorrow.

With everything put away, Annie unlocked her room and went inside. Her daughters hadn't come downstairs yet, and Annie sighed again as she sank into the armchair in the room. Room four was bigger than room three, and Annie realized as she looked at the two queen beds that she couldn't have traded with Colton. Emily and Eden were staying here with her.

Annie changed into her pajamas and went to the door, opening it and peering out before making the move to the bathroom next door. The four rooms down here shared this bathroom, and the one around the corner, and Annie figured she'd run into Colton again sooner or later.

Back in the room and ready for bed, Annie climbed under the covers just as her phone chimed. She picked it up and saw Graham had sent a link to the group string. Everyone at the lodge for the next couple of weeks was in the group text, and Annie knew where the link would go before she tapped on it.

The holiday schedule.

Excitement built within her, because she did love the Christmas holidays at Whiskey Mountain Lodge. They'd have baking competitions, meals together, game night, movies throughout the afternoons and evenings, fancy brunches, snowshoeing, horseback riding, cross-country skiing, arts & crafts, among other things.

Bree tried to add something new to the schedule every year, and since this was only the third year, Annie expected big things. She tapped, but before the website opened, the door did too, and Emily and Eden spilled into the room, both of them laughing.

"Oh, sorry, Mom," Emily said when she turned and saw Annie sitting in bed, the pillows all propped up behind her. "Tired?"

Annie put a smile on her face, because she loved her daughters deeply. "Yeah," she said. "A lot of cleaning in a short amount of time."

Emily came over and hugged Annie, who patted her back. "Thanks for coming up," Annie said.

"Yeah," Emily said, smiling warmly when she pulled back.

"What's Kelly doing the next couple of days?"

"Oh, he's working right up until three o'clock on Christmas Eve," Em said. "He said he'd be up by dinner and the tree lighting though."

"Sounds good." Annie looked at her phone again, and the list of activities stretched before her. She'd forgotten about hunting down the perfect Christmas tree, the signups for decorating, the kid's class for ornament construction, and the children's caroling. Of course. Who wouldn't want all the Whittaker grandchildren to knock on the door and sing a rousing rendition of Frosty the Snowman?

Annie smiled just thinking about it.

"I'm going to go shower," Eden said, taking out her toiletry bag. She disliked talk about Emily's boyfriend, and it had taken Annie six months to figure out why. She'd finally taken Eden to dinner at Devil's Tower and said, "I need you to tell me what's going on with you and Em."

Jealousy, that was what. Eden had cried and cried while they ate their towers of onion rings and stacks of salad. Annie's heart had gone out to her in every way, and she'd moved from across the booth to sit beside her daughter and console her.

Emily was the pretty one, Eden had said. The one who got all the boys in high school and gets them all now that she'd returned to Coral Canyon from college. She'd earned a business and bookkeeping degree, and she ran all the paperwork and money in the cleaning business Annie had founded fifteen years ago. She'd done it for something to do after Eden had started kindergarten, but she'd been relying on the income from Swept Away for a solid decade since her husband had died.

All at once, she knew why she was nervous around Colton. She pushed against the feelings building within her. She'd felt utterly abandoned when Ryan had died, though his death had been an accident.

She hadn't wanted Ryan to fly that day, though. She'd begged him not to go.

She would not do the same again, especially not for a man she'd just met. And he wasn't planning on staying for any significant amount of time in Coral Canyon—and she wouldn't be begging him to stay.

"Eden, wait," Annie said, coming back to the moment. "There's a guy next door." She swallowed, the word "guy" coming out of her mouth oddly. "That man—cowboy—who showed up right before we ate? Patsy put him in four."

"Okay," Eden said, and then she ducked out of the door, leaving Emily and Annie alone.

Emily changed into her pajamas too, pulling her long, blonde hair out of its ponytail and letting it flow down her back. "I told Eden to sign up for an app to meet someone."

"You did?" After Annie had learned why Eden practically ran from the room every time Em mentioned a boyfriend, ex-boyfriend, or even "some guy I went to coffee with once," she'd kept it to herself.

Only when the girls had come to one of the worst arguments of their lives, had Eden looked at Annie with tears streaming down her face and said, "Tell her."

So Annie had told Emily how her sister felt, always being in the shadows. Always being overlooked. Always needing to shop in the plus section while Emily could practically still wear things from the junior department.

"And what did she say?" Annie asked. It had been six months since everything had come out, and while the tension still ramped up from time to time, at least they'd been able to deal with it instead of letting it fester, grow, and then explode.

"She said she's going to look into it." Emily peeled back the comforter and went around the bed, untucking the sheets that Annie had worked so hard to put in. She grinned at Annie. "But I'm on that app, and she signed up *months* ago."

"What else can you see?" Annie asked as Emily tilted her phone toward her. Maybe a tiny part of her wanted to know the name of the app too.

She already knew Eden had signed up for the dating app, even if she didn't know the name of it. In the last few weeks, she'd been talking to a guy named Mitchell, too, and she'd sworn Annie to secrecy.

"I can't see anything," Emily said, and Annie relaxed a little. "Just her profile, and that she's single. I can see when she's active." She peered closer at her phone. "And she's active right now."

"She just wants to find someone," Annie said, trying to play things off as casual. "We need to be gentle with her."

"I *am* being gentle with her," Emily said, but Annie knew Em simply didn't get it. She hadn't ever been passed over for her sister or her best friend. It wasn't her fault; she *couldn't* understand.

Emily tucked her legs underneath her and faced Annie, and the sleep Annie wanted started to fade. She loved talking to her daughters, though, and she'd given up plenty of hours of sleep to stay up late and bond with Emily and Eden.

"What about you?" she asked.

"What about me—what?" Annie searched her oldest daughter's face.

She held up her phone, a twinkle in her eye that Annie did not like. Not one little bit. "*You* should join the dating app."

"Oh, no." Annie scoffed, though she'd literally just thought of doing so twenty minutes ago. "There's not going to be men my age on that thing." She shook her head and left her phone lying in her lap. "And I'm not looking for someone the same age as my *daughter*." She cocked her eyebrows at Emily.

"But you *are* looking." Emily tried to bite back her smile, but she couldn't, and it spread across her whole face.

"Oh, I don't know." Annie leaned back against her pillows and looked up at the ceiling. "Maybe? I don't know." She'd loved Ryan so much, but she didn't want to be alone in her later years. Now that she was closer to fifty than forty, maybe she should get more serious about finding someone to sail into her silver years with.

Silver....

Annie closed her eyes as Emily started talking. "Here's a guy who's forty-two, Mom. That's not too young for you."

"I should hope not," Annie said. "That's only four years."

"This guy is fifty."

"I don't want a 'guy,'" Annie said. "I want a *man*."

"Fine," Emily said, the bed creaking as she got off of it. "Look. This *man* is fifty. And he's cute."

Annie opened her eyes and took her daughter's phone. The man's picture filling the top half of the screen smiled back at her with crinkled, blue eyes, straight teeth, and plenty of charisma.

"That's Will Mayers," she said. "He cheated on his wife, who left eight months ago to live with their daughter in Butte." She rolled her eyes and handed the phone back to Emily. She had caught the name of the dating app, though, and she would consider joining.

She'd pray about it, if Emily would ever stop talking. But she prattled on about another man, and how Annie couldn't expect that every man would cheat just because he had once.

She closed her eyes again, aware when Eden came back into the room, because Emily braided her hair, and the conversation switched to the schedule of activities at the lodge.

Annie conjured up the picture of her husband. Ryan had been a man's man, with big, broad shoulders, dark, sexy hair, and the ability to grow a beard in twelve hours or less. He'd flown a helicopter for twelve years, taking tourists up into the most remote parts of the Grand Teton Mountains. In the winter, when he couldn't fly as often, he worked as a backcountry guide, taking people up to spots of snow that had never been touched by humans before.

He'd loved Annie with his whole heart, and she'd been gloriously fulfilled and happy with him too. He'd always listened to her before, when she said she had a hunch he shouldn't do something, or that the girls shouldn't go to whichever neighbor's house.

But for some reason, the day she'd asked him not to take the tour to the top of Mount Moran, he'd gone anyway.

He hadn't come home.

Annie drew in a deep breath and started a prayer in her mind. *Help me, Lord, to be where I need to be, so I can meet who I need to meet. I would like to…meet a new man. Someone who will love and cherish me, and someone who I can love and cherish too.*

Practical. Direct. Annie didn't need to tell God everything she felt; she believed He already knew. He knew even the knotted bits, the parts Annie didn't understand herself. And He'd always provided a way for Annie to take care of herself and the girls. She didn't need another client, or a way to pay the bills.

She needed someone to start taking care of her heart.

What about Colton Hammond?

The thought ran through her head, and she couldn't help wondering if the Lord had put it there, or if she just had the handsome cowboy on her mind.

CHAPTER 4

When Colton woke the next morning, the tip of his nose felt ice cold. He shivered as he rolled over and pulled the blanket up to cover his face. Being in the basement, the only window in the room sat above the desk, and it was still dark.

He'd been surprised at how sound-proof the room was, and after he'd changed into his pajamas and gone to bed, he hadn't heard anything. No one coming down the stairs. Nothing from next door or across the hall. No footsteps above him.

The little of his face exposed to the air felt the winter's chill, and he knew something was wrong. The furnace had gone out in the lodge, or maybe Mother Nature had blown such a huge storm into the lodge that he was the only one left, the ceiling above him the only thin layer protecting him from the icy air outside.

He always had enjoyed an active imagination, and he told himself to calm down and go back to sleep. He wasn't the only person left in the lodge, the only room untouched by gale-force winds that had carried everyone into the surrounding forests.

His need to use the bathroom prevented him from falling asleep again, and he finally got up, the cold now a tangible being he could not ignore. Something had gone terribly wrong in the lodge.

The blackness around him was absolute, and when he reached for his phone, he found it only had fifteen percent battery life left, despite him plugging it in the night before.

"Power's out," he murmured to himself. "That would explain why the furnace isn't working." Or the pilot light had gone out, or the furnace simply couldn't keep up with a lodge of this size. Anything was possible, and his imagination started running again.

He cracked his door and listened. No one seemed to be up and about. If possible, the air in the hallway was even colder than in Colton's room, and he hurried into the bathroom. After locking the door and taking care of his business, he went back into the basement room. He had no idea where anyone was, besides Annie, and he cast a look at room four, the door of which stood just a few feet away.

An eerie sensation swept over his skin, and he scanned the huge basement room again. He could hear nothing, sense nothing. But he knew he couldn't just go back to bed. If the furnace was out, someone needed to start investigating why, and he'd seen the giant fireplace upstairs. They wouldn't freeze to death— up there.

Colton shivered as he stepped over to Annie's door. He knocked, his fist against the wood sounding like a gunshot in the relative quiet of the lodge. "Annie," he hissed. He leaned as close to the door as he dared without touching it, and he heard nothing.

He knocked again, a little louder this time. "Annie, it's Colton. There's—" He cut off when the door opened, and a woman stood there that was not Annie. She lifted her phone and shone the flashlight in his face.

He held up one hand, instantly annoyed. "I'm sorry," he said. "I thought Annie was in this room."

"And you came to see her?"

"It's freezing," he said. She had to feel it. "I don't know where anything or anyone is. I figured Annie was the best bet to make sure we don't all freeze in our beds."

The woman lowered the light, but all Colton could see now was blackness beyond her. Every time he blinked, he had a large, white spot in his vision.

"Mom, this guy needs you."

Mom rang through Colton's mind. He wasn't sure why he was surprised. Annie was forty-six-years-old, and she'd obviously been married before. His curiosity piqued, and he couldn't believe it. He told himself he wasn't interested in knowing who the guy was, or why Annie was no longer with him.

None of your business, he told himself, mentally folding his arms. That was that. He just needed Annie to help him get this place heated again.

Another shiver racked his shoulders just as Annie appeared, hugging herself. "You're right. It's freezing down here."

"Is it a basement issue?" he asked. "Or is this abnormal?"

"It's abnormal." Annie reached out and pressed the light switch on her wall. The light stayed stubbornly off. "There's no power."

"There's a fireplace upstairs. Should we go build a fire?"

"Yes," she said. "And there's one down here too. But there's nothing on the second floor."

"Heat rises," Colton said. "If you'll show me where things are, I can get started." He thought about waking the others, bringing them all out into the common areas of the lodge so they'd be warm enough.

But they needed to get the fires going first.

"Let me get my phone so I can see," she said. "And we'll need to call Patsy and Bree and find out if their cabins have power. If they don't, they'll be much colder than we are." She ducked back into the darkness, and Colton waited in the hall.

Another shiver prompted him to go grab his coat out of his room, which he did, rejoining Annie in the hallway a moment later. She too wore a coat, and she had her flashlight shining toward the ground.

"The wood is all upstairs," she said, leading the way.

Colton followed her up, where the air was slightly warmer on the main level. But not much. She took him past the kitchen and down a hall that led to a back door. On the left sat a laundry room, and past that, a tiny room held firewood.

He loaded up as much as he could carry, and she lit the way for him to take it into the living room. They made three trips before Annie went into the kitchen and started rummaging through drawers, muttering to herself.

Colton thought of what she'd said while vacuuming. *Maybe you can join one of those dating websites once the New Year starts.*

For some reason, he'd thought that whichever dating site she joined, he'd join too. Which was absolutely *ridiculous.*

He wasn't dating right now. "Ever again," he muttered to himself as he knelt in front of the fireplace and started stacking the wood. He'd been a Boy Scout as a teen, but a lot of years had passed since then. Many of those had been spent in a lab, an office, or a conference room, not out under the starry sky, a campfire lazily flickering in front of him.

In that moment, he wanted the lazy campfire. The starry sky. The easy, laid-back life of a cowboy. He had plenty of money. Why couldn't he become a full-time cowboy? Wear the hat all the time, and go horseback riding, and maybe work on the family farm in Ivory Peaks.

There would be no press out there. No one to care who he'd been dating and for how long. No one to answer to.

Even as he thought that, he knew it would never be, especially at the family farm in Ivory Peaks. There, he'd had to answer to his mother, and his father, and his grandmother.

"Matches," Annie said, finally coming back into the room.

"Thanks." Colton took them from her, his hands almost numb. His fingers stuttered, and he dropped the book of matches she held. They both reached for it at the same time, and the next thing Colton knew, his hand and Annie's hand were pressed together, the book of matches pinned between their palms.

Her skin was cold too, but it ignited a fire inside Colton that actually made him angry.

He pulled his hand away, letting the matches fall to the hearth. Annie picked them up again, extending them out between two pinched fingers. "Sorry," she said, and her voice was so kind and so soft that once again, Colton felt his heart doing something he'd thought it would never do again.

Beat.

Grow.

Confused now, he took the matches and focused on his task. A few minutes later, with enough force and only a few smoking paper towels, the wood caught the flame and started to burn.

He basked in the warmth coming from the fire, closing his eyes and breathing it in. "Mm," he said, noting that Annie had done the same. He wanted to stay right there with her for the rest of the night, maybe to try to explain his erratic behavior. Maybe she hadn't even noticed.

"Let's go downstairs," he said. "This should be okay for a minute."

They repeated the whole process again, hauling wood downstairs and getting a fire going in a fireplace Colton hadn't seen during the brief tour of the lodge.

"Did you get the activities schedule?" she asked as he stuffed a wadded-up paper towel between two pieces of wood.

"Is that what that link was?" He picked up the book of matches and struck one, immediately holding the fire to the paper towels.

"Yes," she said. "Who knows what will happen if we don't have electricity. We won't even be able to make coffee."

"That's not good," he said, glancing at her to find a smile on her pretty face. "We better start praying now that the electricity comes back on."

"Good idea," Annie said, though Colton hadn't actually meant it literally. But he thought Annie had. He tried to remember the last time he'd prayed for something, actually prayed vocally for something.

It had admittedly been a couple of years, and he'd prayed out loud while he drove to the family farm when he couldn't reach any of them who knew how to use a cellphone. He remembered the complete desperation, the utter fear, and he'd turned to the Lord.

Why hadn't he done that more often in his life?

It's never too late to start, he thought, and as he blew on the embers of fire still eating their way up the paper towel, he thought, *Please, God, let the electricity come back on so we don't have to babysit fires all day as our only source of entertainment.*

———

HOURS LATER, COLTON JOLTED AWAKE AS A DOOR SLAMMED somewhere nearby. He heard someone walking in the hall beyond the living room, and he held very still. The bathroom door clicked closed, and he sat up to put more wood on the fire in front of him.

Annie groaned as she sat up too, rubbing one hand down her face and then up into her hair. Colton had dreamt about that pretty face, but now he wondered if it had really been a dream.

"I'll go check the fire upstairs," she said.

"What time is it?" he asked, yawning immediately after getting the words out.

She checked her phone, as his had died after they'd built the fires and gotten their blankets to huddle in front of the comforting flames. They'd set an alarm every hour to check on the wood supply and keep the fires going, and they'd been swapping who had to go upstairs.

"Six-fifteen," she said. "People should be getting up soon.

Well, at least Celia. She starts breakfast early when the lodge is full."

"Maybe not today," Colton said. Annie nodded, got up, shrugged into her coat, and went upstairs.

"Please, Dear Lord," he said aloud, vocally praying for the first time in years. He'd been thinking his prayers all night as he and Annie worked to keep the lodge and all of its occupants from freezing. "Now would be a really great time to get the electricity back on."

His stomach grumbled, and he'd been looking forward to a hot cup of coffee and plenty of pancakes and sausages.

God did not answer his prayer, and Annie came thumping back down the steps. "Still going strong up there," she said. "It's not nearly as cold as it used to be." She discarded her coat and curled into her end of the couch, pulling her blanket all the way to her chin.

Colton said nothing, because he'd just had a terrible, horrifying thought that perhaps God *had* answered his prayer. No, the electricity hadn't come back on, but he felt it arcing through his whole body as he looked at Annie.

What does this mean? he asked the Lord next, but He didn't answer that question either.

CHAPTER 5

Annie took a tray of mugs into the living room, where she found Colton reaching for the coffee kettle hanging over the fire. "Wow," she said, feeling like she sounded like a complete flirt. She tried to tame her voice back to itself when she added, "You're like a real cowboy."

That got a partial smile from the man she'd been up with for half the night, tending the fireplaces. "I think it's hot enough now," he said. "How's it going in the kitchen?"

Annie set the heavy tray on the hearth. "Yeah, the range is gas, so Celia has all the burners going. The sausage is done, and she's got pancakes in every pan now. They're eating in shifts."

Colton nodded and set the tea kettle Celia had given him to make coffee in next to the tray. He hung the second pot on the hook and started filling mugs with coffee. Annie did like watching him work, because his movements were strong and sure, and she had the suspicion that the man could do anything he wanted to do.

He stood and bent to pick up the tray, and Annie marveled at the way his biceps bulged with the weight. So this cowboy worked out. He flicked a look at her, and Annie set a smile on her face. "You're going to be their favorite person."

Colton preceded her into the kitchen, where a cheer did raise up to the roof at the sight of coffee. "My man," Eli said, selecting a mug and handing it to his wife before taking one for himself too.

A variety of flavored creamers sat on the counter, along with sugar and plain cream. The mugs of coffee went quickly, and Colton didn't seem to know what hit him. Annie stifled a giggle and took the tray from him. "I'll be out in a second."

Colton turned and went back to the fire in the living room, and Annie started stacking more mugs on the tray. The scent of sausage and maple syrup filled the air, and Annie listened to Beau and Bree argue about the reality TV show they both liked. A slip of happiness moved through her as Annie basked in the energy at the lodge. If Celia had been able to use electricity, she'd have four griddles on the counter, with nine pancakes on each one.

As it was, instead of making thirty-six pancakes at once, Celia could only make twelve, and she set a plate on the counter. "Pancakes are up."

"Let's say grace," Graham said, and Annie hurried to put the last two mugs on the tray. She didn't pick it up though, and waited for the general chaos to die down in the kitchen so Laney could say grace.

She gave a nice prayer about being grateful for the holidays, for the fireplaces in the lodge, and for food and family. The moment she said, "Amen," and everyone had echoed it, Patsy jumped up.

"And we have a new, updated schedule for today. We need people to watch the fires all day, and we'll need people on firewood duty."

"There's still time to do activities," Bree said. "But we can't do anything with electricity, obviously. So no movies, no baking contests, that kind of thing. But we can still go snowshoeing, and there's a whole closet of games and puzzles upstairs we can bring down." She smiled around at everyone, and Annie picked up the tray to go get more coffee for everyone.

She didn't have to work to feed everyone today, but she didn't have anything else to do, and she liked going out into the living room to spend a few minutes with Colton. She found him loitering in the doorway leading out of the kitchen, and he reached for the tray.

"Let me," he said. "That's heavy."

"Thanks." She smiled at him, a shot of self-consciousness moving through her. She wondered how old she'd be before she had the confidence she needed to hold her head high. In some things, she did. When she met with a potential new client, she carried her mini-clipboard and opened their closet doors as she took notes.

She gave a price for the cleaning they said they wanted, and she signed ninety percent of the people who called her for a meeting to discuss their cleaning needs.

With Ryan, she'd been confident. They'd worked well together as a team, and she could call him as she backed out of the driveway and say, "I forgot to put the trash can out, and they come early. Could you do it?"

And he would. She served him, too, and there was nothing better than getting up early on Sunday morning and making cinnamon rolls just for Ryan. He loved them with a lot of butter and a lot of cinnamon and a lot of raisins. She could almost hear his laughter when he came out into the kitchen and found her rolling out the dough into a large rectangle on the counter.

But with Colton...he made her doubt everything that came out of her mouth, every look she shot his way, just everything. And she didn't like it. She was too old to feel like this.

He set the tray down just as the kettle started to hiss, and he switched out the hot one for the cold one that needed to be brewed. She poured this time, aware that he watched her after he'd hung the kettle over the fire.

"You know, I have made coffee over a fire before."

She glanced up for only a moment, because the last thing she needed was to spill hot coffee all over herself and the hearth. "That doesn't surprise me." She smiled at him. "What activities are you going to do today?"

"I think going outside and getting cold isn't a great idea," he said. "So I don't know. Maybe I'll take a nap to make up for all the missed sleep last night."

Annie nodded, but she didn't want him to disappear into his room. What that said about her, she wasn't sure. "Maybe we could play a game." She finished with the last cup of coffee and left the kettle on the hearth for him. He had a system of putting all the grounds in a filter and tying it closed and letting it brew over the flame, and she didn't want to disrupt that.

He didn't move to pick up the tray, and Annie met his eye. "Just a board game, right?" he asked.

Annie blinked. "Yes," she said. "Can't play video games without electricity, and I can't imagine going outside to play like badminton or anything."

Colton tipped his head back and laughed, and Annie sure did like the sound of it. His laughter didn't last long, and he leaned toward her. "I just meant, you know, we're not going to play games with each other." His dark, stormy gray eyes sparkled at her, and she felt sure he was flirting with her.

Yes, she'd been out of the game for a while, but the connection between her and Colton felt very real.

"No games," she said. "I'm too old for that. But." She hit the T hard. "I'm not too old for cribbage."

"Cribbage?" Colton's right eyebrow went up, and Annie found that downright sexy.

"Don't you dare say you don't know what it is." She poked him in the chest. "Or that it's for old ladies."

Colton grinned and put one hand over his heart. "I would never."

"So look it up before we play." She nodded to the coffee. "If you don't pick that up and take it into the kitchen, we'll be dealing with a riot."

"Yes, ma'am," he said, picking up the tray and following her into the kitchen.

By the time Annie and Colton got their hot coffee and fresh-from-the-pan pancakes, at least half of the people in the lodge had already eaten and left the room. That was just fine with her, and she noticed Colton sticking right next to her through it all. And she didn't mind that at all.

————

LATER THAT DAY, JUST BEFORE LUNCH, ANNIE HAD JUST WOKEN from a two-hour nap when the lodge came back to life. The lights brightened, and the whirring of machines starting up again filled the air. Out in the living room in the basement, Annie heard an outcry, and she jumped up to go join them.

She opened the door and nearly ran into Emily as she came in to get her. "It's back," her daughter said, as if Annie couldn't see the lights shining down from the bulbs in the ceiling.

"I'm so glad," Annie said.

"Graham's checking the furnace, and then Celia's going to serve what she has for lunch." Emily smiled at her, and Annie nodded as she left.

Colton stepped beside her, and Annie startled as he did. "How many daughters do you have?"

"Two," she said.

"Sons?"

"None," she said, tilting her head back to look at him. "Do you have any children?"

"No, ma'am." He shook his head, and she realized he wasn't wearing his white cowboy hat. His dark hair had plenty of silver in it, and Annie wanted to reach up and run her fingers through it. Her hand actually twitched that way, and she cemented it to her side.

"How long have you been single?" he asked. "I mean, I'm assuming you're single. I suppose you could have a boyfriend. Okay, I'm going to stop talking now." He cleared his throat, and Annie suppressed a giggle.

Feeling bold and like she wanted to convey what she'd been feeling for the past twenty-four hours, she slipped her hand into his and squeezed. His fingers warmed the spaces between hers, and he actually squeezed back.

"I don't have a boyfriend," she said. "My husband died twelve years ago in a helicopter accident."

"Oh, wow," he said, his voice reverent and soft. "I'm sorry, Annie."

"Thank you." She released his hand, and he took a step away from her. Annie didn't know what to make of that, and she quickly cleared her throat.

"Okay," she said brightly. "I'm going to go see where I can be the most useful."

"We have a date with a cribbage board later," Colton called after her, and Annie almost stumbled over the smooth carpet at the word *date*.

At least he knows it's a cribbage board, she thought as she started up the steps, ready for some of Celia's homemade chicken noodle soup. The scent of toasty, garlicky bread reached her nose too, and Annie could really use a lot of carbs to make it through her "date" that afternoon.

She'd barely reached the top of the steps when Amanda appeared in front of her. "Hey," she said with a smile. "I just need a yes or no answer." She held up her phone. "Beau just heard Colton say you two have a date later today?"

Annie blinked at Amanda, sure this question was a joke. "We're going to play cribbage," she said.

"So that's a yes."

"No," Annie said. "He's just new here, and you Whittakers can be a lot to handle." Annie gave her a pointed look, but Amanda just scoffed and waved her hand.

"She's right," Finn said from somewhere behind Amanda, and she turned toward him.

"I didn't ask for your input," she said with a laugh. She faced Annie again. "Do you like him?"

"Is this a yes or no question too?" she asked.

"Yes."

"Then sure, I like him." Annie thought of the brief escapade of holding his hand. That had been really nice. "But he's...." She searched for the right word. "Closed off. He's got lots of walls up." And she wasn't sure she had the energy to break them down. She wasn't as young as she once was, and while she was willing to capitalize on her birthday wish, she didn't want to be the one pursuing Colton.

Footsteps sounded on the stairs behind her, and she moved out of the way. "Don't text all your sons about this. Please?"

Amanda looked like Annie had just suggested something preposterous. Annie had known Amanda for years, and she just cocked her head; no words necessary.

"Okay, fine," Amanda said, tucking her phone in the pocket of her slacks. "But they have eyes."

Annie waited for Laney to pass, smiling at the woman who had tamed Graham's most beastly qualities. "If that were true, Amanda, Beau wouldn't have texted you to ask me a yes or no question." She nodded once, her point made, and went into the kitchen to see what Celia needed from her.

She buttered the bread and placed it on a sheet tray for Celia, who chopped fresh garlic like her life depended on having it on-hand all the time, like maybe a troop of vampires could attack the lodge at any moment.

"Need some help?" Colton asked, and Annie dropped the butter knife. It landed on the counter with a clatter, and he picked it up for her.

"Yes," Celia said. "Can you get the bowls out of the cupboard there by your head? And as many spoons as you can find." She started sprinkling the garlic over the buttered bread Annie had put on the sheet tray.

"Spoons," Colton muttered to himself, opening a drawer that had Tupperware lids in it. Annie couldn't help giggling, and she nodded to the counter behind him.

"They're over there by the microwave."

"Oh, look at that," he said. "It's even labeled."

"Yep," Annie said, another laugh coming out of her mouth. And suddenly, she thought maybe she could start kicking at the walls Colton had put around his heart—especially if she knew how they'd gotten there. So she'd just ask him during their friendly cribbage match.

Which was really a date....

CHAPTER 6

Colton didn't usually consider soup a complete meal. It was an appetizer at best, even if it did have homemade pasta and big chunks of chicken in it. But chicken noodle soup was what Celia had made and served for lunch, and Colton wasn't complaining. He hadn't anticipated getting all of his meals for free while at the lodge, especially home cooked meals.

His mother had never been much of a cook, and Colton had been fending for himself since age ten. He could open cans and heat up the contents like nobody else, and he did enjoy a couple of bowls of cereal for any meal.

As he got older and got a job, he became a big fan of fast food, pizza, and delivery. Living in the city made cooking something he didn't have to know how to do, but when Annie bent to pull out a sheet tray of sizzling, toasty, golden garlic bread, Colton thought he'd really like to eat that for every meal for the foreseeable future.

He knew he couldn't get toast like that from the freezer section of the grocery store, and that meant he needed a cooking lesson. The air smelled like salty chicken stock and buttery garlic, and Colton's stomach growled.

Annie looked at him, and he thought of her hand in his. His

pulse had boomed through his veins, vibrating in his muscles, and he'd been numb to the feel of her skin after only a moment.

She scared him more than anything else, and Colton had needed more space from her after she'd released his hand. He wasn't sure what kind of air he put off, but Annie had left soon after that. Colton had stayed downstairs for a few minutes, just so it wouldn't look like he was following her around like a puppy.

Someone came in the back door, and a moment later, a freezing cold gust of air whooshed into the kitchen. Patsy came around the corner, her cheeks and the tip of her nose bright red. "It's still coming down," she said. "But the power is back on at my cabin too."

"Good news," Celia said. "We're ready to eat. Do you want to sound the alarm? Or should we just let people graze?"

Colton would've voted for grazing, but Patsy said, "I'll ring the bell." She stepped back around the corner and a moment later, a *ding-dong-dong-ding* came through a speaker system in the ceiling.

"Lunch is served in the kitchen from now until one o'clock." Patsy didn't beat around the bush, that was for sure. She re-entered the kitchen, and Annie handed her a bowl, then picked up another one and extended it to Colton.

"You don't pray over lunch?" he asked, taking the bowl.

"Not when it's come from now until one o'clock," Patsy said, giving him a smile he would categorize as terse. He wasn't sure what he'd done to make her life harder, but he sure felt like he had. If anyone had been put out by his arrival, it was Annie, who'd had to clean a room after she'd thought she was done working for the day.

He held back as Patsy went through the line, letting a couple of people get between the two of them. He knew when to make his presence known and when to lay low, and this definitely felt like a time to stay off the radar.

Because of that, he filled his soup bowl, took two pieces of toast, and left the kitchen. He felt like both Annie and Patsy watched him leave, but he couldn't make himself go back. He wanted to eat, pack his pajamas, get in his truck, and go.

The lodge had huge, picturesque windows in the front, and one look at them, and he knew he wasn't going anywhere that day.

Maybe tomorrow, he told himself as he settled on the bottom step of the stairs that led up to the second floor. He sipped his hot soup until it was cool enough to take full bites. He enjoyed one piece of toast as-is, and dunked the other in his soup, deciding that with toast like this, soup could absolutely be considered a meal.

Others came into the living room, but he sat around the banister, across from the front door, and they didn't see him. He heard their voices as they talked about presents, their parents, and their kids.

He deduced the women talking to be sisters, and he wondered if they'd be offended if he stood up and passed by them to go get more soup.

In the end, he wanted to stay out of sight, so he waited until they left, and then he got up and took his empty bowl into the kitchen. He snagged one more piece of bread before he went downstairs to get his coat and gloves.

He wasn't sure when he and Annie would play cribbage, but he wanted to get outside for a minute. Maybe he'd be able to breathe outside, as the lodge was already starting to smother him.

Back upstairs, he opted to go right instead of left, which led past the kitchen, and he opened the door at the end of that hall to find a garage. Perfect. He slipped outside without anyone noticing him, and he gazed at the four pickup trucks parked in the expansive garage. His was outside in the weather, getting covered with feet of snow. He'd have a lot of work to do to get out of here tomorrow, and something told him he might not be leaving tomorrow either.

A sigh escaped his lips as he opened the door in the back and stepped out into the blowing, white snow of the storm. He wasn't sure what he expected to find, as he'd experienced blizzards in Ivory Peaks. Colorado was the highest state in the country, and he'd survived plenty of heavy snow winters.

But he'd never seen anything like this. The wind here blew the snow sideways, and Colton flipped up his hood as he stepped away from the door. He stopped immediately, because he couldn't see at all. Not even a little bit, in any direction. He backed into the garage door behind him, relieved it was there.

All at once, the wind died, and Colton could see through the falling snow. It was much more magical now, and the tension in him finally leaked out. The big, fat, fluffy flakes fell slowly, and he stepped away from the garage again.

After walking straight out, Colton could see the tall, majestic pines in front of him, what looked like a barn to his right, and the main backyard to his left. He went that way, because he didn't want to get too far from the house.

A patio expanded from the back door, and the roof extended for several feet over it. But the wind had blown snow over the patio anyway. It was much less, and Colton stuck close to the house, where a bench sat on the other side of a swing. He bypassed that, because the cushions would be wet, and he took a seat on the bench.

His mind seemed sluggish and slow, and he kept his hands tucked into his coat as he tried to find a string of thought and hold onto it. But he couldn't. He felt as numb now as he had when Annie had touched his hand, and that sense of not feeling anything had started when Priscilla had sent her father to say she couldn't go through with the wedding.

Maybe this was just how he had to live now.

The chill had just started to creep through his coat when someone came out onto the patio. Colton looked toward the back door, but the swing was in the way, and he couldn't see who it was.

"That makes no sense," a woman said, and Colton recognized the voice. He'd spoken to this woman before, but he couldn't remember who it was.

"Okay, so you're telling me that we've been dating for six months, and I don't know your real name?"

Colton did not want to hear this, but he felt trapped just like he had on the steps. He really just needed to stay in the basement until the roads were safe enough to travel. His heart pounded in his ears, but he could still hear the woman—Bree! Her name was Bree—when she said, "I don't know what to think, but I do know one thing, this relationship, or whatever it was, is over."

With that, Bree marched out into the snow just as a gust of wind picked up. Colton couldn't see super clearly, but he knew Bree wasn't wearing a coat.

A scream rent the air, and he flinched. His heartbeat accelerated. He jumped to his feet and watched as Bree stumbled and slipped in the snow, righted herself, and turned as if she'd go down to the barn.

"Bree," Colton called, because it was not safe for her to be out in this storm. As if on cue, the wind swooped down from the sky again with a mighty roar, and he lost sight of Bree for a moment.

He didn't hesitate as he took off after her. He couldn't let her wander in the Wyoming wilderness in this weather, that was for dang sure.

"Bree," he called again, passing the spot where she'd slipped and fallen.

She'd heard him, and she turned back to him. "I'm fine," she called back to him.

"You can't be out here," he said. "You don't even have a coat on."

"My house is just down there."

"Then let me walk with you." Colton reached her and took her arm in his hand. Not a single spark moved through him, and he hadn't expected any to. But with Annie, he had felt something. So maybe he wasn't completely dead inside.

They walked in silence, and Colton's feet felt like bricks of ice by the time Bree said, "It's right there. I can make it."

Colton wasn't an expert, but he knew what code she'd just spoken. *I'm fine now. You can't come in.*

He walked her all the way to the front door, and she went inside with a "Thank you, Colton."

Colton stayed on the porch for a minute, trying to stomp some warmth back into his feet. He'd walked for ten minutes to get here, and he figured he might as well get started on the way back. He kept his eyes on the ground, because the wind hadn't swept away the footprints yet, and he needed them to get back to the lodge.

When he finally arrived at the back door, pure relief filled him. He released his tension with a sigh as he entered the warmth of the lodge. After shedding his soaking wet coat and boots, all he wanted to do was shower. He made his way downstairs, where he found Annie sitting on the couch with her daughters.

"There you are," she said, perking up. Her eyes scanned him from top to bottom and returned to his face. "You're—where have you been?"

"I had to…." Colton didn't want to tell anyone what Bree had said on the patio. "I went outside for a little bit."

Alarm crossed Annie's face. "Did you still want to play cribbage?"

"Can I shower first?" he asked, his hands starting to shake with cold.

"Sure." Annie watched him though, and Colton had the very real feeling that she saw and knew more than she let on. He couldn't speculate on what she saw in him right then, and he nodded and went to get some clean clothes to change into after his shower.

He didn't want to lie to Annie, but it really wasn't his place to give away Dree's secrets. On his way out of the room, he grabbed his phone, which he'd plugged in once the power had come back on.

Wes had texted, and Colton's chest filled with a heartbeat. His oldest brother ran Hammond Manufacturing, and he'd been kind when Colton had said he needed some time away from the city, the company, his job. He'd said to take the time he needed, and Colton had been gone from HMC for seven weeks now.

Once he'd locked himself in the bathroom, he checked the text, and all Wes had said was *Call me when you can please.*

At least he'd said please, but Colton didn't want to deal with family things or business things right now. He didn't want to deal with anything right now, and he wondered when that would wear off.

He decided his brother could wait. Colton needed to get his core body temperature back to normal, and then he was going to play cribbage with Annie. He wasn't sure when a shower and a card game he'd never heard of had become the things he was most looking forward to, or what that said about him.

He'd once known who he was and what his life was going to be. But now, Colton Hammond had no idea who he was, or where his life would take him.

CHAPTER 7

B reeann Richards shed her shoes, then her jeans, which had heavy, wet cuffs. She peeled the soaking wet sweater off and let it fall to the floor as she entered the kitchen. She shivered, because the power had only been on for a couple of hours or so, and the cabin had grown cold while the furnace hadn't been running.

She'd made it from the lodge to her cabin without breaking down, but that was mostly because Colton Hammond had come out of nowhere to escort her.

She supposed it wasn't smart for her to rush out into a Wyoming blizzard without her coat. But Jay had called, and she'd been giddy to see his name on the screen after issuing an invitation for him to come up to the lodge as soon as the roads were cleared. She'd been bold in sending the text, and she'd fretted about it for several hours before he'd called.

She'd been dating him for six months, and she really wanted to see if they were ready to take their relationship to the next level. Bree was, she knew that.

Tears leaked down her face, and Bree went into the small kitchen in the cabin. This place belonged to Laney, and it actually sat on her property. But since Graham had married Laney, the fence between the two properties wasn't enforced.

She shared the cabin with Elise Murphy, the full-time groundskeeper and animal specialist, but Bree didn't expect to see her roommate for a while. A movie had just started in the basement theater room, and Elise loved Celia's caramel corn more than almost anything else the woman made.

So when a sob erupted from her throat, Bree didn't try to swallow it back down. "Jay," she said, her voice much too high. She hated that this man had reduced her to a blubbering mess, leaning over the sink in the kitchen.

"What a stupid name," she said, and she could say it because Jay wasn't the real name of the man she'd been dating for half a year. That was why he'd called, not to accept her invitation to the lodge.

But to say, "Listen, Bree...."

She still didn't know the man's name. How embarrassing. What was she supposed to tell people? Oh, I ended things with...Jay, Kay, El, because I didn't know the guy's name?

She cried harder, finally reaching for a clean glass next to the sink that she'd washed that morning before going to the lodge, where they had a fireplace blazing with heat.

"Okay, enough," she told herself, straightening. She hiccupped as she filled the glass with water and took a sip. It went down ice cold, stinging her throat, but Bree didn't mind. She needed the shock to bring her back to reality.

And the reality was, she no longer had a boyfriend. It wasn't the first time she'd broken up with someone or been broken up with. In fact, in the past decade, she'd had ten boyfriends that hadn't worked out.

"Maybe it's just not meant to be," she said to herself. Maybe she should be content with what she had. She had a great place to live, with a woman she got along well with. She had a great job, with a family she loved. They loved her too. And she knew all of their real names.

Bree stepped over to the fridge and opened it, though she'd eaten lunch only an hour ago. She often turned to a snack to help her through hard times, and she saw no reason to deviate from that now.

She pulled out a container of vegetables and the ranch dip that went with them and retreated to her bedroom. Elise wouldn't bother her there, no matter what time she came home. Bree couldn't stomach the thought of going back to the lodge for dinner, but she also had no desire to cook in the cabin either.

She didn't have to think about that right now. After setting her favorite rerun on her computer, she sat on the end of the bed and snacked her way through an entire episode.

Then she crawled beneath the comforter and pulled it all the way to her chin. She let the TV show run, and she closed her eyes and fell asleep.

She had no idea how long she napped, but she woke when Elise said, "Bree? Are you okay?"

Light shone into the dark bedroom from the hallway, and Bree's TV show had stopped playing at some point. She groaned as she rolled over, and Elise sat on the bed.

"I found your clothes."

"I'm sorry," Bree said, her voice right on the edge of breaking. "I got wet on the way here, and I just had to get them off."

"I get it," she said. "I did the same thing." Her unsaid words were, *But I picked mine up.* Elise knew she wasn't okay, and Bree appreciated that she reached out and stroked her hair off her forehead. "What happened?"

Bree's tears came instantly, and she hated them. "I broke up with Jay." Technically, if Bree had been thinking clearly, she'd say that Jay had ended things with her. When a man called and started the conversation with the word, "Listen," he was breaking up with the woman on the other end of the line.

"Oh, no." Elise leaned down and hugged her. "I'm sorry." She didn't pry for more details, which Bree appreciated. Of course, they'd been living together for about a year and a half now, and Elise knew that Bree would tell her eventually. She'd heard all about Martin, whom Bree had been dating when Elise had first been hired at the lodge. She'd been around when Bree started dating David—and when she'd broken up with him. Now, this thing with Jay had started and stopped too.

"When am I going to meet a good guy?" Bree asked, though she knew Elise didn't have the answer.

"You will," Elise said, because she was a good friend. She peered at Bree with a special intensity in her green eyes. "You really will, Bree."

She reached up and hugged Elise again, saying, "Thank you, Elise."

"Of course. Colton sent me down here to make sure you were okay. I'm glad he did."

"Colton did?" Bree pulled back and looked at Elise. She was a petite kind of beautiful, with soft, wavy blonde hair and those bright green eyes. The first time she'd met Elise, the word *fairy* had come to Bree's mind. She was just so cute, and so tiny, with such a sweet voice.

Bree had thought she wasn't real, but she actually was. What she'd always seen from Elise was exactly who she was. Bree had learned a lot from her about being herself, and Bree had been trying to do exactly that with everyone she met.

"Yes," Elise said. "He was really worried about you." She stood up and extended her hand toward Bree. "Come on, sweetie. Let's get you up and get you dressed for dinner. It'll be ready in about twenty minutes."

Bree groaned as she got up, letting her whole head roll instead of just her eyes. "Maybe I'll just put a pizza in here," she said.

"Nope," Elise said. "Celia made the meatloaf you love just for you." She smiled and drew Bree into another hug. "No one's going to ask you any questions."

"Okay," Bree said. "I'll be out in a minute."

Elise left her alone to get dressed into dry, fresh clothes, and

Bree did just that. She wasn't going to let Jay ruin her holidays. He didn't want to come up to the lodge, where he would be fed three meals a day, have access to all the snacks he wanted, and have multiple activities to choose from every day?

No problem.

She and Elise linked arms and walked back to the lodge. The snow had stopped, thankfully, and the storm had blown out during the afternoon. The dark sky was clear, and that meant the temperatures had dropped considerably in a short time.

If she'd come out in this weather without a coat, as she had earlier, she would've definitely frozen on the ten-minute walk back to the cabin.

They made it back to the glowing energy in the lodge, and Elise gave her a quick smile before slipping away to help Annie get plates and cups out. Bree felt a little lost, because she didn't have a job at the lodge right now. None of them did, but Annie and Elise seemed to know exactly what to do.

"Hey." Someone touched her elbow lightly, a quick tap that was there and then gone.

Bree turned toward Colton and looked up at him in that white cowboy hat. "Hey." She tried to give him a smile, but it felt a little shaky. "Thanks for helping me get back to my cabin okay."

"Of course," he said. He didn't smile either, and Bree wished she felt even the glimmer of a spark with him. But she did not— and besides, she'd seen the tension and chemistry between Colton and Annie as they'd sat on the couch to eat dinner last night.

"I feel kind of useless," he said, turning to face the activity in the kitchen.

"Yeah, I hear that." Bree nodded to the other doorway that led into the other half of the kitchen, where most of the family gathered. "None of them feel like they need to help get the meal ready, though."

"None of them crashed the party," Colton said.

Bree did smile then as she shook her head. "It's impossible to crash a Whittaker party," she said. "They love everyone, and they have the attitude of the more the merrier. Trust me."

"They are extremely kind," he mused, almost like he couldn't believe that people could be so kind.

"Do you have brothers?" she asked. "Sisters?"

"Four brothers," he said.

"Where are you from?"

"Colorado."

"Time to eat," Annie said, poking her head out into the hall, where Colton had approached Bree. She looked between the two of them and then ducked back around the corner.

Before Colton could move, his phone rang. Bree saw the name Wes on it, and noticed the way Colton's eyebrows drew down into a frown.

"Brother?" she asked.

"Yes." He swiped on the call and put the phone to his ear. "Give me five minutes, please." He didn't sound upset or frowny, and he'd said please. He listened to Wes say something, and then he nodded before hanging up.

Colton gestured for Bree to go into the kitchen first, almost the beginning of a smile on his face. Bree stepped into the kitchen with Annie and several others, immediately migrating closer to Elise than Colton. She didn't want Annie to think there was anything happening between her and Colton, because there wasn't.

In fact, Bree wasn't going to have anything happen between her and any man for a long time. *Maybe never again,* she told herself as Celia started detailing the food and what they had to choose from and Colton slipped out of the kitchen again, silent and unnoticed by most.

Maybe never again.

CHAPTER 8

Wesley Hammond didn't have five minutes, but he was honestly surprised Colton had picked up the phone in the first place.

He stood at the window of his office, which wasn't hard as it filled the entire back wall of the expansive space. He needed his executive marketing director back, and Wes's stomach squirmed as if someone had filled it with snakes.

He'd given Colton the benefit of the doubt for the past two months. Yes, his brother had been stood up by his bride on their wedding day. Yes, the press had been relentless and cruel, resurrecting the story after weeks and weeks. Colton should've expected as much, as the media had been following generations of Hammonds.

Wes sighed, because he was tired of sneaking out side doors and meeting bodyguards at the elevator just so he could get to his car without getting mobbed by reporters—or worse, women.

He'd been engaged twice himself, but he'd always ended things long before it came time to stand at the altar. So he didn't truly know what his brother was going through. He just knew he needed Colton here to go over the new logo for the company, as well as put the last touches and approval on the catalog that had to be finalized by January third.

Impatience beat against the back of his throat, but Wes clenched his phone in his hand so he wouldn't call his brother again.

Gray, the brother that sat between Wes and Colton, had said he was in Wyoming, at a place called Whiskey Mountain Lodge, and all Wes could think about was what his life would be like if he allowed himself to drink.

He didn't, because his mother would be horrified, and his father would disown him. Bad things happened when people got drunk, and the last name of Hammond was simply too high-profile for Wes to even take a sip of alcohol. He didn't mind all that much, because he liked being the only businessman in the group with all his wits about him. He'd managed to get several lucrative deals because he'd been present while someone else was hungover.

His phone rang, and he checked to make sure it was Colton as he raised it to his ear. "Exactly five minutes."

"They were just sitting down to dinner," Colton said. "And there are a ton of people here, and if I don't get anything to eat because of this call, I'm going to send a curse to that office of yours."

Wes burst out laughing, because Colton meant every word of the threat he'd just issued. Thankfully, Colton chuckled too, but Wes knew better than to stand between the man and his dinner.

"I'll be quick," he said. "When will you be back?"

"I'm not sure," Colton answered, calm and confident, as always.

"I have projects that need your stamp of approval."

"Kacey said she was going to email me everything." Colton wore a frown in his voice. "Wes." He blew out his breath. "I don't know if I'm coming back."

"What?" Wes laughed again, but Colton didn't join in this time. "Dear Lord, you're serious." He immediately sent up another prayer that the Lord would please, please, *please* help Colton see that he was needed here. Wanted and needed, no matter what Priscilla had done.

"Yes," Colton said. "I'm serious."

"Dad and David want me to run for governor," Wes blurted, all the panic and anxiety he'd been holding in exploding out with the words.

"Wow." Colton let out his breath slowly, ending the exhale with a whistle. "Well, we knew that was going to happen."

"In five years," Wes said. "I don't want to run for governor right now."

"Stacey is a weak candidate," Colton said, and Wes had already been over all of this with his father and the public relations director at HMC. "That's why they want you to step in now."

"Yeah," Wes said. "The timing is right, they said. We could sweep the primaries and basically have no competition all the way to the seat." He sighed, wondering why he'd never aspired to anything political.

He loved running the multi-billion-dollar company his great-grandfather had founded and grown. Then his grandfather had brought them into the twentieth century with sophistication and billions more in profit.

His father had survived the changes in technology, invested in all the right things, and retired to leave Hammond Manufacturing Company in Wesley's hands, poised to make them the largest producer of dozens of products in the twenty-first century.

Wes liked that work. He liked pushing himself to meet ridiculous goals and raise the bar ever higher. But he'd never wanted to be governor.

It had been David Pointe who'd first come up with the idea, about three years ago, and Wes had gone along with it, because the possibility of it actually happening had felt far off in the future.

But the future was here now.

"So just say no. Cite them some number or data fact about how the company can't survive without you, or outline whatever project you're right in the middle of." Colton made such a thing sound so easy.

Wes knew it would not be as easy as simply texting, *You know what? I don't want to run for governor. Thanks for the offer.*

He'd have to handle this delicately, though his first thought had been to jump in his truck and follow Colton right out of town.

"I don't know," Wes said, and something scuffled on Colton's end of the line. He said something to someone else, and a loud clunk almost broke Wes's eardrum.

"Sorry, sorry," Colton said. "Listen, can you talk to Bree for a second?"

"What?" Wes said. "Who's Bree?"

"Um, hi," a woman said, and Wes's annoyance sang like a bird. "Colton had to run after—he had to take care of something real quick."

Well, Wes wasn't thirteen, when he'd used to like to talk to random girls on the phone. His memory flashed to a time when he, Gray, and Colton had all been home alone while their mother was out with the younger boys, and Gray had called a girl he liked. They'd all talked to her, and since Wes was the oldest— and three years older than Gray—he'd asked Marta out.

Yeah, that hadn't gone well at all.

"Where are you guys?" Wes asked, thinking he could at least get some information out of this woman.

"Whiskey Mountain Lodge," she said. "It's been snowing for hours and hours."

"Yeah, I think we're supposed to get that storm tomorrow," Wes said, realizing how fruitless his attempt to get Colton home really was. He gazed out the window at the gray sky in the west, kicking himself for talking about the weather. The *weather*.

This was what his life had come to—talking about the weather on the phone with a stranger.

Maybe he *should* run for governor.

"Anyway," Bree said. "We think we'll be able to start digging out tomorrow. Where are you? Somewhere warm, I hope."

"Denver," he said. "How well do you know Colton?" His suspicions fired, and he couldn't help it. Everyone wanted something from Wesley Hammond, and perhaps this Bree woman was a reporter who'd followed Colton as he'd left town.

"I just met him yesterday," Bree said, trilling out a high-pitched laugh afterward. She had a good vibe in her voice, and Wes found his shoulders relaxing. "He showed up at the lodge just before the snow hit, and we served him cake and dinner and somehow got him to stay."

"That is amazing," Wes said, though he would never air his brother's dirty laundry. "Tell me about this lodge."

Bree started to talk about the thirteen rooms at the lodge, and how she was the activities director, and she planned "amazing hikes" into the foothills of the Grand Tetons, and horseback riding, and archery.

"Horseback riding?" Wes asked, trying to remember the last time he'd been out to Ivory Peaks to ride a horse—or see his parents and grandmother.

"We have seventeen horses here now," Bree said, and she sounded a bit like a brochure. "You should come, Wesley."

He chuckled, thinking it had been a very long time since he'd put on a cowboy hat and spent an afternoon in the mountain sunshine. And he needed that escape. Maybe then he'd know what to do about this governor's race.

"Oh, Colton's back. Here he is. It was nice talking to you, Wesley."

"You too," he said, but Colton said, "Sorry," over him, so Bree was already gone.

"Whiskey Mountain Lodge, huh?" Wes asked.

Colton groaned, and Wes chuckled. "Don't worry," he said. "I won't come up there and crash your party."

"You know what?" Colton asked. "You should. It's a great place, and it's relaxing, and you'd like it."

"I'm sure I would." Wes didn't say the things streaming through his mind. As the CEO, he didn't get to just jaunt off to Wyoming for an afternoon of horseback riding. As the oldest brother, he carried more responsibility than Colton.

"Anyway," Wes said. "I guess I just needed to find out when you'd be back."

"I don't know that," Colton said. "I can approve stuff via email. I'll talk to Kacey and find out where the break-down happened."

"Just don't leave me hanging."

"I won't," Colton said. "And Wes, seriously, you do a ton of stuff you don't want to do. Running for governor isn't a little thing. It's not something you can call off if you ultimately decide you don't want to do it."

And Wes knew why he'd called Colton. "You're right," he said. "Thanks, brother."

"Anytime," Colton said. "Except for dinnertime, bro. Aren't you ready to eat?"

Wes laughed, though he nodded. "Yeah, I suppose it's time for dinner."

"Past time, Wes. Go eat. *Text* me later if you need to."

"Have fun with Bree," Wes said, but Colton just laughed and hung up. Wes sighed as he twisted and tossed his phone on the desk behind him. The sky settled deeper and deeper into darkness as Wes's thoughts went round and round and round....

And he hadn't even told Colton about the cousins who wanted to take over the company, and how seriously Wes was considering letting them.

CHAPTER 9

Foolishness filled Annie from head to toe, and she couldn't get herself to leave the bedroom she was sharing with her daughters. She'd felt so much in the past hour, but the worst thing of all was how out of control she felt. How immature.

Jealousy had flowed through her when she'd seen Colton and Bree chatting in the hall just outside the kitchen. She'd interrupted them just so she could hear what they were talking about.

Colton had left while Celia explained the food, and Bree had scampered off after him. Annie really thought something was going on, and she'd ducked out right after the prayer to see where they'd gone.

It's nothing, Annie.

She heard those words in Colton's voice after she'd found him and Bree on the front steps. He'd been on the phone, and he'd practically shoved it at Bree and followed her downstairs as she'd fled from him.

Literally, she'd run away from him.

And he'd followed.

Annie drew in a slow, deep breath through her nose, thinking of the confrontation that had happened in the living room only steps outside of her bedroom.

"Can you wait?" he'd said, and she'd spun back to him.

"If you like Bree, it's fine."

"What? I don't like Bree. I mean, I like Bree, but it's...." He'd never said what it was, and Annie's heart beat irregularly just thinking about it.

"Listen," he said. "If you saw something between Bree and me, it was just friendly."

"Okay," Annie had said, and she knew Colton could see that what she wanted between the two of them was more than friendly.

And that was when the foolishness had started. He'd said he needed to talk to his brother, and he'd gone back upstairs, tossing her a small smile from the landing before turning and leaving her in the basement.

Annie had waited until her heartbeat had evened out, and then she'd gone upstairs too. Dinner had started by then, and she'd been able to blend into the crowd. Bree had come in before Colton, and he'd integrated himself into the crowd without a big scene.

She'd escaped the moment she'd finished eating, despite Laney announcing that the four Whittaker brothers were going to have their ice cream making contest that night, and a winner would be chosen by anyone who tasted all four concoctions.

Annie normally loved the cooking contests at the lodge, and she didn't hide out in her room. She drank in the energy, cheered for everyone, and usually tasted everything but rarely voted.

"Mom," Eden said, poking her head into the bedroom. "They're trying to set up some tables on the landing, but the closet is locked."

"I'll come," Annie said. She turned back to her purse and fished out her keys for the lodge. She followed Eden upstairs to the main level and then to the second one. The storage closet in the hall opened easily with her key, and she stepped out of the way as Vi and her husband Todd rounded the corner.

"Thanks, Annie," Todd said with a smile. "We're going to set up a puzzle at the end of the landing."

"And Colton wanted a table for cribbage," Vi said, almost smiling afterward. Annie wanted to return the smile, but something had frozen inside her with the words "Colton" and "cribbage."

Todd slipped by her and pulled out a table, taking it around the corner. "Just around the corner," he said, and Colton appeared there. He froze, his eyes locked onto Annie's, and her heart did a full spin and then stopped in her chest.

"They said we could put a table up here," he said, moving toward her and adjusting his cowboy hat. She followed the movement, trying not to think how the whiteness of it cast a reflection into his eyes.

But she did think it, and she couldn't make her mind *not* think he was the most handsome man she'd ever laid eyes on.

Vi left, and Annie had no buffer between her and Colton. "You can," she said.

"You'll still play with me, right?" he asked, pausing and peering into the closet.

"If you want." Annie knew she sounded cool, but she couldn't help it.

"I do," he said, edging past her and pulling out another table. "Do you have the game?"

"It's in the closet downstairs," she said. "I'll go get it if you'll get the table and chairs ready." She walked away without waiting for him to answer, and Annie honestly wondered how she'd managed to get married the first time.

Everything between her and Colton felt ten shades of awkward, and she knew it was because of her. Forty-six-years-old and acting like a complete fool. She shook her head as she went down the stairs, and she determined that this game of cribbage would clear the air between them.

She collected the game and climbed the steps again. Colton

unfolded the second chair, and he'd placed them so neither had to sit with their back to the railing.

"Annie," a little girl said as she came down the hall. Annie paused and grinned down at Chrissy, Andrew and Becca's little girl.

"What's going on?" She glanced down the hall as Averie came running toward her too. She crouched down and hugged the two little girls; Chrissy, who was five, and Averie, who'd just turned six. "Ooh, you girls smell good. Did you get baths?"

"My mom has perfume," Averie said, and a quiet alarm went off in Annie's head.

"Oh, I see." She smiled at the girls. "Did you ask your mom if you could use it?"

The two little girls exchanged a glance, and Annie had her answer. She never quite knew what to do in a situation like this. These weren't her children or grandchildren. But she'd been a young mother once, and if her children had been in her perfume or makeup, she would've wanted to know.

"Maybe you should go tell your mom," Colton said, and Annie looked up at him.

"Okay," Averie said, though she didn't look happy about it. She took Chrissy's hand, and they went down the steps.

Colton extended his hand toward her, and Annie let him pull her back to standing. "Thanks," she said, a zing shooting up to her elbow from his touch. "Sometimes I forget I'm not as young as I once was."

Colton barely cracked a smile, and Annie wanted to know why. "Do you ever smile?" she asked.

"When I have a reason." He turned and went to the table.

Annie picked up the cribbage board and followed him, her nerves rattling through her veins as she walked. She sat down in the chair facing the steps and looked at him. "I told you about my husband."

Colton gazed evenly at her. "And?"

"And I like you," Annie said, her throat closing in on itself.

"And I don't know, maybe you don't like me, or you're just… closed off." She lifted her chin, almost challenging him. "You feel like you have walls up, and I'm wondering what they're about."

She turned the board over and slid open the compartment to get out the pegs. Then the next one where the deck of cards was kept. During that, Colton said nothing. Annie felt him watching her, but she didn't look at him.

"What if I'm not ready to share that with you?"

Annie glanced at him, her eye skating past his face. "Okay, yeah. That's okay." She righted the board and stuck the pegs in the start. "Do you know how to play cribbage?"

"No, ma'am."

She paused again, because she definitely felt a flirty vibe coming from across the table. When she looked at Colton, though, he still hadn't allowed himself to smile. Not even a little bit. He definitely had something deep and dark and dangerous inside him, and Annie's curiosity burned through her.

But she'd already asked, and she wasn't going to do it again.

Annie started explaining how she'd deal, and what they needed to count, and Colton wore a look like she was speaking a different language. "Let's just start," she said with a smile. "You'll pick it up." She dealt six cards and picked up her hand. "You choose two to put in the crib."

"Any two?" He looked at his cards like they might bite him.

"Yep."

He laid two cards away, and Annie cut the deck and laid a card on top. She tried to walk him through every play, but about ten minutes in, Annie burst into giggles and laid her cards down. "I don't think cribbage is going to be your game."

Colton sighed and laid his hand down too. "Thank goodness."

She laughed, and she even got Colton to crack a smile.

"Ah, there it is," she said, grinning at him. Clearly flirting with him. She thought she could see a spark in his eyes, but he extinguished it so quickly, she wasn't sure.

A call of "Ice cream is almost done," came from downstairs, and Annie stood up.

"Feeling like ice cream?" she asked.

He picked up his phone and looked at it before standing too. "Yeah, I just need to call my assistant first." He barely glanced at her before turning and walking away.

Annie watched him go, a sting moving through her chest. He paused at the top of the steps and turned back to her, a half a smile on his face. He reached up and touched two fingers to the brim of his hat, expanded that grin, and started down the steps.

Annie fell back into her chair, because that man's smile had the power to knock a woman backward.

She felt redeemed after acting like a fool in front of Colton. "Thank you, Lord," she whispered. "And if possible, could You help him break down his walls?"

Maybe Annie was asking too much of the Lord in that regard, but she did want to get to know Colton better, and she felt like she'd never be able to without some divine help.

CHAPTER 10

Colton retreated to the basement, fully intending to call Kacey and find out about the things Wes needed him to approve. He knew intellectually that he couldn't leave HMC forever. At the same time, he wondered if he could.

He had all the right contacts for the job, and until he'd been stood up at his own wedding, Colton had enjoyed his job a whole lot. His home away from home had been on the twenty-fourth floor of the HMC building. He'd pulled many an all-nighter there, but the thought of going back had every defense in him firing.

He'd run from Denver and Ivory Peaks, hoping for some rest and relaxation. Some time to find himself. But Annie already knew who she was, and she wanted Colton to talk to her. He really didn't like talking.

Fine, he liked it when he didn't have to do any of the sharing. He wasn't even sure he'd said out loud to anyone that he'd been left standing at the altar in the deepest, darkest, blackest tuxedo money could buy.

He turned toward the mirror in the room and opened his mouth. "See, here's the thing...." But the right words didn't come.

Sighing, he lifted his phone and tapped to dial Kacey. Though it was after dinner, and she wouldn't be sitting at her desk outside his office, she still answered on the second ring. "Colton," she said. "I've been trying to call you for two days."

"I haven't gotten a call," he said. "The reception must be bad here."

"We've got a couple of things to go over."

"Lay 'em out for me," he said, reaching for his laptop backpack and pulling out his computer for the first time since he'd left town. He wasn't even sure if this place had Wi-Fi, but he imagined they did. They claimed to be a luxury lodge, after all.

"First, we have the spring catalog," Kacey said, and Colton bit back his irritation. He did not care about the spring catalog, though he'd literally combed through every page of previous catalogs. He listened to Kacey detail the pages she had concerns about, and Colton promised he'd get back to her no later than tomorrow night.

"The graphic designer came back with four designs for the new company logo," she continued. "Wes and Gray have marked their favorite two, and they're waiting on you, sure you'll be the one to break the tie."

"Oh, I see that email," Colton said, as he'd finally gotten his computer up and connected to the Internet. "I can do this in the next five minutes." One minute really, as he'd spent plenty of time in meetings with his brothers about the new face of Hammond Manufacturing Company to move them into the future.

He'd been the one to send the concept notes over to the graphic design company they'd hired, and he clicked to download the zipped file so he could see his choices. "I won't keep you," Colton said as the download circle spun. "Thanks, Kacey. I'll go through my email and get you everything you need."

"Thanks."

"I didn't mean to leave you to Wesley the Wolf."

Kacey laughed, and Colton smiled thinking about the blonde

who kept everything straight for him. "Please," she said. "I can handle Wes." And she could. Colton had seen her put his brother in his place a couple of times, despite Wes being the CEO of the entire family-owned operation.

Colton allowed himself to chuckle. "Yes, you can."

"Okay," she said. "I won't bother you until after the holidays unless it's an emergency."

"Looks like email is going to be the best way to get me," Colton said. "I honestly didn't get any calls."

"Email it is," she said, and Colton let her end the call so he could click on the freshly downloaded zip file. The folder came up, and he double-clicked to get the images open. All four popped up, and he dismissed the first one in the corner immediately. It had way too much blue in it, though he'd specifically said the logo must have blue.

They all did, and he gravitated toward the green and gray one, with the navy something he liked a whole lot. But the one with a sort of reddish-magenta, with a deep, ocean blue, and hints of yellow was nice too.

Wes would like that one the best, Colton knew. He liked the font on the HMC, as it looked a bit more abstract with all the straight lines in the H and the M, with the C around them both—and the fact that it said family-owned underneath it.

Gray had definitely chosen the green and gray and navy one, because he liked blocky letters more than an abstract concept, and Gray was more of a straight-shooter when it came to everything. He'd gone to law school and returned to the company to be the corporate lawyer, doing a bang-up job for the past nineteen years. He knew more than anyone Colton knew, and he wouldn't want anything too frilly.

Not that the more abstract design was frilly. Hammond Manufacturing wasn't frilly—another specification delivered to the graphic design team. They made plastics and electronics, pharmaceuticals and components for aircrafts that flew across the globe.

Colton sided with Gray on this one, and he sent his choice to Kacey, checking the time on his phone. He'd been down in the bedroom for fifteen minutes, and with the size of the crowd at Whiskey Mountain Lodge, the ice cream could be gone by now.

Part of him wanted it to be. The other part didn't want to leave Annie hanging like that. He'd definitely felt something between them.

Had he felt something *for* her?

Colton wasn't in the habit of lying to himself, so he nodded and said, "Yeah, you felt something for her." Especially when she'd thought he and Bree were starting something romantic behind her back. He'd managed to put that fire out, and he wanted to kindle a different kind of spark between him and Annie.

He took his cowboy hat off and smoothed his hair back. Suddenly feeling self-conscious, he hurried into the bathroom to brush his teeth, noticing how much more gray he had growing in his beard and on his head now. He wasn't sure if that had increased since Priscilla's departure from his life almost seven weeks ago. He just knew he looked older than he remembered.

He looked tired.

He brushed his teeth while the water heated, and then he washed his face with a warm washcloth. With his cowboy hat back in place, Colton went upstairs, feeling like he might be able to say something to Annie that would make her happy.

He pulled back on the thought, because he didn't want to do things only to make her happy. He needed to be happy too, and he decided to just play it by ear.

He stepped into the hallway at the top of the steps, the chatter coming from the kitchen echoing toward him. He'd never thought he'd want to be around so many people, but he actually found it somewhat comforting. It reminded him that while he wasn't with family, he wasn't alone. He realized in that moment that what Bree had said during his first meal with the Whittakers was true.

When you work for the Whittakers, you become a Whittaker.

He didn't work for them, but he definitely felt like they'd be glad to see him when he walked in the kitchen. He did, and no less than three men leapt from their chairs. "Yes," Graham said. "Colton's here."

"Don't influence him," another—Beau—said. "Hey, Colton." He smiled while the third brother had to come around the table.

"Neither of you even blink," Eli said. "You're such cheaters." He joined his brothers, the fourth—Andrew—getting up much slower. He held a baby boy in his arms, and he definitely seemed the least threatening.

"We have a tie," Graham said. "And we need just one more taste-tester. Whichever ice cream you choose will win." He grinned, though an anxiousness existed in his expression too.

"I don't know if I can handle the pressure." Colton grinned back at them, this formidable wall of cowboys who had somehow found women who came to the altar and formed families.

Maybe Colton had given up on women too soon.

"Too late," Annie said, stepping through the wall of cowboys with a tray in her hands. He met her eye, cemented his smile in place, and then looked at the four small glass bowls on the tray, each featuring a different flavor of ice cream.

Beau suddenly had four different spoons, and Colton realized he wasn't going to get a relaxing evening at the table eating as much ice cream as he wanted. He took a spoon and dipped it into the chocolate bowl.

He tasted coconut, and chocolate, and something else that made his mouth rejoice. "That's good," he said.

An uproar filled the kitchen, and Colton actually took a step back.

"You don't say anything," Annie said, grinning at him with more flirtatiousness in her gaze than he'd seen from any woman for a long, long time.

"I can't say anything?"

"No," several people said.

"It's a tie-breaker," someone added, and Colton wanted to say he'd missed the explanation of the rules.

"You taste," Annie said. "Take your time. Then you can proclaim a winner."

He took another bite of the chocolate ice cream, because it was good, and Colton didn't want just four bites.

"Oh, he's liking the chocolate," Eli said, his grin widening.

"I think you all need to go sit down," Celia said, stepping between Colton and the cowboys. Also, she blocked the ice cream. "Now."

"Fine," Graham said, nudging the brother closest to him. But none of them moved.

"Let's go in the living room," Annie said, stepping around Celia. "You keep them here."

"Wait a second," Beau protested, but Celia acted as a bouncer, and she did not let them by. Colton chuckled as he followed Annie into the living room.

"Are they always like this?"

"When there's a title at stake, yes."

"There's a title?"

"And a trophy." Annie laughed as she handed him the tray with the ice cream so she could collect a TV tray for him. "Stockton and Bailey made it, and you should've seen those men's faces when it was a tie."

"I honestly don't know if I can handle this pressure."

Annie set up his tray and gave him a sly smirk before she took the ice cream back from him. "You can. Sit."

Colton sat, finding her strong and sexy as she stood in front of him. When he let go of his reservations and unlocked the doors he'd built around his heart...maybe he could allow another woman into his life.

He pulled the TV tray closer to him and picked up another spoon, this time diving into the white ice cream. He became aware of the audience he'd drawn, though they'd congregated in the doorway and hadn't come all the way into the room. None of them were the Whittaker brothers though.

"Oh," he said when he found the flavor to be toasty, warm marshmallow, with a hint of something spicy beneath it. He ate that whole bowl, liking it more and more with every bite.

He ate the third bowl too, which had mint, chocolate, and pine nuts, all things he loved. The fourth bowl also had a chocolate base, but this one had peanut butter and the hint of raspberry jelly. Colton had never eaten chocolate and peanut butter together and not fallen in love, and he wanted more of that one right now.

And that was his answer. "That one," he said, tapping the bowl that had the PB&J—with chocolate. "It's amazing."

A cheer went up from a few people, and he heard footsteps running back into the kitchen, where someone said, "He chose Beau's!"

Cheers and boos filled the air, and Annie said, "Let's get back in there to see the trophy awarded."

He stood and followed her, arriving in the kitchen just as two teenagers lifted a tall structure made of mostly egg cartons and empty aluminum cans. Colton recognized a crude rendition of an ice cream cone at the top, and they presented it to Beau, who lifted it above his head and shook it while he bellowed.

Colton had never seen anything like it, and while the other Whittaker brothers looked at him and shook their heads, in the end they clapped and grinned too. They even went up and hugged Beau like they were really happy for him.

Colton inched closer to Annie and touched her hand with his. She flinched, but he held on tight and leaned down. "Can I have more of that chocolate ice cream?"

She giggled and nodded. "I'll get it for you. Which one?"

"Both of them," he said. "Whose was the other one?"

"Eli's," Annie said. "I voted for his." She squeezed his hand and went into the other side of the kitchen to get his ice cream, and they retreated to the living room again. Several other people did too, including the two girls he'd seen her with throughout the day.

"Colton," she said as they sat nearby. "These are my daughters. Emily is the oldest. Eden is the youngest." She beamed at them, and they smiled at her too.

"Nice to meet you," he said. "I'm right in the middle of my family."

"How many siblings?" Emily asked easily.

"Five boys," he said. "Third in line. I was always the swing vote, so you'd think I'd be used to what just happened, but nope." He put another spoonful of ice cream in his mouth.

"What do you do?" Emily asked, and Colton had a suspicion that her mother had put her up to asking all these questions. Annie sure was sitting silently beside him on the couch, and she just watched him.

"I'm the executive marketing director for my family company." Before she could ask him something else, he asked her, "What do you do?"

"I do all the accounting and bookkeeping for Mom's business."

"Oh?" Colton switched his gaze to Annie. "What business is that?"

"I own a cleaning company," she said. "It's called Swept Away. We all work it together. It's a family company."

Colton knew it wasn't as big as his family company, but he was impressed anyway. "That's great."

Thankfully, a phone rang, and Emily jumped to her feet. "It's Kelly." She hurried away, leaving Eden there with Annie and Colton. He wasn't sure what happened next, but he looked down for more ice cream, and Eden got up too. "I'm going to go take a shower." She left too, and Colton looked to the little kids sitting on the other couch, all of them piled around a device one of them held.

Colton smiled looking at them, because this was the kind of situation he wanted. None of his brothers had gotten married for good yet, though Gray and Cy had both been to the altar before. Cy's marriage hadn't lasted very long, and he had no kids.

But Gray had been married for five years, and he had a ten-year-old son who lived with him full-time. His wife had left town in the middle of the day one day, and Gray hadn't found out until the principal at Hunter's school had called to see who was supposed to pick the child up.

Gray had picked him up, and then tried to pick up the pieces of his life too, putting them all back together into a new life where he was a single dad, a corporate lawyer, a good son, and the best brother of them all.

Colton could learn something from Gray, that was for sure. With his ice cream finished, and no audience for his conversation with Annie, he looked at her and said, "My fiancée left me standing at the altar about seven weeks ago. That's why I have a lot of walls up right now."

CHAPTER 11

Annie looked at him, blinking as she absorbed what he'd just said. A quick glance toward the doorway revealed that no one stood there watching, and she reached over and took Colton's hand in hers. "Wow. I'm so sorry."

He nodded, the brim of his hat moving up and down. He kept his eyes and chin down, and she couldn't see his face.

"I wanted to apologize," she said.

That got him to look up, and their eyes met. Sparks flew through her chest, and she hoped he couldn't tell how handsome she thought he was.

"For what?"

"Pushing you," she said, humiliation streaming through her. "I'm not normally like that, and you've literally been here for twenty-four hours."

"Well, I'm pretty sure I got here before dinner last night," he said with a sexy smile. Annie knew he'd be downright devastating with that exact grin on his face. She pulled it into her memory, so she could picture him while she fell asleep at night. "So it's been more than twenty-four hours."

Annie knew she'd have to explain to her daughters about Colton, but she found she didn't care. When Emily had left,

Annie had nudged Eden to go too, and thankfully her youngest had gotten the hint. A yawn pulled through her, and she didn't want anyone to see her sitting there holding Colton's hand.

So she said, "I'm exhausted. I'm going to head to bed."

"Hopefully we won't have to babysit any fireplaces tonight," he said.

"If the furnace goes out," Annie said. "I'm calling Graham." She gave a light laugh, let go of his hand, and stood up.

He joined her, and said, "I've got a bit of work to do before I can go to bed. What time is breakfast?"

"Usually eight," Annie said. "But really, you can get food whenever."

"I hope so," he said. "Because I'm not going to make up here by eight."

Annie led him downstairs, and she stepped to her door and knocked while Colton went past.

"It's open," Eden called, and Annie went inside without looking at Colton. She could do it. She wasn't fifteen, or even twenty-five.

Or even thirty-five, she told herself. Another hint of foolishness threaded through her as she stepped inside and closed the door. Both of her daughters faced her, their eyes full of questions.

"I'm sleeping until I wake up," Annie said. "No alarms." She turned toward the door and added, "I have to use the bathroom. Be right back," hoping that would be it before she went to bed.

"You're telling us about him," Emily called after her as Annie closed the door. She hurried next door to the bathroom and pressed into the door behind her, a sigh moving through her body, accompanied by a fair amount of giddiness.

Once those emotions passed, Annie could face them. She didn't want to admit that her heart had run away from her already, but it kind of had. So she pressed on the brake, and she'd pull back a little bit. She didn't need to push Colton into a corner he didn't want to be in, and he'd just been through a terrible trauma.

She'd had years and years to heal after her husband's death. He'd had seven weeks. "*Almost* seven weeks," Annie reminded herself. She washed her face as she thought about him and what his plans for his life moving forward were. He hadn't said and while Annie wanted to know, she wasn't going to ask. Oh, no, she was not.

She racked her memory for what he'd said last night when he'd arrived, but she couldn't remember. The older she got, the less her brain could retain, and she'd simply have to take one day at a time. He wasn't going to leave the lodge tomorrow.

She finally returned to the room, unable to hide from her daughters for long. They both lay in bed, looking at their phones, and Annie peeled back her own covers. Eden put her phone down with a clunk and said, "Start talking."

"He's handsome," Annie said. "And close to my age. And I like him, and maybe we've been flirting."

"More than maybe," Emily said, still swiping on her phone.

"Yeah, Mom, you kicked me in the back to get me to leave."

"I *nudged* you," Annie said. "And thank you for getting the hint." She climbed into bed and pulled the blankets over her.

"Are you going to date him?" Emily asked, sitting up and looking at Annie.

Annie saw the worry in her daughter's eyes. "I don't know. I'm not sure how long he'll be here. I just know he's the most interesting man I've met in a long time, and we're getting to know each other."

"Good for you, Mom," Eden said. She'd always had an easier time with the men Annie dated. For some reason, Emily felt responsible for making sure whoever Annie went out with wasn't leading a dangerous life. Or something.

"He's a marketing something-or-other," she told Em. "The most dangerous thing he probably does is drive to work."

Emily nodded, gave her mother a small smile, and laid back down. "No alarms," she said. "And let's pray that the furnace stays pumping all night long."

"Will you say a prayer?" Annie asked. "We can stay in bed."

"Sure," Em said, and she waited a couple of seconds before beginning, giving the others time to close their eyes and be ready. "Lord, we thank Thee for this Christmas season, where we can celebrate the birth of Thy Son. Bless us to be safe. Bless us to be kind. Bless us to get along with all of those around us. Bless Mom that she can have a clear head when it comes to Colton. Bless Kelly that he can arrive safely on Christmas Eve."

She went on to offer gratitude for the blessings they had, and Annie smiled all the way to the end. "Thank you," she said, reaching over to snap off her lamp. She loved it when her daughters prayed for her, and she did need the blessing of a clear mind when it came to Colton. She was grateful for all the Lord had given her over the years.

She closed her eyes, that smile of Colton's dancing through her mind the way sugarplums did in the famous Christmas poem, and fell quickly to sleep.

———

THE NEXT DAY, ANNIE WOKE FEELING LIKE SHE'D CAUGHT UP ON THE sleep she'd missed the night before. Neither of the girls lay in the bed next to hers, and she sat up, somewhat surprised. Her phone said nine o'clock had just come and gone, and Annie couldn't believe it.

She dressed quickly and went upstairs to get a cup of coffee and see what she could find for breakfast. The kitchen was the hub of the house, and at least half a dozen people milled about, coffee mugs in front of them as they chatted and finished feeding their children.

"Morning," a few people chorused to her, and she said the same back to them.

She poured herself a cup of coffee and spied a couple of pans of breakfast casserole sitting on the stovetop. She served herself and took a seat at the table to eat.

"Are you going out to get the tree?" Lily asked, reaching to help Charlie down from his chair. "Stay upstairs, bud," she said to him before looking at Annie.

"No," she said. "I'll stay here and help with lunch or pull decorations out of storage."

"Would you mind watching Charlie if Beau and I go?"

"Of course not." Annie smiled at her, glad she'd have someone to keep her entertained. She'd always wanted grand-children, though her daughters were still young.

"I think Andrew and Becca wanted to go too, but they were going to ask Amanda to help with their kids."

"I'm sure we can manage all the kids if they're left here," Annie said. "I'll make white chocolate popcorn and put a movie on in the theater room. Done." She took a bite of eggs and sausage, so grateful Celia kept them all fed here at the lodge.

Lily put her arm around Annie's shoulders and squeezed. "Thanks, Annie. You're the best." She stood up and reached for Charlie. "Come on, bud. Let's go find Daddy and see what time they're going to get the tree."

Annie glanced at Rose and Vi, who both sat by their kids, making sure they all got enough to eat. She wanted to ask if they'd seen her girls or Colton, but she didn't.

As if drawn by her thoughts, Colton entered the kitchen, with Bree right beside him. He was smiling at her, and Annie's jeal-ousy reared instantly. Her mouth turned dry as she watched the two of them together, despite the reassurances from both of them that they were just becoming friends.

"There you are," Bree said. "Did you sleep well?"

"Yes," Annie said with a smile. "Have you seen Em or Eden?"

"They went out to help dig out the sidewalks and cars." Bree exhaled as she sat down. "Colton and I just got back from doing the sidewalks out to Patsy's and Sophia's, and Graham has the tractor to clear the path for me and Elise."

Annie nodded, because she'd learned over her lifetime of

living in Wyoming that shoveling snow came with the territory. Today, she was glad she had all these big, strong cowboys to dig them out from underneath what Mother Nature had dumped on them for the past couple of days.

"Are you going to go pick out the tree?" Bree asked as Colton sat on the other side of Annie with a fresh cup of coffee.

"No," Annie said. "I'm staying here to babysit some of the little kids so their parents can go." She glanced at Colton. "We'll have to wait until later to try cribbage again." She gave him what she hoped was a flirty smile.

"Oh, I'm not doing that again," he said. "It's literally the most confusing game in the world."

"We didn't even make it through one game."

"That's because it's too confusing." He kicked at grin in her direction and added, "We should raid the pantry here until we find a bag of chips and then put a movie on."

"There's a movie later today," Bree said. "It's at four-ten." She tapped on her phone. "There are still some slots for tree decorating. And let's see…Celia is doing a kid's cooking class just before dinner, which is pot roast and baked potatoes." She glanced up at Annie and Colton. "There's always games and whatnot, and I think the weather is nice enough for snow-shoeing."

"I'm not a hugely outdoor person," Annie said.

"You're not?" Colton asked. "I love being outside in the mountains."

"In the winter?" Annie cocked her eyebrows at him.

"Definitely more in the summer."

Annie finished breakfast and got up to put her dishes in the dishwasher. Patsy came over the speaker system and said, "Anyone who would like to go pick out the Christmas tree, please meet in the front circle drive."

The activity in the house increased, and Amanda and Finn came into the living room, grouping kids onto the couches.

"You're sure?" Rose asked. "There's three of them."

"We can handle it," Amanda said, glancing at Annie. "Annie's here, and Celia, and Patsy."

"They're naughty."

"Oh, go on," Annie said, picking up one of the boys who was trying to get off the couch. "They're fine." The two-year-old in her arms started to cry and reach for Rose, whose face fell. "Just go," she said. "He's fine."

Rose blew them all kisses, and she and Liam made a hasty exit.

"Come on," Amanda said. "I've got play dough, but you can only use it in the kitchen." She picked up another two-year old, and Finn did too. "Come on Daisy. Mary." The little girls slid off the couch and went with her, and Annie reached for Charlie.

"Come on, sweetheart. Do you want to play with play dough?"

"Yes," Charlie said, putting his hand in hers. Her heart melted, and she went into the kitchen, only to find Colton standing there.

"You didn't go to get the tree?" she asked, putting a still-sniffling Jackson in a highchair. "You want a cookie, baby?"

The little boy looked up at her, his eyes wide and hopeful. She smiled down at him. "I know where Celia keeps the cookies." She used a hushed voice, but Charlie still said, "I want a cookie, Aunt Annie."

"And you will get one," she said, beaming at him. "Get up in that chair, and I'll be right back." She stepped away from the table and rounded the counter into the area where all the cooking took place. She took out a box of animal cookies and handed them to Colton.

"You give them those, and these kids will do whatever you want."

"Oh, I see how you do it." He gave her a sparkling look and stepped over to the two little boys waiting at the table. He gave them each one cookie, and Amanda arrived with a chunk of green play dough for both of them.

"Don't eat the play dough," she told them. "Only the cookies."

"Grandma?"

Amanda turned toward Averie and Ronnie. "What, my sweets? We're doing play dough and cookies in here."

"Can we put a movie on in the big bedroom?" Ronnie asked.

"Of course."

"Can we have some cookies too?" Averie asked.

Colton didn't miss a beat as he stepped over to them and filled their six-year-old hands with cookies.

"Don't get those on the sheets," Amanda called after them. "Finn and I are sleeping in there."

"We won't," Ronnie yelled back to them.

Annie sat down next to Jackson and helped him make his dough into a circle and then a square. She liked talking to Amanda and Finn, and Colton didn't say much but he had a calming presence and when they took the littles downstairs to put on a movie, little Collin climbed right into his lap as if they'd known each other their whole lives.

Annie's heart softened toward him, and she caught him snuggling the little boy back too.

When their parents returned, so did the chaos, as it was also lunch time. She stayed in the basement as the children went with their parents, and when she and Colton were all that remained, she looked at him. "Thanks for helping."

"That was actually fun."

"You were great with them." She moved over and slipped her hand into his. "Do you want little children?" Because she couldn't give him little babies of his own, and maybe he wanted a woman who could.

"I haven't thought much about it."

"No?"

"I mean, I don't really have a lot of faith in marriage right now, so I haven't thought about kids." He spoke casually, as if he didn't realize what he'd just said.

But Annie heard him. And it sounded like Colton didn't want to get married. That he didn't want to commit to a woman.

Annie really didn't want to spend the rest of her life with just herself and her cleaning clients. She wanted another husband.

And Colton didn't believe in marriage, let alone have the desire to get married.

CHAPTER 12

Colton watched Annie recede right in front of him, and he wondered what he'd said. His stomach grumbled for food, though he'd had a few animal cookies too. "Should we go up to lunch?"

"You go," she said, removing her hand from his. "I'll be up in a minute." She flashed him a tight smile and headed toward the bathroom. The door clicked closed with a very final sound, and Colton stared after her.

He took a couple of hesitant steps toward the staircase, wondering if he was making a mistake by going. But she clearly didn't want to keep talking to him, so staying would definitely be a bad idea too.

Footsteps came down toward him, and Colton paused as a couple of teenagers thundered down to the landing and then jumped the last three steps to the basement.

"Sorry," the girl said, but she didn't stop. She continued into the theater room while the boy followed, saying something about how it wasn't fair she got to choose every time. Colton knew exactly how he felt, because Gray and Wes had always been bigger and faster than him. He never got the good tennis racquet, never got to pick the best water shoes, never had a plate of food first.

Colton smiled and shook his head as he went upstairs, the scent of spicy salsa hanging in the air. Mixed with that, a chill permeated the house, and a distinct earthy smell met his nose too.

"No, it has to go that way," a man said from the living room, while someone else said, "We're not eating until they have the tree set," from the kitchen.

Colton hardly knew which way to go, but he chose the living room, because it seemed like they wouldn't be eating until whatever was happening out there finished up. He made it through the doorway far enough to see people everywhere. Several clustered in front of the fireplace, watching, while a couple of cowboys stood on the stairs, holding the largest, tallest, and most beautiful pine tree Colton had ever seen—and he'd grown up in the Rocky Mountains.

"Back up, Andrew," Finn said, and the cowboy on the lowest stair did what he said. Eli, who stood a few steps up did too, and Zach moved sideways, as he stood on the walkway of the second floor, holding nearly the top of the tree.

Graham, Beau, Todd, and Liam worked at the base of the tree, adjusting something Colton couldn't see. A metallic sound filled the air as it scraped against the floor, and Graham groaned as he strained against it.

"Hold it there," he said, his voice full of urgency.

"Should Zach lift it?" Beau asked.

"Yes," Graham said. "I can't get it."

"Up," Beau called, and Colton wondered how on Earth one man was going to lift that tree. It had to weight hundreds and hundreds of pounds, and there was just no way.

"Let me put the handles in better," Zach called, and he made some adjustment that Colton couldn't see.

Todd and Liam bent and if Colton thought he could get his broad shoulders under that tree to help lift it, he'd do it. Graham was already down there, and only Beau stayed standing while the other men positioned themselves.

"Ready," Zach called, and Beau counted down from three.

They all lifted, and to Colton's surprise, the tree moved. Graham flew into action, and another scuffling sound came before he said, "Okay, that's it."

The tree dropped, and Zach let out a huge sigh and shook his hands out.

"Tighten on that side, Liam," Graham said, and Beau turned to look at Finn.

"Is it straight?" he asked.

"Looks good," Finn said. "Hold it tight, boys."

A minute or two later, they all fell back from the tree, moving farther away until they could look all the way to the top of it.

"It's great," one of the country music sisters said.

"Best yet," Laney said.

"Definitely the biggest," Annie said, and Colton's attention flew to her. He hadn't noticed her come in, and he wondered what that meant. He knew he had more fear in his heart than excitement, and that it pulsed out of control because he felt like he'd done something wrong downstairs.

She was nothing like Priscilla, and Colton wondered if he was reacting to her with his wounded heart and not who he really was. And was that even fair to Annie?

"Is the tree done?" Celia asked, pressing into the room too. "Oh, you boys. It's amazing." She touched her palm to her heart, and in that moment, Colton felt like he'd come home.

Celia was so much like his mother, though she was probably a decade younger than the mom he'd left in Ivory Peaks. But Celia's emotions filled the massive space, and Colton also had a moment of pure peace.

He hadn't been to church in a while, but he liked how this family prayed over the meals, how they cared about each other, how competitive they were with each other. He liked that they seemed to have the Lord at the center of their lives, and he knew he was missing that in his.

"Okay," Bree said over the speaker system in the lodge. "Celia wants to serve lunch, and our first slot for decorating isn't until two, so let's move this party into the kitchen."

Colton wanted to eat, but he kind of wanted to stay in the living room with the feelings that existed there. In the end, he followed the others into the kitchen, sticking to the side out of the way.

"Where's Bailey?" Laney asked, reaching for her son's hand. "Have you seen her?"

"Just leave her," Graham said. "She's off with Stockton somewhere, and they've done nothing but argue today." He looked at Laney. "Let's enjoy lunch without them."

"Maybe we should separate them for a bit," she said. "We could go back to the house tonight to get a little distance."

Graham nodded as Celia called out, "Today we have taco-dillas. Some are beef, some are black bean—those are the vegetarian ones—and some have pork. There's chips and salsa, plenty of guacamole, and tortilla soup. The little kids can have plain cheese quesadillas, and those are on the sheet pan on the stove." She looked around at everyone and added, "I feel like I'm forgetting something."

"Let's eat," someone said, and Celia smiled.

"Yes, let's eat." She looked around. "Graham?"

"Finn's in charge of the prayers today," Graham said.

"Ronnie's gonna say it," Finn said, and Colton saw most eyes move to the little boy who stood near him.

The boy closed his eyes and opened his mouth, and the sweetest prayer came out of the child's mouth. Colton's emotions swelled and swelled, and he had the desire to flee before anyone saw that he was choked up.

"Amen," the boy said, and everyone chorused it through the house. Activity happened as the crowd surged forward. Colton went the opposite direction. He hadn't been outside yet today, but several others had, and he didn't want to go downstairs and get his coat.

He'd taken a couple of steps toward the back door, but someone came out of the other doorway leading out of the kitchen, and he plowed right into them.

"Oh, gosh," he said. "Sorry." He grabbed onto her, trying to find her name. She lived with Bree, but the name eluded him at the moment.

"Sorry," she said too. "I just…."

He released her, and she turned and went down the hall he'd been planning to go down. He followed her, because the air inside the lodge held too many scents and too many people.

When the door had closed behind both of them, he said, "I just needed some air. Can I be out here with you?"

"Yeah," she said. "Colton, right?"

"Yes," he said. "I don't remember your name, sorry."

"Elise," she said. She gathered her white-blonde hair into a ponytail and bound it with a rubber band. "I just get over-whelmed with so many people," she said.

"Don't you work here?" he asked.

"Yeah." She pushed out her breath, which wafted in the air in front of her in a white cloud for a moment. "It's different during the holidays, though. When guests stay here, they don't stay inside all day, and I spend a ton of my time working outdoors. I can't really do that in the winter."

"I just feel completely out of my element," Colton said.

"Oh, trust me," Elise said with a light laugh. "I totally know what you're feeling right now." She migrated to his side and they both gazed out at the winter landscape in front of them. The snow glinted in the sunlight, and it lay everywhere. On every branch, every roof, every square inch of Wyoming.

The air definitely held bite, but it couldn't sink its teeth into Colton's skin. "I love being outside too," he said. "There's just something about being able to *breathe* out here, you know?" He looked at her and found her nodding slowly.

"Where are you from?" she asked.

"Colorado," he said. "Big mountains there like here."

"I love the mountains."

"Are you from here?"

"No, I grew up in Prince Edward Island," she said, crossing her arms and pressing them tightly against her body. A half-laugh and half-scoff came out of her mouth. "I followed my boyfriend to Idaho, and then this side of the Tetons, only to have him fall in love with someone else."

"Oh, no," Colton said. "Well, trust me, I know what *that* feels like." He grinned at her, glad when her laugh became full, her nervous energy flying away into the sky.

"Men suck," she said, still giggling.

"Yeah, well, women suck too," he said, and he sensed in Elise a kindred soul. A little sister he'd never had.

"Not all of us," she said.

"And not all men." He nudged her with her elbow. "So did you just come out here because there are too many people inside? Or someone particular?"

"Well, all the men in there are married," she said. "So it's not one of them specifically." She sighed and drew in a big breath. "But my ex-boyfriend rode bulls like Todd, and every time I look at him, I see Brandt."

"That stinks." Colton would've slept in his truck in the snow if anyone in the lodge had reminded him of Priscilla. Hands down. And he'd have left this morning for sure. "So can I ask you a question?" he asked.

"You can," she said. "I don't know if I'll be able to answer it, but you can ask."

"So talk to me about Annie…."

Elise turned her bright green eyes to him. "That's not a question."

"I think I messed up with her, and I don't know how to fix it."

"Ah, I see." Elise focused on the tree line again. "Well, Annie is a straight shooter. She says things how they are, and she likes it when people do the same. So you just go to her, and you say, 'whatever I did, I'm sorry, and I think you're so pretty, and will you please tell me what it is so I can fix it?' And then she'll tell you, and then you'll fix it."

Colton burst out laughing, though he believed everything Elise had just said. "Wow," he said, chuckling. "You make it sound so easy."

"It is." She turned and patted his arm. "With women, Colton, it's just that easy." She smiled at him and added, "I'm headed back in. You take your time, and you'll see I'm right." She left him standing on the back patio, which had been cleared of snow, his mind arcing in a dozen different directions.

CHAPTER 13

E lise Murphy took one last breath of the fresh, Wyoming air before she went back into the lodge. What she hadn't told Colton was that not only did Todd remind her of her ex-boyfriend, but that he knew Brandt too.

Colton was easy to talk to though, and he gave off the air of an older brother, the way Malcolm, her real older brother did. He'd been thrown into the Whittaker family celebration, and Elise knew that wasn't very easy.

She'd almost quit—more than once—because she came from a family of three, and being around so many people really did induce levels of anxiety inside her that she couldn't deal with. There were more Whittaker brothers—just brothers—than she'd ever had to deal with, and they then had spouses and children and parents too.

She opened the door to a wall of warm air and loud talking. She wanted to walk right back out and go back to her quiet, solitary cabin out in the middle of a snowy field. Elise forced herself to stay, because she wanted to eat and help Patsy and Celia. She wanted to decorate the tree during her slot, and then she'd escape back to her cabin to call her mom to find out how the trip to Las Vegas had gone.

Her mom had recently started dating someone new, and Elise hadn't met him yet. His brother lived in Vegas, and they were going there for Christmas. She expected a picture at any moment from her mom, because they were so close.

Growing up, it had just been her mom, Malcolm, and Elise, and the three of them had relied on each other for so much and for so long. But Malcolm had gotten married last year, and somehow, that had given their mother permission to start dating too.

She pushed away her insecurities and rounded the corner to the kitchen. It wasn't as busy as she'd expected, and she took a beef taco-dilla, chips, and guacamole and even found a spot at the table. Thankfully, Todd wasn't there and the triplets were. Elise loved the little two-year-olds, because they had a ton of personality. Loud voices, sure, but a ton of spunk she just loved.

"Did you get chips?" she asked Clover, who looked up at her with the widest eyes the color of dark chocolate. She had the cutest chubby cheeks that Elise just wanted to pinch or poke. She grinned at the little girl, who held up a chip.

"Yep, you eat it," she said, pointing to her own plate. "I have my own chips."

Clover put the chip in her mouth, smiling soon after. Elise giggled at her and looked at the other people at the table. She knew she connected better to kids, even two-year-olds, but she didn't know what to do about it.

She told herself she was only thirty years old, and she had plenty of time to meet the right man. She *wanted* to meet him. She didn't get a lot of chances to meet men at the lodge, and she worked a lot.

She hoped he was out there, looking for her too. She knew that was probably too romantic, but she didn't want to let go of that idea. She liked the idea of two people exactly meant for each other, looking for that other person, and just knowing the moment they met them that they were The One.

She actually sighed at the table, and then she pulled herself together for long enough to eat lunch.

She'd just set her plate in the sink when someone yelled something from somewhere outside the kitchen. She spun around as she tried to make sense of what had been said.

Had it been help?

Elise's heart bounced in the back of her throat, because someone had definitely called for help.

Becca appeared in the kitchen, holding her oldest daughter in her arms, her eyes wild while Chrissy's silence meant a tremendous scream was about to come out.

There was blood everywhere. Absolutely everywhere, and Elise just froze.

And Chrissy screamed, the sound chilling Elise all the way to the bone.

CHAPTER 14

Annie had heard someone yell, and she'd left the office, where she'd been meeting with Patsy, instantly. The other woman's footsteps sounded right behind her as they both hurried down the hall.

A scream filled the air, and Annie's heart froze.

Around the corner, Becca held her daughter in her arms, plenty of blood marking the way they'd come. Annie blinked at the scene before her, quickly commanding herself to *slow down. Think.*

She'd taken plenty of first aid classes as a young mother, and then again after Ryan had died. She never wanted to be in a situation where she didn't know what to do, and that had spurred her attendance in the courses.

"Becca," she said, stepping around the woman. "Let me have her." She took Chrissy from her mother, both of them crying quite hysterically. "Tell me what happened." Annie turned toward the sink, only to find Elise gripping it tightly.

"Patsy," she said over the crying. "Elise needs to sit down. She looks like she's going to faint." Annie couldn't do anything but step next to Elise, hoping she could at least cushion the fall if she did go down.

Thankfully, Patsy arrived, and she escorted Elise away from the sink. "I'll get towels and rags," she said briskly, walking out of the kitchen.

Annie flipped on the water in the sink and moved the handle to make the water warm. She twisted to look over her shoulder, adding, "And grab the first aid kit would you?"

Colton appeared in the doorway, his eyes wide and anxious. Annie held his gaze for a moment, and then she turned back to the crying, wiggling, bleeding five-year-old. "Shh, baby," she said. "Tell Auntie Annie what happened."

But Chrissy couldn't, and in the next moment, Annie heard cowboy boots slapping the tile. Colton appeared at her side, his arm around Becca. "I think she said she fell."

"Against the stone table upstairs," Becca said. "I have her teeth." She opened her hand, and in her palm sat two bloody teeth.

Annie looked away. She could handle the sight of blood better than lost teeth, and she'd always made Ryan play the Tooth Fairy for Emily and Eden when they were younger.

"Okay," she said, balancing Chrissy on the edge of the sink with one arm and her body while she wetted the other one. "Let's see what we have, should we?" She looked at Colton. "Will you take Becca out into the living room? And then find Liam Murphy. Rose's husband. He's a doctor."

"Oh, dear," Elise moaned, and Annie swung her attention away from Becca and Colton. Elise swayed in her seat and put her head down on the table.

"Elise," Colton said, taking Becca with him as he moved away from the sink and into the other half of the kitchen where Elise sat. "Come with me." He practically picked her up with one arm, and he took both of them out of the kitchen.

Chrissy still fussed a lot, and Annie started singing softly to her. "I'm going to touch your head, okay, baby?" She wiped her wet fingers along the child's hairline, smoothing the hair back and out of the way.

Nothing wrong with her head that Annie could see.

"Rags and towels," Patsy said, dropping a mound of them next to Annie. She picked one up and got it wet, squeezing out as much water as she could against the side of the sink.

"Now your face." Annie wiped the girl's face carefully, moving down both sides. She started to quiet, and Annie began singing again. She quickly mopped up as much blood from Chrissy's chin and neck as she could, gradually getting closer to her mouth.

"Annie," Andrew said, rushing to her side.

"She's all right," Annie said. "Don't act upset." She kept her gaze on Chrissy's eyes as they started to crinkle again. "Shh, baby. It's okay."

"Liam's on the way. He was down at Graham's."

"She's gonna be just fine." Annie resumed her singing as she took a clean, freshly wetted cloth from Patsy and put the soiled one in the sink. She put the whole thing right over Chrissy's mouth, not putting any pressure on it at all. Her lips came away clean, and Annie could see the damage in her mouth.

"Yes, you lost two teeth, sweetheart." She smiled at the girl. "You're going to get a visit from the Tooth Fairy soon."

Chrissy tried to say something, but Annie couldn't tell what. At least she wasn't sobbing or screaming anymore. She reached for her father, and Andrew took her one tiny hand in both of his. "It's okay, baby. Annie is taking good care of you."

Colton returned to the kitchen. "I don't know where Liam is."

"I called him," Andrew said, glancing at Colton. "Thanks, though."

"Anything else I can do to help?" He looked at Annie, the weight of his gaze on the side of her face so heavy. She'd escaped from him earlier, and she knew it. He likely did too. They hadn't had a chance to talk yet, as he hadn't come to lunch with everyone else, and then Annie had moved on to talk business with Patsy.

"My wife's in the living room?" Andrew asked.

"Yes," Colton said. "With Lily and Beau and your mother."

"Can you stand here with Chrissy?"

The little girl whined, and Andrew leaned down and placed a kiss on her forehead. "I'm just going to go check on Mommy. I'll be back in two seconds. Hold Colton's hand." And just like that, Andrew stepped away, and Colton stepped into his spot.

Annie's heartbeat went wild, but she managed to get one more cloth and wipe away the last of the blood. "Lean your head back, Chrissy. Let Auntie Annie look in your mouth."

The little girl did what Annie said, and she found there was more than just a couple of missing teeth. The roof of her mouth looked like ground meat, as did the inside of her lip. She whined, and Annie dropped her lip back into place. "Uncle Liam should be here soon," she said. "He'll tell us what we need to do."

"Should I make it cold?" Patsy asked, and Annie nodded. She switched the water and prepared another cloth.

Chrissy actually seemed to sigh at the colder touch of the rag to her mouth, and Annie asked, "Can you hold it there, baby? As tightly as you can."

The little girl lifted up her free hand, wobbling a little until Annie balanced her, and held the rag against her lips and teeth. She did not let go of Colton's hand, and he stayed right at Annie's side, his hand covering Chrissy's.

"You're doing great," he said. "Once, when I was a little boy, I fell out of this tree house my brother built." He put a warm smile on his face, and Annie couldn't help melting at the sight of it. "He had no idea what he was doing, and I just went *poof!* Down through the floor."

Chrissy looked at him with wide, hazel eyes, clearly entranced with the story. Truth be told, Annie was too.

"It was close to the trunk, but I had nothing to hold onto, and I just went right on down. The bark scraped up my whole body, and when I landed, I bit my own tongue. It hurt so bad." He chuckled and shook his head, the sound quiet and the move-ment slow and soft.

Annie sure did like him, her feelings for him so strong they made no sense. She barely knew him and had only met him a couple of days ago. But somehow, she sensed that they were cut from the same cloth, and she wished he could feel it too.

Who says he can't? she wondered. But he'd spent most of his time here frowning, and Annie didn't want to push him into somewhere he didn't want to go. And that was also how she felt —that she was ready for a new, wonderful relationship, but he was not.

And he'd admitted that he might never be.

Annie swallowed and looked away as Colton continued his story, claiming he'd had to get a stitch in his tongue because the gash was so deep.

Chrissy pulled the rag away from her face. "Wow. Can I see?"

Colton opened his mouth and stuck out his tongue. The little girl examined it, her own injuries clearly forgotten. "Can't see it, can you?" he asked.

She shook her head, and Annie took the cloth and exchanged it for a new one. "Hold it on there, sweetheart." Chrissy did, and Annie heard chatter and talking coming from the living room.

"It healed up real good," Colton said. "So don't worry. You're going to be just fine."

"Chrissy?" Liam asked, and Colton stepped to the side as he and Andrew both arrived at the kitchen sink. Liam's gaze swept the sink, which held plenty of gory cloths, and he added, "Oh, we've got some mouth bleeding." He grinned at her, though he was extremely calm. "Your mom showed me your teeth. Let's see what else you've got."

Annie stepped out of the way, and Liam took her place, easily balancing Chrissy against his body too.

Her adrenaline ebbed, and she turned away from the medical examination, sighing. Before her sat the trail of blood, and thankfully, everyone who'd come in and out of the kitchen had possessed the wherewithal not to step in it.

"I'll get the bucket," she said to Patsy.

"I'll start the laundry," she said. "Then I'll come help clean up."

"I can help," Colton said too, hopping over the line of blood. "Point me to the bucket, and I'll get it started. You might want to go change your clothes." He let his eyes slide down the front of Annie's body, and she followed his gaze.

Her entire shirt had blood soaked into it, and Annie gave another sigh. "Okay, let me show you." She took him around the corner to the closet, where more cleaning supplies were kept. "There's a bathroom right down the hall there, around the corner on the left. I'd use the tub there. Mop here. Cleaner here." She plucked the pine-scented floor cleaner from the shelf and handed it to him. "I'll be right back."

His eyes burned into hers, but all he did was nod. Annie wanted to say something more to him, but there was simply too much going on right now. So she turned and left him to get the mop bucket ready.

By the time she returned, all traces of blood had been removed from the kitchen. Colton now worked in the living room, and Patsy had the spot cleaners out as well.

"It's on the rug," she said. "I thought we might be able to get it out one drop at a time, but for every one I get, I find five more."

"Just throw it away," Colton said, swiping the mop back and forth two times. "I'll get them a new one for Christmas."

Annie thought that was a fine idea, and she said, "I agree with Colton. It's just a rug. Not worth the effort." She glanced into the kitchen, then to the empty couches. "Where is everyone?"

"Liam said they should go to the dentist, just to make sure everything is okay," Patsy said. "He went with Andrew and Becca, and Beau and Lily went for moral support."

Annie nodded, her mind cloudy as to what she'd been doing before the emergency. Patsy started spraying the bloodstains on the hard floor, making it easier for Colton to swipe them away with the mop.

"Where'd you put Elise?" she asked. "She didn't look good."

"Uh, she was right here," Colton said, looking around as if he could possibly miss a human being in the living room.

"Maybe she went down to one of the bedrooms," Patsy suggested.

"I'll go find her," Annie said. "She probably shouldn't be alone."

Colton's eyes once again weighed on her as she left, but Annie kept her back straight as she disappeared down the hall. Only when she knew he couldn't see her did she allow the stress to pull through her body.

She found Elise in the guest bedroom next to the bathroom, her eyes closed as she lay on the bed. "Elise?" she said quietly as she entered. "Are you okay?"

Elise opened her eyes slowly and nodded. "Yes, I'm okay now." She sat up, and Annie reached for her hand. Elise worked hard around the lodge, and Annie had always liked her.

"I didn't know I couldn't handle that much blood," she admitted. "I nearly fainted."

"Good to know now," Annie said with a smile. Elise was fifteen or sixteen years younger than Annie, and she had a charming, fresh-faced look about her that said innocent and pure.

"How is Chrissy?"

"She's doing okay," Annie said. "They took her down to a dentist."

"I think I'd have been okay if I hadn't just eaten," Elise said. "Honestly."

"I understand." Annie enjoyed the quiet stillness of the bedroom, the barely-there scent of flowers hanging in the air, the presence of a friend beside her.

"Hey," a man said, and Annie blinked a couple of times before she recognized Colton's voice. "Sorry to interrupt. Can I talk to you for a minute?"

Elise patted Annie's knee and said, "Go on. I'm feeling fine, I swear."

Annie looked at her, all of her excuses gone. So she got up and nodded at Colton. "Sure."

CHAPTER 15

C olton led Annie down the hall and down the steps too. He wasn't sure where he was going, but he ended up in the theater room. Annie followed him like he was in charge, and she closed the door behind them.

"There's a movie in here in forty minutes," she said. "*Gulliver's Travels.*"

"Oh yeah?" Colton didn't want to talk about the family activities at the lodge, though. He still hadn't even eaten lunch, and with the sight of all that blood, he wasn't sure he could stomach anything right now anyway. "I think I'll be skipping that."

A smile slipped across Annie's face. "Me too. Not my favorite movie."

"Bree does a good job with having things for people of all ages, though," Colton said. "I signed up for a slot to decorate the tree."

"Did you? I still haven't done that."

He reached for her hand, his heartbeat thrashing against his ribs now. Their skin touched, and a spark flared up his arm. He settled his fingers right between hers, the fire accelerating and singeing his shoulders and down into his chest now. "Maybe you could help me during my slot."

"I don't know," she said, her eyes still too hard though she'd let him hold her hand. "I'll have to see what the girls are doing."

Colton thought fast, trying to remember what Elise had said to say to Annie. "I'm sorry," he said, knowing he needed an apology in there somewhere. "I know I said or did something to upset you, but I'm not one-hundred-percent sure what it was. If you tell me, I'll fix it, so you're not upset with me."

He really didn't want anyone to be upset with him, but least of all Annie. What that said about him and their relationship he wasn't sure. He wasn't even sure he'd known they *had* a relationship until that moment.

She simply looked at him, and Colton blurted, "I think you're really pretty," right as he remembered Elise had said it.

Annie blinked once and then burst out laughing. Colton wasn't sure if he should join her or unleash the humiliation threatening to drown him. He pushed against that so hard, it prevented him from laughing with her.

Thankfully, she quieted quickly, taking a small step toward him, though they already stood very close together. "You said you didn't believe in marriage."

Colton tried to remember when those words had left his mouth. "I did?"

She nodded solemnly. "You said you didn't really have a lot of faith in marriage right now, so you didn't know if you wanted kids."

Colton's throat stung, the fire now burning through him in a very bad way. It moved down into his chest, making his bones tingle and his organs shrivel up. "I dated Priscilla for four years," he said. "We were engaged for another year. Before her, I hadn't dated in a while. She's basically been my entire dating pool of knowledge for a decade—and she ditched me while I was in the dressing room, tying my bowtie for our wedding."

Annie got what he was saying, didn't she?

"So, right now, in this very minute, I don't have a lot of faith in marriage. It doesn't mean I don't *believe* in it."

"So you do want to get married."

"Eventually," he said. "Of course. I believe in marriage and family. I'm not really cut out for the bachelor life, and I'm not into just hooking up with whoever." Heat filled his face. "I'm just…still really embarrassed, and still trying to figure out who I've become in the past ten years."

Annie stepped right into his personal space then, releasing his hand and wrapping her arms around him. "I know a little bit about who you are."

"You do?" Colton let himself hug her back, and wow, that felt so, so nice. He'd missed the touch of another human being, and the steady way her heart beat with his, and the presence of another soul so close to his.

"A little," Annie said. "You're kind, I know that. You're not afraid of very much, I know that. You work hard—I think I know that from listening to you on the phone with your brother. You're smart, though maybe not with cribbage."

Colton chuckled then, mostly to get her to stop talking. He didn't want her listing all these things about him as if they were facts. The truth was, he wasn't always kind. He did get scared of things. He hadn't worked since the wedding, and he'd literally never be able to figure out cribbage.

He pulled away slightly and looked down at her. Those honey-soft, dark green eyes smiled back at him. He liked the smattering of freckles across her cheeks and nose. He reached up and brushed her hair back behind her ear, his eyes drifting down to her mouth.

And yep, there came the fear. A bolt of it like lightning to his chest. He couldn't kiss her. The very idea was *ridiculous*. His heart groaned as it tried to re-erect the barriers that had somehow formed there on his should-be-wedding day, and he pushed against them just as hard.

"I think you're pretty amazing too," he managed to say. "You know right where everything is, and you deal with stress better than anyone I've ever seen. You're obviously a good mother, and you're great with kids too. Watching you with Chrissy was like bottling magic."

"I'm trained in first aid, that's all," she said, her eyes focusing on his mouth too.

Colton had no idea what to do. He wasn't even sure how to kiss another woman. Maybe he'd been doing it wrong for years and years, and that was one of the reasons Priscilla had left.

But he found himself leaning toward Annie, and she tipped her face toward him, creating the just-right angle for a kiss.

"No fair!" a child yelled as the door swung open. It banged into the wall behind it, and Colton felt sure he'd find a divot in the sheetrock when he looked.

Annie jumped out of his arms as a couple of children came running inside. "You never let me pick," the girl said.

"No one's picking," Annie said, sweeping the few DVD cases from the shelf where the little boy was reaching. "It's *Gulliver's Travels*. Bree said so." She put the movies in a cabinet that was much too high for the kids while Colton tried to fade into the last row of recliners so he wouldn't be seen.

But what did eight-year-olds know about kissing? Surely they wouldn't read anything into him being in the room with Annie…alone…with the door closed. Not the same way any of the adults here would.

"Aw, I don't like that movie," the little girl said.

"Well, Averie," Annie said with a warm smile. "Take it up with Bree. She sets the movies during movie time. You can only pick during non-movie time." She herded the little girl toward the door. "Come on, Ronnie. You can't be in here without someone older than you."

He looked longingly at the cabinet one more time, groaned, and followed Annie out of the theater room. Colton knew how the kid felt, and he grinned at his unhappiness. He wanted something from this room too, and he hadn't gotten it.

Maybe later, he thought as Annie stood at the bottom of the steps and shooed the kids back upstairs, telling them, "Go put some popcorn in the microwave. The movie doesn't start for another half an hour anyway."

She turned back to Colton with a hopeful look in her eyes, but the moment had long since fled.

"So," he said, leaning in the doorway to the theater. "You'll decorate the tree with me in thirty minutes?"

She ducked her head and tucked her hair behind her ear. "Yeah, I'd like that."

"Great." He approached her, sliding one hand along her waist and giving her a side-squeeze. "Now, I'm going to go see if it's too late for lunch."

"You didn't eat?"

"Not yet."

"It's never too late for lunch," Annie said. "I'll sit with you."

Colton would like that, and as they climbed the steps together, he told himself not to think too hard about Annie. He'd wanted to get away from his real life, and ultimately himself. He simply needed to rediscover who he was, and Colton had never been afraid to tell a woman how he felt.

He'd just put the last bite of his third taco-dilla in his mouth when Amanda came into the kitchen with Celia and Rose. "You get the hazelnuts going," Celia said to Amanda. "And I'll get the chocolate melting."

"I really think we should add vanilla to it," Rose said. "I'm telling you, it makes the flavor so much deeper."

"We'll try it," Celia said, banging around as she got out a pot.

"I think mocha would be nice too," Amanda said, and Colton looked at Annie with his eyebrows raised. "Oh, hello," Amanda added as if she hadn't seen Colton and Annie sitting side-by-side on the far side of the table.

Annie smiled in her direction, and Colton looked at the older woman too. "Hey. I'm just finishing lunch, and we'll get out of your hair."

"You're fine," she said, her smile as warm and as inviting as anyone's could be. She reminded him of his mother, and Colton couldn't help returning the gesture. "We're just experimenting with our hot chocolate recipe for tomorrow's contest."

"Ah," Colton said, glancing at Annie again. She was shaking her head no and shooting lasers from her eyes. He looked back at Amanda, whose face transformed right in front of him. The two of them were clearly communicating about something, and Colton had missed the memo.

"You guys have a lot of contests," he finally said, almost yelling the words. Annie actually flinched, and Amanda tore her gaze from her.

"Yes," she said, turning. "It certainly keeps things lively around here."

"I think things are plenty lively around here," Annie said, getting up and taking her teacup with her. He'd declined the tea, as he'd never really been into drinking anything that could taste like flowers or soap. "Have you heard from Andrew or Becca?"

"Not yet." Amanda went into the other half of the kitchen and put some sort of appliance on the countertop. "How much alcohol did we decide goes in this?"

"A quarter-cup," Celia said, and Colton watched as Amanda opened a bag of hazelnuts and put them in the bowl of the cooker first. She then painstakingly measured and poured the quarter-cup of gin into the pot too. Satisfied with her work, she latched the lid on tight, and said, "Forty minutes...low pressure...hazelnuts are going."

Colton took that as his cue to get going too, and he managed to get his plate into the dishwasher and escape the kitchen while the three of them chattered about how much chocolate to put in with the cream, and if they should try powdered milk too.

"Wow," Colton said once he made it into the living room. "Who knew so much went into hot chocolate?" He looked up at the tree, the sheer magnificence of it overcoming him. Someone had started putting balls and stars on it, and he stepped over to the boughs. "These stars are cross-stitched."

"Crocheted," Annie said, correcting him gently. "And then starched. They're actually my mother's."

He turned and looked at her. "I thought you said you hadn't signed up to decorate the tree."

"I haven't." She gazed happily at the stars. "We just have all the decorations here, and whoever wants to put them up, can." She faced him, linking her arm through his. "Should we see what other stuff we can find?"

"Definitely," he said. "Tell me about your mother and father. Are they still here? Did you grow up here?" He followed her to the wall separating the kitchen from the living room, where an assortment of boxes had been stacked.

"My parents live in Coral Canyon," she said. "In the same house where I grew up with my two sisters." She smiled and opened a shoebox. "Oh, here are some more stars. Do you want to put one on?"

Colton took it from her, suddenly wanting to know everything about her. "Sure. Your sisters, older or younger?" He turned back to the tree and bypassed hanging the ornament at a comfortable level. The teenagers and kids could decorate the bottom fourth of the tree, but this thing needed adornments all the way to the top. He pulled a chair over to it and stepped up, hanging the star as high as he could.

"One older and one younger," she said. "I'm right in the middle."

"Hey, me too." He grinned at her and accepted another star. "But I only have brothers. Two older and two younger."

"Yes, you told me yesterday while you ate ice cream."

"Oh, right."

"And you all run the company?"

"Oh, heavens, no," Colton said with a light laugh. "Wes is the CEO. Gray is the corporate lawyer. I do the marketing. The twins...well, the twins don't do much with the family business." He thought about Cy and Ames, and he finally added, "Ames is a cop in Aurora, just north of Denver. And Cy has kind of done everything. He acts like he doesn't have a job, but he sure has a lot of motorcycles, and I think he's on the West Coast somewhere right now, as it's warm there."

"You don't know where your brother is?"

"They don't know where I am," he said. "Well, Gray and Wes do, but that's it."

"Interesting," she said. "How can he support himself with no job?"

Colton got down from the chair and scooted it around the tree a little further before he took another ornament from Annie. "Well, the thing is...." How did he say this? He'd never really had to explain his family financial situation before, because well, he just hadn't.

Priscilla had known he was wealthy long before he'd even known her name. Everyone in Denver and the surrounding areas did. Hammond Manufacturing was a massive company, employing over twenty thousand people in the city and its surrounding suburbs. It seemed like he couldn't go more than a block in any direction without seeing his surname on something.

"The thing is," Annie prompted.

"I'm a Hammond, right?" he asked, as if she knew what that meant. She clearly didn't. "And well, Hammond Manufacturing is the leading employer in the entire state of Colorado, and my grandfather was the mayor of Denver twice. And well, when we turn twenty-one, we get two billion dollars and the charge to do something with it." He deliberately took his time finding the perfect bough to hang his starched, white angel on before he looked at Annie.

She stared at him, her eyes wide and her mouth slightly open. "Do something with it?" she finally asked.

"Yeah, you know, invent something or invest in something lucrative. Start our own company. That kind of thing." He extended his hand, ready for another ornament, but Annie didn't have one ready.

She flew into action then, threading a silver hook through the top of a birdcage with a bright red cardinal inside. She handed it to him, asking, "What did you do with your two billion?"

"I went to school," he said. "I thinkered with some apps and web development."

"Thinkered? I think you mean *tinkered*."

"No, I thinkered," he said with a grin. "I, uh, worked with some men and women smarter than me, and we worked through the sequencing of all of the human genomes." Surely she'd heard of that. The Human Genome Project had been one of the biggest achievements in science in decades.

But Annie looked like he'd spoken another language.

"I majored in biology in college," he said.

"But you're a marketing director."

"Yeah, most of us come back and work at the family company for at least a little while," he said. "I've been there for twelve years."

"So you went from sequencing genes to tweeting?"

Colton laughed, the sound flowing easily out of his lungs and throat. Way easier than it had in years and years. That felt really nice too, and he couldn't help letting it go on as long as it wanted to. "I guess so," he said. "I enjoyed the Genome Project, and it opened a lot of doors for medicine, and treating diseases, and all kinds of stuff. Evolution."

"And here I thought you were literally a cowboy who writes press releases."

"Well, I do that too," he said, reaching up to adjust his cowboy hat. "And you should know something about me. I don't—"

"Mom!" A blast of cold air accompanied the excited shriek from Annie's daughter. She held up her phone as she ran inside, not bothering with closing the front door behind her. "He did it. He finally asked me out!"

"Mitchell?" Annie abandoned the box of ornaments and hurried to meet Eden.

"Yes!" She waved her phone and started jumping up and

down as she squealed. Her happiness carried on the air like a strong scent, and Colton couldn't help smiling as Annie celebrated with her daughter.

He simply had no idea a woman could be that excited about a date, but as he watched Annie, he had the distinct feeling that she'd probably be very happy with a date from the man she liked too.

Colton stepped off the chair and went to close the front door, because there was no sense in heating the outdoors. As the door clicked closed and Annie and Eden continued to chatter behind him, he realized he'd turned into his father.

No sense in heating the outdoors? He shook his head and caught Annie's eye as he went up the steps. He had no idea what the rest of the day's activities were, but as soon as Annie had a free moment, he hoped she'd come find him at their cribbage table.

CHAPTER 16

A nnie couldn't have been happier for her daughter. Eden had been flirting with Mitchell Starting through a dating app for the past month. They'd met a couple of times in town, but always with a group of other young single adults.

"Praise the Lord," she whispered to herself as she bent to get another box of ornaments. Eden had taken over Colton's job of hanging the baubles on the tree, and even when Annie glanced up, she couldn't see where Colton had gone.

"So what are you going to do?" Annie asked after Eden had detailed how he'd finally called her and asked her to dinner. Eden had even been bold enough to ask him specifically, "Just the two of us?" to which he'd confirmed yes, just the two of them.

"He said he knows a great place that's pretty new," she said. "But he wanted it to be a surprise."

"There are a lot of new places that have gone in," Annie said. "What are you hoping for?"

"Honestly, I don't care," Eden said. Annie hadn't seen this glow in her daughter's face in far too long, and she sent up another prayer of gratitude that Eden had gotten this date. *Please don't let him break her heart,* she added in her plea to the Lord.

The front door opened again, and Emily walked in, laden with shopping bags. "Thanks for waiting for me," she said with plenty of acid in her voice. She kicked the door closed behind her and glared at Eden as she pranced through the living room.

Annie watched both of her daughters, hoping that one day they could learn to get along. They'd fought like cats and dogs growing up, their teens years especially hard. Everything had been hard for Annie in those years, because Ryan had died when Eden was eleven and Emily fourteen.

Eden kept her nose in the air, and Emily rolled her eyes just before she stepped through the doorway to take her gifts downstairs.

"Eden," Annie said. "How was shopping?"

"Great," she said. "We finished today, thank goodness."

"I hope you didn't spend too much." She hadn't been able to focus on any of the bags Emily had been carrying.

"We didn't, Mom. Don't worry." She jumped down from the chair, apparently done with the decorating. She picked up her phone from where she'd set it on the side table, and she collapsed onto the couch and started texting.

"Maybe you should go see if you can help Em," Annie suggested, not sure how to parent adult children.

Eden didn't even look up from her device. She didn't respond either, and awkwardness descended into the huge living room, stuffing the silence all the way to the top of the two-story ceiling.

The front door opened again, and this time, Andrew entered, carrying his sleeping daughter. Annie left the ornaments where they lay and went toward him. "How is she?"

"Good," he said. "No issues with the teeth." He stepped out of the way as Becca and Lily came inside, followed lastly by Beau.

"She's wearing a retainer, just to protect the roof of her mouth," Becca said, smoothing her daughter's hair off her forehead. "Let's take her upstairs so she can sleep."

Annie smiled fondly at the little girl as everyone started moving through the house. "I think Laney has all the littles down at her house."

"Yeah, she's going to keep them until dinner," Becca said. She turned back to Annie and grabbed her in a tight hug. "Thank you, Annie. You knew exactly what to do, and I appreciate it."

Annie hugged Becca, warmth moving through her. "You're welcome. I'm glad I could help."

"Let's go practice our hot chocolate," Lily said. "While Charlie is down at Laney's."

"Practice hot chocolate?" Beau asked, following her. "Why do we need to do that?"

Annie couldn't help smiling to herself, and she cast one more look at Eden texting on the couch, and she went upstairs too. Colton sat at the table they'd set up to play cribbage, but he didn't have the game out. He didn't have his phone out.

He sat leaned over, with his head cradled in his hands, as if he were asleep. She made sure Becca and Andrew had gone down the hall and there were no prying eyes, and then she put her hand on his back. "Colton?"

"Hmm?"

His back was strong and sturdy, and Annie's hormones fired. "The recliners in the theater room are super comfortable."

"But *Gulliver's Travels*," he whispered.

"Come on." She got him up and down two flights of stairs to the basement. Only Averie and Ronnie seemed to be around the lodge today, and Annie had missed the memo of going down to Laney and Graham's farmhouse. Not that she minded. She wouldn't have gone even if she had known.

Neither of the six-year-olds cared that Colton and Annie slipped into the back row of recliners, and Annie nudged Colton all the way to the corner, where a two-seater loveseat sat. She really wanted to sit in that with him, and she settled a little too close to him to be friendly, and she took his hand in hers.

"You're right," he whispered. "This is so much better." He

put up his leg rest, and Annie cuddled into him more, wondering if they would get their kiss in the theater room after all. She really, really wanted it—the same way Eden had wanted a date with Mitchell.

Her nerves accelerated, and she had no idea how to tip her head back and kiss him. His breathing stayed as even as calm water, and she hoped he hadn't fallen asleep again. The music in the movie annoyed her, and she focused on the picture playing on the wall for a few seconds.

"This is a really dumb movie," Colton whispered.

Annie turned toward him to find him taking off his cowboy hat and setting it on the armrest on his left. "No kidding. I'm just not sure where else to go."

"I thought you said this place had activities all day." He grinned down at her and ran his free hand through his hair. The light from the movie caught on his silver hair, and Annie found him so, so handsome.

"They do," she said, returning his smile. "But there's plenty of downtime too."

"Obviously." He reached for his hat. "Maybe if I cover my face, I can fall asleep again."

"Before you do that," Annie said, pushing herself up and putting her right hand on his chest. She didn't want to blurt out that he needed to kiss her first, and Colton hadn't participated in the Human Genome Project and run the marketing for the largest employer in Colorado by not connecting the dots.

And this time, he dropped his cowboy hat and used that hand to cradle her face. He studied her for a long moment, and Annie couldn't tell what he was thinking because of the flickering lights.

Then he lowered his mouth to hers, and Annie pulled in a breath through her nose as she kissed him back.

She expected him to kiss her quickly and settle down for his nap. After all, she'd seen the fear in his face earlier, under proper lighting here in the theater. But he kissed her, and kissed her, and kissed her, truly taking his time. She hoped he liked kissing her and wasn't trying to decide if she was worth his time.

Because she sure did like kissing him, and when their connection finally broke, she giggled and laid her head against his chest. He released her hand and put his arm around her shoulders, and Annie had never been happier to be in the strong arms of this sexy cowboy.

———

"WHAT ARE YOU GIRLS DOING?" ANNIE ASKED AS SHE SAT NEXT TO Bree and Eden, who hadn't moved from the couch in the living room. Someone had been decorating the tree while she'd been downstairs in the theater room, kissing Colton.

She wiped the smile from her face, because she wasn't eighteen years old, and she didn't want to provide any explanations to either woman in front of her.

"She's helping me get set up with my dating profile." Bree glanced up at Annie, and she'd obviously seen something, because she didn't look back at her phone. "Where have you been?"

"Oh, I watched the movie with Averie and Ronnie." She nodded to Bree's phone. "You're ready to jump into the pool again?"

"Heavens, no." Bree looked down and started tapping on her phone. "I just want to lurk. Eden said she lurked for months before she even swiped on someone."

Annie had hesitated on the online dating app for a few reasons, one of them that one could never really be sure who was behind the screen. She'd heard that Bree's latest boyfriend had broken up with her with the news that he hadn't been using his real name. So why she'd want to use an app—where anyone could use any name—Annie wasn't sure. But she wasn't Bree's mother—or even old enough to be Bree's mother—and she only wanted the best for her friend.

"Okay, well, I'm going to go help get dinner on the table." Annie got up and left the two of them there. She entered the kitchen, where Celia had a pair of grill pans on the stovetop, hot dogs covering half of one and burgers covering the rest of the surface.

"Indoor barbecue," Annie said. "Do you need help with lettuce and tomatoes?"

"Yes," Celia said. "Condiments. Stir those onions, if you could. And I have the buns ready to go in the oven, but we won't do that until five minutes out."

Annie surveyed the work Celia had done. Down the counter a ways, Finn stood with a knife and an avocado in his hand. Annie thought they were the sweetest couple, and she smiled at Finn when he looked up from underneath his cowboy hat.

"There's bacon in the oven too," he said. "I bet it's done."

"I'll start there." Annie got to work, and before she knew it, she and Finn had plates and bowls of toppings for the hamburgers and hot dogs, as well as a big bowl of green salad and a bowl of potato salad, on the counter facing the half of the kitchen with the giant dining table.

"Call 'em, Patsy," Celia said when Patsy poked her head into the kitchen. A moment later, her voice came over the intercom, and everyone started gathering in the kitchen. She didn't see Bree or Colton, and she worked against the jealousy surging against her voice box. She wasn't even sure why those emotions existed. Colton liked her; she knew that. They'd just spent several minutes downstairs kissing, for crying out loud.

So it seemed very strange that she felt like crying out loud when Colton and Bree appeared in the kitchen together, side-by-side, laughing about something. In Annie's mind, she could see the two of them as a couple, and that was the biggest problem. She wanted to only see herself with a man, but she could see Colton and Bree together, and that bothered her a whole lot.

She pushed the feelings away and caught Colton's eyes. He gave her that sexy smile, and she hadn't seen him flash that at Bree. In fact, when she said something to him, his smile changed to an entirely different one, and all of Annie's fears withered away.

At least for now.

CHAPTER 17

Bree sat beside Colton after she got her food, as she felt a kinship with the cowboy. He didn't have anyone to sit by anyway, and she didn't want him to feel out of place. Annie stayed in the kitchen and worked with the kids until they'd all gotten the hamburgers or hot dogs they wanted.

"What is that?" he asked, looking at her plate with plenty of disgust.

"It's a black bean patty," she said, slipping the top of her bun over the nearly black patty on her plate. "And it's delicious, and you can keep your judgements to yourself, Mister." She flashed him a playful smile and picked up a potato chip.

"Are you a vegetarian?"

"Yes," she said. "I mean, sometimes."

"Sometimes?"

"I just don't really like red meat," she said. "Or hot dogs. I mean, those aren't even meat."

He picked up his hot dog, which he'd drenched in ketchup, mustard, and relish, and took a big bite. His eyes grinned while he chewed, and Bree shook her head.

"They're good though," he said after he'd swallowed.

"Disagree," she said, cutting her "burger" in half. She picked up one half and took a bite of it. The black beans had great flavor, and Celia had introduced Bree to the concept of grilling the veggie burger, so it had some charred flavor too.

"That has to be so dry," Colton said.

"Oh, I put on plenty of sauce," Bree said, not wanting to admit that without the mayo and ketchup mixture she drowned the patty with, he'd be right.

"Can I try it?" he asked.

"Sure." She watched him use a knife and fork to cut off a piece of the half she hadn't touched yet, and delicately put it in his mouth. He wore a stone mask, that was for sure, and Bree had no idea what he thought until he rolled his head slightly and shrugged.

"It's not bad."

"Ah-ha."

"It's not *good*," he said. "So don't get too excited."

"What are we not getting too excited about?" Annie asked as she sat on the other side of Colton.

He turned and beamed at her, and Bree could see the fireworks of attraction between the two of them. Sharp jealousy pulled through her, because she wanted a man to look at her the way Colton looked at Annie. She wanted to watch his eyes light up when he saw her, and smile like he'd get to kiss her later, and lean slightly toward her like he wanted to touch her.

Jay hadn't done that.

Bree ducked her head and focused on her potato chips and her potato salad while Colton said something to Annie she couldn't hear above the others talking at the table.

She just needed to find another man. Get another date. Then Bree wouldn't be jealous of Annie, but happy for her.

She *was* happy for her. Annie hadn't had hardly any luck with men in the last few years, and Bree knew what it was like to go home alone, something Annie had been doing for years.

Yes, she had her daughters, and Bree had Elise. But it was

different to have a loving boyfriend or husband, and Bree knew it.

Everyone knew it.

She only ate half of her burger, laughed when Colton teased her that she wouldn't eat the other half because he'd touched it, and then told him, "No, I only ate half, because I have chocolate-dipped crispy treats in my cabin."

The interest in Colton's eyes doubled. "Is that right?" He leaned toward her, ducking his cowboy hat away from Annie. "What does one have to do to get invited down there for a midnight snack?"

"Maybe check with your girlfriend," Bree whispered back, smiling at him.

Colton straightened as if Bree had electrocuted him, the smile falling right off his face. Ah, so he and Annie might be flirting, but they hadn't quite defined the relationship yet.

"Did Annie make them?" He turned to her. "Did you make chocolate dipped crispy treats for Bree?"

Annie blinked at him a couple of times and looked past him to Bree. "No, I think Elise makes those. She and Bree are roommates."

"Yeah, I know." Colton looked back at Bree, who didn't get what his confusion was about. "You said to ask her."

All at once, understanding bloomed in Bree's mind. And she now knew Colton *did* think of Annie as his girlfriend. "I meant, you should ask Annie if she's okay with you coming down to my cabin for a midnight snack."

Colton's face turned red in about five seconds, and he ducked his chin to his chest, trying to hide it. Bree burst out laughing and picked up her plate. "But hey, at least now I know what you think of her." She walked away as Annie asked, "What do you think of me?"

Bree couldn't help giggling, and her good mood got her through helping with the dinner dishes. Then she escaped out into the cold night air, drawing a big lungful of it down into her chest.

The chill stung, and she didn't waste any time standing on the back patio. She walked, grateful the paths had been cleared so she and Elise didn't have to traipse through the snow to get to the lodge and back.

The minutes passed under the soft light of the moon. Every so often, that light would mute, and Bree watched the clouds chase each other through the sky. It felt like snow would arrive again soon, and Bree determined to check her weather app once she got back to the cabin.

Inside, the warmth from the furnace caused a sigh to pull through her, and she did get out her phone. But she forgot completely about the weather app and went right into Singles Spark, the dating app where Eden had met a man she'd just gotten a date with.

Bree forgot about the chocolate dipped crispy treats, and the passage of time as she looked at profile pictures and read bios of the men behind them.

She was old enough to know that anyone could literally put anything on the Internet, and that included apps. She saw a few men she was attracted to physically. But she wanted more than that. She wanted fun conversations. She wanted deep conversations. She wanted someone who would look at her the way Colton looked at Annie.

With Annie in her mind, she sent her friend a quick text. *I hope I didn't make anything too awkward for you.*

Not at all, Annie said almost instantly. *If anything, you got Colton to say I was his girlfriend. So thanks!*

Bree smiled and shook her head. She didn't know Colton Hammond super well yet, but she hadn't pegged him for the type of guy to show up somewhere and have a girlfriend two days later. But Annie *was* quite the catch, and he'd be smart not to let her get away.

So you like him, then?

Yes, I like him, Annie said.

Never one to gossip much, Bree left it at that, and Annie didn't add any more to the conversation. She got up when she realized how dark the house was and flipped on the lights in the kitchen and the hall leading down to the two bedrooms.

Elise often stayed at the lodge later than Bree, and she decided to take a shower to warm up her feet. She'd just finished putting on her pajamas when she heard voices in the house.

Two voices.

A male and a female. Bree went down the hall, recognizing them both. But it wasn't until she entered the kitchen that she realized Elise had brought Colton to the cabin with her.

"Well, well, well," she said, nudging Colton with her shoulder as she sat beside him at the kitchen table. "You got Elise to give you the good stuff."

He put the last bite of a chocolate covered crispy treat in his mouth and just grinned at her before chewing it.

"He has a real weak spot for sugar," Elise said as she turned back to the sink from where she stood in the kitchen. She brought over three mugs and set them on the table. "Coffee?"

"Yes, please," Bree said, because she knew Elise brewed some of the best coffee on the planet.

"Not for me," Colton said. "I can't sleep if I drink coffee this late at night."

"It's seven-thirty," Bree said. "What time do you go to bed?"

He looked at her with coolness in his gaze. "Early enough not to drink coffee at seven-thirty." His eyes turned into lasers. "And thanks for embarrassing me at dinner."

"Oh, I didn't embarrass you."

"About what?" Elise asked. "I was late, because this guy came to the lodge looking for a room, and I had to hunt down Patsy and then stay with them while she explained there was no room for him."

"You guys didn't turn me away," Colton said.

"You didn't smell like vodka," Elise said with a pointed look.

Bree giggled again, glad for the friends she had in her life. *Thank you for making sure I'm not alone*, she prayed, a measure of gratitude for the people the Lord had put in her life seeping through her.

"And anyway, you did get the last room," Elise said. "So we weren't lying."

"What if he doesn't have somewhere to stay?" Colton asked.

"It's not snowing," Bree pointed out. "He'll make it down the canyon just fine. There are plenty of places down there."

"Especially now that we're growing so much," Elise added.

"The town is growing?" Colton asked.

"Like crazy," Bree said. "Has been for a couple of years now. Maybe longer. We have about ten thousand more people here now than we did when Liam came, and that was what? Three years ago?"

"I moved here three years ago," Elise said, pouring coffee into Bree's mug and then her own. "The clinic had just opened."

"Yep, Liam did that." Bree picked up her coffee mug and her spoon and started stirring in sugar and cream, until her coffee was just how she liked it.

Her phone made an odd noise, drawing the attention of all three of them. "What was that?" Elise asked. "I've never heard your phone make that noise before."

"Neither have I." Bree swiped open the screen and looked at the solid white heart in her notification bar at the top of the phone. "What is that?" She pulled down and tapped on it, and Singles Spark opened up.

"Oh...dear."

"What?" Elise peered over the top of the phone as Colton tried to see the screen too.

"Someone wants to make a love connection," he said. "Who's Cayden Jackman?"

"I have no idea," Bree said, almost dropping her phone. A love connection? That couldn't be true. Could it?

"It's not called that," Elise said, saving her. "It just means he swiped right on you, Bree. He's interested. If you swipe right on his profile too, then the two of you can chat."

"I don't want to chat," she said, her voice a bit higher than normal. She tapped on his name, and his profile opened up, complete with emojis and a picture of him.

"You don't?" Elise's voice held plenty of curiosity and surprise. "Why'd you join the dating app then?"

Bree looked up from the handsome, chiseled face of Cayden Jackman. He wore a tan cowboy hat and had other pictures of himself riding a horse, a four-wheeler, and a roller coaster. What she was supposed to get from those, she wasn't sure.

"He doesn't seem like my type," she said.

"What's your type?" Colton asked. "And that still doesn't explain why you joined a dating app if you don't want to chat with men."

She looked from him to Elise, both of them expecting an answer. "I don't know," she said. "I just don't meet many available men here, and I thought it sounded like a good idea when Eden told me about it." Now, she wasn't so sure.

"So swipe right," Colton said, peering down at her phone. "He looks nice enough."

Bree looked at Cayden again, trying to decide what to do. In the end, she didn't want to swipe right. She wasn't sure she was really ready to start another relationship—even just a chatting one—with someone else.

What if Cayden Jackman wasn't this guy's real name? What if he had lied about who he was and what he liked to do?

Bree hated the thoughts in her head, but they didn't flee just because she wanted them to.

"So what happened with you and Annie at dinner?" Elise asked, lifting her coffee cup to her lips. She'd just saved Bree, and Bree knew it.

"Oh, nothin'," Colton said, his face already turning red again. "I'm going to head back to the lodge. Thanks for the sweets, you guys." He grinned at them, tipped his hat all proper like cowboys do, and headed out the front door.

Elise sighed as the knob clicked into place. "It's too bad he feels like my brother," she said. "If I saw his picture on a dating app, I'd definitely swipe right."

"He and Annie have a thing," Bree said without really thinking.

"They do?" Elise asked.

Bree looked down at Cayden Jackman again. "Yeah," she said, already distracted. "I teased him about it at dinner." She looked up again, determined not to look at this silly app again that night. "I didn't really realize it until he turned the color of a beet."

"You mean like he did just now?" Elise laughed. "But good for them. Annie needs someone like him in her life." And Elise meant it, because Elise was the nicest person on the planet.

"Yeah, I'm happy for her," Bree said, telling herself she really was. She just wanted a Colton Hammond for herself.

Could it be Cayden Jackman?

She'd never know if she never swiped right....

CHAPTER 18

Colton had eaten breakfast—stuffed French toast with homemade peach preserves—and had just committed to going snowmobiling with Annie and several others when his phone rang.

Wes's name sat on the screen, and Colton felt his whole day changing right in front of him. He glanced at Annie, apologies already forming in his mind.

"I'm sorry," he said. "I have to take this. I could be a minute."

"It's fine," she said, though she already wore a pair of snow pants and highly waterproof boots. She smiled him out of the mudroom, where he answered the call.

"Wes, hey," he said. "Is this a long call or a short call?"

"Long," Wes said. "We have a huge problem here, Colton, and it affects you."

He sighed, wondering why business couldn't wait until he was back in town. Or at least until the holidays had ended.

"Okay, give me two minutes." He covered the receiver of the phone and stepped back into the mudroom. Annie helped one of the Whittaker kids—maybe Stockton? Colton couldn't remember all of their names—step into a different pair of boots and start to feel around the toe to see where his foot hit.

"These are going to work, Stocky."

"Annie," Colton said, causing her to turn. "I'm not going to make it snowmobiling." He held up his phone. "Family emergency."

Alarm crossed her face, and Colton wished he'd phrased it differently. There was probably no emergency, at least not a medical one.

"Is everything all right?"

"It's a long conversation," he said, and that definitely meant things weren't all right. Annie didn't get the Hammond vernacular though, and she simply nodded.

"Okay," she said. "I'll catch up with you later then. Let me know if you need anything." She didn't look terribly upset that he wouldn't be going with her, and Colton was glad for that.

He left the mudroom, glad he hadn't chosen any boots or pants yet. "All right, Wes," he said, heading for the basement bedroom where he could have some privacy. "Tell me what's going on."

"Jill, Kent, and Laura want to take over HMC."

Colton's step faltered, right there on the stairs. He'd been wrong; this was a true family emergency. "What? They just came out and said that?"

"Laura is a piece of work," Wes said, and that was putting it mildly. Colton put up with his cousins, because they had Hammond blood. Otherwise, he'd probably have stopped thinking about them and talking to them years ago.

"But she's over research and development."

"It's another prod to get me to run for governor," Wes said. "She didn't say that. Wouldn't admit to it, actually. But she did recently just finish her Ph.D. in corporate finance, and she knows what she's doing."

Colton continued down the stairs, trying to hear what Wes was really saying. "Have you spoken to Gray?"

"Yeah, he's working with both of us. You know, contracts and legal crap I don't care about. He cares, and he knows what he's doing." Wes sighed, and Colton could picture him at the huge windows that overlooked the city and the huge Rocky Mountains in the distance. His oldest brother sounded tired. Beyond tired.

"You know," Colton said, heading for his bedroom now. "Maybe this isn't so bad. Maybe it's time for you to be done there. Do something else."

"What?" Wes asked. "What else am I going to do?"

"I don't know," Colton said. "It's not like you have to work."

"Yes," Wes said quietly. "I do."

Colton knew what his brother meant. It didn't seem to be in the Hammond genes to sit idly around and do nothing. Even Cy and Ames, while Colton didn't understand their brand of "investing," didn't just do nothing. Cy had started a custom motorcycle shop when he'd inherited his money, and Ames had bought custom cars before he went into the police academy. They both worked like dogs too, because all of the boys had been raised to work. Be industrious. Do something with their lives.

"We're meeting next week," he said. "Closed doors. No staff in the building."

"And you want me there." Colton unlocked his door with the keycard and went inside. He wasn't asking his brother if Wes *needed* him there. Wes didn't need Colton, and they both knew it.

"Yes," Wes said. "I want you here. I think they want your job too."

"Why would they want my job?" Colton sank onto the bed. "Not that I want my job, but Kent knows machines, and Jill knows how to drive everyone insane. They don't know social media marketing, or even regular marketing."

"Let's table that for a second," Wes said. "You don't want your job?"

Colton couldn't believe he'd said that out loud. "I mean...I could take it or leave it. I've been thinking it might be time for a change for me too."

"And we're going to leave Gray here to deal with Hansel and Gretel? And the Wicked Witch?"

Colton burst out laughing. "I still don't get why you call Jill and Kent Hansel and Gretel, but I guess. Gray can do what Gray wants to do."

"Because," Wes said. "They literally killed that old woman, and I think Kent and Jill would do the same if they had to."

"Oh, boy," Colton said, not wanting to get into the finer points of the fairy tale where "that old woman" had kept the kids locked up for days.

But he got Wes's point. Jill and Kent would do whatever they had to do if they felt backed into a corner. If they felt trapped, the way Hansel and Gretel had been, they'd literally set fire to anything to get free.

Everyone in the family had seen them do it for years.

"What is Gray saying?" Colton asked.

"You know Gray," Wes said. "He doesn't say anything." And Wes didn't sound happy about it. Colton understood. Gray was as political as the President of the United States, and he never said anything to truly give away how he felt about something. He never took sides. He thought like a computer, and his brain was so analytical, that Cy had once teased him and asked, "Do you have any emotions at all, Gray?"

To which Gray had socked Cy in the mouth, so he could definitely get mad.

Colton smiled just thinking about the altercation between his brothers. Growing up with four of them had been an adventure, that was for sure.

"When's the meeting?"

"December thirtieth," Wes said. "We're out for Thursday, Friday, and Monday, since the first is on a Saturday."

"I should be able to make it by the thirtieth," Colton said, thinking of what he'd say to Annie. They hadn't talked about anything long-term, that was for sure.

After he'd gotten back from Bree's and Elise's last night, he'd found her sitting on the couch in the living room just down the hall from their bedrooms. She'd claimed her daughters were watching a TV show and keeping her awake, but she'd been on her phone, not trying to sleep.

Colton knew she was waiting up for him, and he'd sat beside her and held her hand. He'd already admitted to her at the dinner table that Bree had called her his girlfriend, and he hadn't denied it.

He wouldn't have given her that label quite so soon, but he was kissing her, so he thought it probably fit just fine. And Annie certainly didn't seem to mind the label.

He'd kissed her last night on the couch too. A lot. Probably more than he should've.

"Are you there?" Wes asked.

"Yes," Colton said, pulling himself out of his personal life. He'd just talk to Annie about being gone for a few days. Maybe a week.

But transferring titles was one thing. Having a new branch of the family take over the whole company was quite another, and that didn't happen in a few days or a week.

"I was thinking we should have a little New Year's celebration at Ivory Peaks," he said. "I can call Cy and Ames and see if they can make it."

"Sure," Colton said. If he was going to be there anyway, he might as well go to a family party.

"Great," Wes said. "I'll see you on the thirtieth."

"Wes," Colton said, before his brother could hang up. "Keep me updated, okay? About anything."

"Will do." The line went dead, and Colton stared down at the dark gray carpet. His thoughts twisted and twined, and he couldn't separate them enough to think any single one.

All he knew was that his life suddenly had the potential to change drastically in only eight days.

COLTON STAYED IN HIS ROOM AND LOOKED UP HIS COUSIN'S COLLEGE degrees. He answered Kacey's questions and emails. He took the lunch Annie brought him and asked her to come sit with him for a while. But she'd said, "The girls and I have a practice slot in the kitchen right now. Maybe after?"

He'd nodded, but she hadn't come back yet. He'd been too distracted to ask her what she and her daughters were practicing for, but when her light knock sounded on his door again, he opened it to find her holding a steaming cup of hot chocolate.

"You're missing the tasting," she said, extending the cup toward him. "And you love chocolate."

Everything that had gone cold since Wes's phone call warmed again. He took the mug and inhaled the chocolatey and slightly orange scent of the steam. "That I do." He took a sip, and sure enough, this tasted like a cup that someone had melted a chocolate orange into and then whisked in some cream.

"There are eight more flavors upstairs," she said, trying to look past him and into the room. "Are you okay? You don't look okay." She took a step toward him, and Colton backed up into the room, hoping she'd enter and let the door close behind her.

When she did, he instantly felt like the space was too small for the two of them. Or like they were doing something they shouldn't be.

"It's just a family thing," he said.

"Maybe I can help."

Colton took another sip of the liquid chocolate orange and set the mug on the desk beside his laptop. "My cousins want to take over the company my brother currently runs."

"Oh, wow." Annie pressed one palm to her chest. "Can they do that?"

"Yeah, I mean, in theory, yes, they can." Colton simply looked at her. She was so calm, and so beautiful, and he had the very strong feeling that he didn't want to leave her here in Coral Canyon while he went back to Denver and Ivory Peaks.

He wasn't sure what that meant. Was he not going to go back, ever? That had never been the plan. He'd simply needed some time away from his job after the failed wedding. Then he'd needed some time away from his aging parents, his family, everything that had to do with Denver, Ivory Peaks, or Colorado.

He sure hadn't made it very far, but he reasoned that God had stranded him here in Wyoming, at this lodge. He'd have kept going north and west had it been safe to do so.

Now what? he asked the Lord, something he hadn't done in a long time.

"Is there going to be a big legal thing?" Annie asked.

"Honestly?" Colton shook his head. "No. We get together as family and we work it out. The lawyer—who's my brother in this case—draws up new contracts and new salaries and all of that, and we all sign it."

"And since you got that two billion...."

"I don't really need the job," he said, the ghost of a smile touching his lips. He stepped toward her and gathered her into his arms. She held him as tightly as he held her, and while Colton didn't *need* his job, he was comfortable there.

Change wasn't comfortable. Change made him stretch in ways he hadn't before, and he rarely liked that. Change brought the aspect of the unknown with it, and Colton would rather know what was going to happen over being surprised by something, good or bad.

"I don't deal well with change," he whispered in her ear.

"That's what hot chocolate is for," she whispered back, and Colton chuckled with her.

She stepped out of his arms, and twisted as if she'd open the door to leave. He increased the pressure on her hand, and she turned back to him.

He didn't ask, and he didn't hesitate. He simply leaned forward and kissed her, glad when she received him with seeming enthusiasm.

He sure did like her, and that was strange for where Colton was in his life right now. He'd told himself last night that the amount of time he'd spent cooped up with Annie in the lodge was equal to at least ten dates, and that he wasn't really moving that fast. It just felt like it, because the time they spent together was really close together.

Besides, they were both consenting adults, and he knew people who'd fallen in love at first sight, managed to make it to the altar together, and had been married for decades.

He could kiss Annie as much as he wanted—as much as she'd let him.

So he did, only stopping when she whispered, "If we don't go upstairs soon, someone's going to come looking for me."

He pulled away then, his heart beating like hummingbird wings in his chest. "And I need to taste all that hot chocolate. What if there's another tie?"

She smiled at him and reached up to push her fingers through his hair. He liked the boldness in her touch, though her hands were gentle too.

Their eyes met, and Colton lost all track of time in that moment.

"Mom?" A knock sounded on the door, and Annie leapt out of his arms. Colton backed up a couple of steps, his legs knocking into the desk chair where he'd been sitting. Down he went, bashing his knee into the leg on the desk.

"Ow," he said with a groan, and Annie opened the door.

"There you are," one of her daughters said. "Is he coming or what?"

"He's coming, yes," Annie said, practically running from the room. Colton rubbed his leg and looked up at Emily, Annie's oldest daughter.

"Sorry," he said. "We got distracted with something."

Emily narrowed her eyes at him, as if she were the mother and she'd just caught her daughter making out with her boyfriend. Which, honestly, wasn't that far off.

"Mm hmm," she said. "I bet." She turned and followed her

mom, and Colton flinched as his bedroom door swung closed with a *slam!*

He rubbed the pain out of his knee, collected his cowboy hat, and followed the ladies upstairs. After all, he didn't want to miss out on the hot chocolate.

CHAPTER 19

A nnie's humiliation accompanied her up the stairs and into the kitchen. Emily came behind her after a few seconds, and Annie stepped over to the sixth canister to help Averie, who couldn't get the spigot to work properly.

"Let me help you," she said, ignoring her daughter. Annie had forgotten that Emily had taken a phone call from Kelly and left before Annie had nudged Eden away from her and Colton.

He entered the kitchen a moment later, and Ronnie ran over to him. "Come taste, Colton," he said. "I helped my mom make one of them."

"Don't tell him which one," Laney said, and Annie backed out of the way so she could watch Colton from a safe distance. He held Ronnie's hand and let the little boy hand him sampling cup after sampling cup.

Colton had gotten better at keeping what he liked a secret, and he glanced at Ronnie as he filled out his ballot and dropped it in the box that Charlie had made.

"Did you make that?" he asked Ronnie.

"No, Charlie did," Ronnie said, pointing to the almost-five-year-old. "We don't always have a box, but he wanted to make one this year."

"Nice," Colton said, smiling at the little boys. "Is that it? How long is the voting open?"

Ronnie looked at his mother, and Laney smiled at him. "Until whenever," she said. "There aren't rules for that."

"Seems like you guys would have rules for everything," he said.

Laney laughed and nodded. "You're right. You should see us when we do the cupcakes. There are a lot of rules for that."

"Annie's told me a bit about that," he said, casting her a look. Annie could only think of his hands in her hair and his lips stroking hers.

She finally managed to smile, and she went to the third canister and filled another cup with the hot chocolate she and her daughters had made. It was a vanilla and chocolate concoction, with melted vanilla ice cream in it, with a bittersweet chocolate mixed with milk chocolate.

She loved the mouth feel of it, because it was thick like the store-bought chocolate milk, but it wasn't so rich that she couldn't have more than one or two mouthfuls.

"What's this one?" Colton asked, and Annie handed him her cup.

"I'll get another one." She picked up one of the cups still stacked on the counter and filled it.

"Let's go sit by the fire," he said, and Annie went with him, the weight of several pairs of eyes on her. She decided she didn't care. She didn't have to answer to anyone at the lodge, least of all her daughters. Well, maybe her daughters. She probably owed them an explanation.

But she didn't have to give it right now. Emily had gone out with Kelly half a dozen times before she'd even mentioned him to Annie, so she was probably getting close to that with Colton.

"Ah," Colton said as he sat on the stone hearth. He grinned at her as she sat beside him and lifted her cup to her lips.

"Which one did you vote for?" she asked.

"Which one was yours?"

"Nice try," she said with a smile.

"I voted for number four," he said, taking a sip of hers. "But this one is delicious too. It's really smooth."

"Hmm," Annie said, determined not to tell him which drink she'd made until it was time for the reveal.

"Which one did you vote for?" he asked.

"This one," Annie said, taking another sip. "It is really smooth. There's nothing worse than having a bunch of chocolate left at the bottom of your cup when you finish."

"Totally agree," Colton said. "Although, I literally have never made homemade hot chocolate. I didn't even know you could do that." He grinned and reached for her hand. "I just use the powder at home."

"For shame," Annie said, nudging him with her shoulder. "And I don't peg you for a hot chocolate drinker at all, actually."

"You're right. I don't drink hot chocolate in my real life."

Annie's heart throbbed in her chest. She knew they needed to have a hard conversation, but she just wanted to enjoy the afternoon.

"We should talk about your real life," she said.

"We should?"

"Don't you think?" she asked. "I mean, you don't live here. I do live here." She squeezed his hand. "And then there's this."

"Yes," he said, lifting her hand to his lips. "There's this."

"And you're...."

Colton took a long breath, held it for a moment, and then let it out. "I have to go to Denver for a meeting on the thirtieth," he said.

"For the cousin coup," she said.

"The cousin coup." Colton laughed, and Annie was glad she'd been the one to make him do that. "That's great. And yes. For that."

"And then?" Annie pressed. She didn't want to put too much pressure on him, but she felt herself walking on slippery ground, and she could fall at any moment. Fall hard—in love with Colton Hammond.

And if he wasn't going to be in town past the New Year, Annie better bind her heart up and keep it from getting punctured by his dashing good looks.

"And then I think I'll be unemployed," he said. "And able to go wherever I want, and do whatever I want."

"Ah, I see." Annie gazed up at the tree, trying to tame her smile. If he could go anywhere and do anything, maybe he'd come back here and keep her company while she did her books and scheduled clients.

She didn't want to think too far ahead, but Annie had done exactly that her whole life. She didn't know how to live a day without a plan, a checklist, or a schedule.

She reminded herself she didn't need one for a relationship, and she stood up when she heard someone call from the kitchen, "The results are in."

"Let's go see who won," she said, reaching for his hand. They went back into the kitchen together, and Annie scooted on over to where Emily stood next to Eden. They smiled at one another, and Annie looked at Laney, who was in charge of this contest.

"Ronnie has the results," she said, smiling at her son. He handed her an index card, and Laney looked at it and then out at the crowd. Annie's hand tightened in Colton's, and he inched a bit closer to her.

"The Pruitt girls," Laney said, applauding as she grinned at Annie and her daughters.

"Oh, my goodness," Annie said, covering her mouth with both of her hands. She turned toward her girls and hugged them, going forward to accept the giant paper cone Ronnie extended toward her.

The excitement died down, but Annie couldn't stop smiling.

"Congratulations, Annie," Colton said, pressing his lips to her cheek in a quick kiss that left her feeling overheated and like everyone was staring at her.

They weren't—only Eden and Emily were. She tried to convey to them that she'd talk to them later, and she turned back to the kitchen to help get cleaned up so Celia could lay out dinner.

———

THE NEXT MORNING, SHE WOKE LATE, BECAUSE SHE HAD BEEN UP late talking to her girls about Colton. She'd dated other men in the past, so they weren't shocked about that.

"It's just, you've known him for three days," Emily had said.

"I know," Annie said. And that was all. She didn't have to defend herself, and she wasn't worried about falling too fast. In fact, she wanted the sweep-her-off-her-feet love story, and if she fell in love with Colton by Christmas, she'd be happy.

She'd kept all of that to herself, though.

By the time she got to the kitchen, the scent of sausage hung in the air, but there was no evidence of the food.

There was coffee though, and Celia leafing through a cookbook that was dedicated to bowls. Literally every recipe was served in a bowl, and Annie hoped she'd get to taste something from it.

"I heard a rumor," Celia said when Annie sat at the table.

"Me and Colton," Annie said in a deadpan.

"So you're not denying it." Celia flipped the page without looking at it.

"Why would I?" Annie asked.

Celia smiled at her. "Good for you, Annie. You shouldn't deny it. That man is gorgeous."

"Talking about me?" Zach asked as he came into the kitchen with one of the triplets. "Jackson wants a cookie."

"Mm hmm," Celia said. "I think Zach wants a cookie."

Zach just smiled and took the two-year-old into the kitchen and opened a high cupboard. He took down a box of cookies and handed one to Jackson before taking several for himself.

"I think he went upstairs to start a puzzle," Celia said, and Annie wondered how she knew that Annie was wondering where Colton was that morning.

"I heard it's supposed to snow again tonight," Annie said instead of rushing up to the table where she'd tried to teach Colton how to play cribbage.

"Yeah, I heard that too."

"Maybe I should have Em text her boyfriend. I think he was going to try to come up tomorrow."

"I think they'll close the roads," Celia said, pausing on one recipe.

"I'll let her know." Annie finished her coffee and put her mug in the sink before going upstairs, where she did find Colton sitting at their table, hundreds and hundreds of pieces in front of him.

"Do you like puzzles?" she asked.

"As well as anything else," he said.

She sat down across from him as the screen of his phone brightened. He looked away from the pieces and texted whoever had messaged him.

"It's my brother," he said. "I guess the cousins are in the building today."

"I thought that wasn't until the thirtieth."

"So did Wes." Colton put his phone back and tapped the box. "It's a fairy garden."

"I see that," she said. "Not very Christmassy."

"That it is not." He fitted a piece into the outer edge and glanced up at her with a smile.

Annie warmed from the inside out, and she started looking for the edge pieces too. He hadn't sorted them out at all when he'd turned the pieces over, and Annie started making a pile of them.

They'd talked about their families, and his job a little bit, and her cleaning company. Her phone chimed, and she looked at it to see Emily had confirmed the bad weather and she'd texted Kelly to see if he could come up that evening.

"I think my daughter's boyfriend is going to propose to her this Christmas," Annie said. "And I don't know how to deal with it."

Colton looked up, compassion and surprise in his eyes. "Is that right?"

"I think so," Annie said.

"Does she think so?"

"I don't know," Annie said. "I think they've talked about it a little bit, but not much."

"Do you like the guy?"

"Yes," Annie said. "He's a good man, and he has a good job."

"You sound like being a good man and having a good job is a bad thing." Colton watched her with an interest in his eyes she hadn't seen before. "And you like a man who's about to lose his job."

"But has billions in the bank," she said, the perfect comeback.

He chuckled and shook his head. "A man still has to have something good to fill his time."

"So what will that look like for you?" she asked.

"Honestly? Right now, I don't know." He looked at her pile of edge pieces. "Have you been hoarding those?"

"I *sorted* these," she said. "Don't you know that's how you do a puzzle?"

Colton's eyebrows went up, and he reached for the box. He opened it and looked inside, making a big show of trying to find something.

"Huh, there aren't any instructions inside." Annie rolled her eyes, really enjoying flirting with him.

His phone went off again, and he busied himself with texting for several minutes. Annie had the bottom of the puzzle put together by the time he put his phone down again.

She saw what stressed looked like on his face, and she wished there was something she could do to erase it. At the same time, it made the smile he gave her so much softer and so much sweeter.

"I told my girls about us," she said.

"Yeah? And?"

"And nothing. I've dated before."

"Do they think I'm a good man with a good job?"

Annie giggled. "Does it matter? They're not in charge of who I go out with."

"To be technical," he said. "We haven't really left the lodge together at all." He looked up from the array of puzzle pieces on the table. "We should fix that as soon as we can."

"We should."

"Dinner? Tonight? We can drive down to town."

"It's supposed to snow."

"I have a four-wheel-drive truck."

Annie didn't want to say no to him. It couldn't snow that much in the time it took to get dinner, could it?

Her stomach flipped, because she'd always been so nervous sending Ryan out into bad weather. Sometimes good weather made her anxious.

But Colton's dark eyes called to her, and she really wanted a date with him, away from all the craziness of the lodge. Who knew? Maybe she wouldn't even like him when she wasn't in such a comfortable place, surrounded by her support system.

"All right," she said. "Dinner, tonight. Me and you. In town."

"Perfect." He picked up his phone again, though his brother hadn't texted. "Now, we just need to find the perfect place."

"I know lots of places," she said.

"Nope." He shook his head. "I get to pick, and it's going to be a surprise."

CHAPTER 20

W es woke to a text, but it wasn't Jill or Laura or Kent. "Thank you, Lord," he muttered as he lifted the phone to look at it.

Colton had messaged him, saying, *Too much snow to go out with Annie. I'll have to tell you about her once we do go out.*

Wes marveled at the fact that Colton had another girlfriend already. Wes had thought his brother would never date again, but Colton had gotten right back on the horse. Wes hoped he wasn't rushing things, but Colton usually didn't.

He'd dated Priscilla forever it seemed, and their engagement had lasted for over a year. So he was probably fine.

Bummer, he sent back to his brother. *Do you think she has any friends up there interested in a soon-to-be unemployed man with no ambition?*

Haha, Colton sent back. *And actually yes, there are single women here in Coral Canyon.*

Wes scoffed at the idea.

He hadn't dated anyone seriously in probably two years, and he only went out when society deemed it necessary for him. And then, he asked someone he'd known for years that he could enjoy the fundraising dinner with, or the complimentary theater tickets, or whatever else black tie event he'd been invited to.

He only went with women he knew he wouldn't fall for. Wes had done that twice, bought the diamond ring twice, been down on one knee twice.

And then he'd cancelled both weddings after only a few weeks. He wasn't sure if he was afraid to commit, or if he just hadn't been able to see himself with Claire or Lauren long-term.

He got up, because once Wes woke up, he wasn't going back to sleep. He moved over to the windows in his bedroom, and looked out over the city. Or at least he tried. The snow had arrived in Denver too.

But instead of it making his heart sink to the soles of his shoes, the way it probably had for Colton, Wes seized the opportunity this snow gave him.

He returned quickly to his bedroom to get his phone from the nightstand, and he texted Jill, Laura, and Kent.

Lots of snow this morning. I'm headed to Ivory Peaks for the holidays, so can we reschedule this meeting?

He hated that he'd asked, but he could put his foot down in a second text if he had to.

Thankfully, Kent responded first, and he said, *My front door is frozen shut, so yes, let's reschedule.*

Relief flowed through Wes, and he jumped in the shower before anyone else added their thoughts to the group text. He packed a bag quickly, checked his phone and found that both Laura and Jill had agreed.

Not that he cared. He hadn't dressed for a meeting, but for a drive through the snow as he ventured northwest to Ivory Peaks.

His parents were getting older, and if Wes thought about it, so was he.

"Forty-seven," he told himself as he walked toward the elevator that would take him from the penthouse on the thirty-first floor to his truck in the parking garage.

Forty-seven was almost fifty, and Wes hadn't quite thought about his age in those terms yet.

He got behind the wheel of the boxy truck that was more sport utility vehicle than pickup, tossing his bag on the seat beside him. He wondered what it would be like to just drive. Drive until he couldn't drive anymore, the way Colton had done.

And look at him—he'd found another girlfriend. Wes reminded himself he didn't want another girlfriend, and he made the appropriate turns at the appropriate times to get out to his parents' farm in Ivory Peaks.

The familiar town square shone through the snow, and Wes slowed to take in the beauty of it. Lights filled the sky, creating an eerie environment with red, green, blue, and white filling the sky like so many alien spaceships.

He'd enjoyed the drive, where there was no pressure to have his clothes pressed into perfectly straight lines. No one was looking to him for the eloquent statement. He didn't have any appearances to keep up.

As he approached the small farm with the big house in the center of it, some of the expectations descended onto his shoulders again.

His father would want to talk about the campaign, though Wes hadn't confirmed nor committed to anything yet. He pulled into the driveway and dashed through the snow to the front door.

"Ma," he called as he stomped the snow from his feet just inside the house.

"Oh my goodness," she said. "It's Wes." She came bustling out of the kitchen to hug him, and Wes smiled as she did. "Hey, Ma. How are you?"

"Staying warm," she said.

"Where's Dad?"

"What are you doing here?" she asked. "I didn't think you'd come until tomorrow."

"It's snowing," he said as if that explained it all. And in Colorado, it should.

He thought about what life might be like if he didn't have to worry about what the weather was like. He could stay home if he wanted to, doing whatever it was that people did when they didn't leave their houses.

And he knew in that moment that he wouldn't fight Laura to keep HMC under his management. He'd done great things at HMC; he knew that.

And he was ready for something else.

What that something else was, he didn't know. But Wes would figure it out. One thing he'd always done was land on his feet, and he would this time too.

"So," his mother said. "Come get some coffee."

"I brought some," he said, as he'd driven through on his way out of the city. But that didn't matter. His mom would pour him a cup anyway.

As she did, she asked, "Are you seeing anyone new?"

Wes didn't roll his eyes. He didn't automatically deny it. His mother had asked him that same question so many times, he'd thought about recording an answer to play back for her.

"You know what?" He reached for the coffee mug. "I'm talking to a woman, yes."

She didn't need to know he'd only spoken to Bree on the phone one time, or that he didn't know her last name.

"Is that so?" his mother asked, and she sounded like she didn't believe him. "Who is she?"

"I'm not ready to say," he said, putting a diplomatic smile on his face. He hated this smile, but it worked, and he really needed it to work right now. "When is Gray coming?" He sipped his coffee though his blood was already zipping through his veins.

"He's supposed to be here by noon," she said. "And he's bringing lunch, so I hope you're not too hungry."

"I'm fine, Ma." He looked around the kitchen and into the family room. "Where's Dad?"

"He's in his office."

"I'm going to go talk to him," Wes said. He took his coffee with him, glad he'd been able to escape from more of his mother's questions.

She might have turned seventy a few months ago, but she was still as sharp as a tack. And she really wanted her sons to get married, and one of Wes's biggest regrets was that he hadn't been able to give her that yet.

Gray had been married before, but he'd since divorced, and Mom still didn't have a daughter-in-law to go on shopping and lunch dates with.

He knocked on his father's open office door and entered. "Hey, Dad."

His father looked up from something on his desk, and Wes wondered what in the world it could be. All of the Hammond boys had gotten their work ethic from their father, who still had plenty of good to do in the world.

Wes wanted to tell his father that he wasn't going to run for governor, but the first thing his dad said was, "I've got a spec sheet on Hancey," and he sifted through a couple of papers before finding the one he handed to Wes.

He didn't look at it, and his father had his back turned as he went back to his desk. "Dad," Wes tried again. "I'm not sure I want to do this." He should've been stronger, just like with the text that morning.

And his dad wouldn't give him the out Kent had.

"Oh, everyone feels like that," his dad said. "Study the specs and draft a speech, and you'll start to feel it." He gave Wes a smile, but Wes didn't return it. His dad was already back to his work, and he didn't notice that Wes didn't return the smile.

Pure exhaustion pulled through him, and he wished he hadn't come to the farm quite so quickly. He didn't want to stay in the office and discuss politics, but he didn't want to join his mother in the kitchen and talk about his non-existent girlfriend.

Thankfully, his phone chimed, and he said, "I have to take this."

He left the office and went down the hall to his old bedroom to check the text from Colton.

Just tell Dad you don't want to be governor.

How did you know I was just talking to him? Wes asked.

Gut feeling.

Wes sighed as he sat on the twin bed, the frame creaking under his full-grown weight. His phone rang, and Wes swiped on the call from Colton. "Hey."

"Did you tell him?"

"You texted ten seconds ago."

"So you're not going to tell him."

Wes sighed, wondering how he could harness happiness again. He hadn't felt it for a while, and he hadn't even known it until that moment. "It's Christmas."

"Oh, brother."

"And I need a gift from you."

"What's that?"

"Uh...Bree's number?"

"Bree who?" Colton sounded genuinely confused. "Wait a second. Bree—*Bree*?"

"I may have told Mom I was talking to a woman, so she'd stop badgering me about not having a girlfriend."

A couple of beats of silence passed, and then Colton burst out laughing.

"All right, all right," Wes said. "Can I have her number or not?"

"I'll have to ask her first," Colton said. "But I think I can give you that gift this Christmas."

"Great," Wes said. "Merry Christmas, Colt." The call ended, and Wes flopped back on the bed and stared up at the ceiling. Gray and his son, Hunter, couldn't arrive soon enough.

His phone chimed, and Wes wanted to turn it off. He held it above his head and looked at it.

The text had one name: Breeann Richards.

And one number.

For the first time in a long, long time, a real smile spread Wes's mouth.

Number one, he wouldn't be a liar now. And number two, he knew Bree's last name. Now he just needed to figure out what to say to her when he talked to her for the second time ever.

CHAPTER 21

Colton woke on Christmas Eve, wishing the snow hadn't kept him from taking Annie to dinner the night before. He'd wanted to walk the shops on Main Street she'd told him about, looking for a few gifts.

The Whittakers had been kind and gracious to let him crash their holidays, and he wanted to get them a little token of his appreciation. But the weather would likely make it impossible for him to have gifts for anyone by Christmas.

Frustration built behind his tongue, and Colton stayed in bed, trying to breathe deeply to get the emotions to loosen and leave his body.

He literally didn't waste time trying to control something he couldn't control. He'd learned that at an early age, when all his friends had made it onto the Academic Olympiad—except for him. They had class together, and worse, lunch right afterward. So they'd talk about their competitions, and what they were learning, and about all the cool science experiments they got to do—without him.

Yes, tenth grade had been miserable for him. He'd gone to as many of their tournaments as he could, cheering them on as they won and won and won—until the championships.

Then, the question that Quinton Dean had missed had been one Colton knew. A biology question about the rate of respiration. Colton could still hear the groan from the team at Peaks High. Ilima Orion had even glanced back at him in the audience, as if she'd known that their team would've won if only Colton had been on it.

But he couldn't control that situation, and he certainly couldn't control Mother Nature. "Bless them all," he whispered up to the ceiling. "Bless them with health and wealth and happiness." That was a good gift, right? A prayer in someone's behalf?

Colton thought so, because his faith in a loving God had been coming back to him slowly over the past few days. This family possessed something magical, and Colton couldn't help feeling like the Lord had led him up this dead-end road to this lodge, right before the snow had gotten so bad that he couldn't get out.

Had God also led him to Annie?

It was hard to push against that, because all the signs seemed to point to yes, He had. After all, Colton believed he'd been led to the lodge, and Annie had been at the lodge....

He shut down the line of thought and went to get in the shower. The first bathroom door was locked, though, and when he tried the second, he found it locked too. He retreated a few steps to lean against the back of the couch while he waited.

A few minutes later, the door opened, and Annie's youngest daughter came out wearing a bright blue bathrobe. "Sorry," she said. "I hope you weren't waiting long."

"Nope," he said with a smile.

Eden smiled too and took a step toward the bedroom she shared with her family before turning back to him. "You like my mom, right?"

"Yes, ma'am," he said, hoping he wasn't about to enter into an extreme session where he had to identify and define how he felt about her mother.

"She likes you too," Eden said with a smile. "I think it's cute."

"Cute?" Colton repeated, not sure what was cute about, well, anything at the moment.

"Yeah," Eden said, not picking up on his guarded tone. "Reminds me of my first boyfriend. Those first few weeks are magical." She gave him another smile and went down the hall.

Colton couldn't move. Her *first* boyfriend? What did that mean? He was forty-two-years-old, and Annie was older than him. Were they acting like teenagers? Was she saying he'd feel differently about Annie after a couple of weeks, once the relationship wasn't shiny and new?

Maybe she wasn't saying anything at all. Colton shook his head and went into the bathroom, but his thoughts wouldn't stop. They pestered him relentlessly until he'd decided he'd keep some distance between him and Annie that day. Her daughters were here for the holidays, and he didn't want to intrude on that.

When he entered the kitchen, he immediately saw the unfamiliar face. He cataloged that the man sat next to Emily, and Colton deduced this must be her boyfriend. He had an open face without a stitch of a beard on it, and a very loud laugh. Beside him, Emily practically disappeared, and Colton watched them for a moment while he doctored up his coffee and took a breakfast croissant.

He took his food out the back door without encountering Annie, and from the patio, he texted Bree.

What are you doing this morning?

Nothing.

Can I come down to your cabin? The lodge is loud this morning.

Sure.

So Colton went that way, eating his warm sandwich before it got too cold. Bree opened the door when he knocked, and he glanced at her. "Thanks."

"Something's wrong," she said.

"Just thinking about my brother," he said, though that wasn't all the way true. He had been thinking about Wes, and he'd told his brother about Annie last night, that he was taking a woman to dinner.

He'd texted to say he hadn't been able to earlier, and Wes hadn't been nearly as distracted by the takeover this morning. He'd said some things about having no ambition that had bothered Colton, and he pulled out his phone and texted him to just tell their father that he didn't want to run for governor.

"My dad wants my brother to run for governor," he told Bree as he followed her into the kitchen. "And he doesn't want to."

Wes's next text came in, and he wanted to know how Colton had known what he was thinking.

Colton didn't know how he knew, he just did. *Gut feeling,* he sent back to Wes. He'd also told Wes earlier that there were a lot of single women in Coral Canyon.

He sat down, looking at one. "Hey," he said. "This might be way out there, but I've got four single brothers...."

Bree's eyes widened. "Are you trying to set me up with your brothers?"

"Well, not all of them." He grinned at her. "Definitely not Ames. He's so not your type."

"No?" She folded her arms, her eyes sparkling with a challenge. "What's my type, cowboy?"

"Well, he's like, this hard-nosed cop. I don't see you with him." His phone buzzed again, but Wes could wait a second.

"Who would you put me with?" she asked.

"Wes," Colton said. "For sure, Wes." He got up again and said, "I have to call him. Be right back."

"Call him why?" Bree asked, following him. "Don't set me up with him."

Colton waved to say he'd heard her, and then his brother answered. He'd talked his brother through plenty of difficult situations, and this one was no different. But when Wes said he wasn't going to tell their dad about not running for governor because it was Christmas, Colton didn't have anything else to argue with.

And then Wes asked for Bree's number.

Pure giddiness filled Colton, and he turned away from the window where he'd been having his conversation.

"Merry Christmas, Colt," Wes said, and he didn't sound merry at all.

Colton couldn't get back into the kitchen fast enough. "Bree," he said, causing her to turn from the stovetop. She held a spatula, and she was definitely pretty enough for Wes.

"Guess what?"

"What?" she asked. "You look like you just won the lottery."

"Well, maybe you did," he said, grinning even harder now. "My brother just asked for your number."

"*My* number?" She looked shocked, and actually leaned against the countertop as if she couldn't stand by herself.

"Yeah," Colton said. "He said he liked the sound of your voice." He hadn't actually said that, but he couldn't tell Bree that Wes had told their mother he was "talking to a woman" just to get her off his back about never dating.

He held his phone in front of him, just waiting for her to give permission. But she didn't seem to get what he was waiting for. "Can I give it to him?"

"I mean...I guess. Can I see a picture of him?"

"Sure," Colton said, his thumbs flying now. He sent Wes Bree's name, and then attached her contact info. "Come look."

She left whatever was frying on the stove and joined him at the table. He swiped to get to some pictures, finally pulling up one of him and Wes from a company party over the Fourth of July.

"Here we are. He's the taller one, obviously." He gave Bree his phone, and she analyzed the picture like it held national secrets.

"He is cute." She handed the phone back and got up so quickly, Colton couldn't see her face.

"Cute?" he echoed. "Okay, don't call him *cute* when you talk to him. He's forty-seven-years-old, not a puppy."

"And he's the CEO?"

"Yes," Colton said, though Wes could technically be jobless soon. So could Colton. "He's really smart, Bree. And *handsome*. The word you're looking for is handsome."

"Probably humble too," Bree said dryly. "Just like you."

Colton blinked and then burst out laughing. "Hey, we have good genes. What do you want me to say?"

Bree shook her head and brought over a pan with fried eggs in it. "Eggs?"

"Yeah, sure," he said, and she slid a couple onto a plate in front of him.

"What's he going to do? Call me?"

"I have no idea," Colton said. "He just asked for your number."

"Did you show him a picture of me?"

"Nope." She'd let the eggs cook too long, and the yolks weren't runny anymore. Colton didn't complain, though, because he'd distracted her.

Bree sat at the table with him, completely silent. A minute later, she jumped to her feet. "We better get over to the lodge, or we'll miss the tree lighting."

"Tree lighting?"

"It's a *huge* thing," she said, scrambling with her plate over to the sink. "Come on. Actually, come help me with my gifts."

Colton did, but it only added to his unease that he didn't have presents for anyone. He carried one of Bree's boxes and followed her into the living room, which had been transformed since the last time he'd been in it. Which was last night.

But now, stockings hung all along the fireplace, and at least a dozen had been tacked to the wall too. The Christmas tree had been fully decorated over the past couple of days, and Colton picked out the few ornaments he'd hung before Annie's daughter had burst into the house with news of a date.

"Those have names on them," she said. "Find the right stocking, and put it inside, if you would."

Colton did what she said, jostling with a few other people as they came into the room to distribute their gifts too. Everyone seemed to know exactly when to congregate in the living room, and by the time Colton had put the last gift in the last stocking, the room had filled.

He tossed Bree's empty box into the hall and stood at her side while Graham got up in front of everyone. Colton glanced around for Annie and found her squeezed into the corner of a couch, with her two daughters and Emily's boyfriend. She did not look in his direction, and Colton didn't know what that meant.

Maybe it meant nothing. He really was tired of trying to read into a situation, that was for sure.

"Welcome to Whiskey Mountain Lodge," Graham said, his voice warm and loud at the same time. "Every year, we have a tradition of lighting this tree and handing out small gifts." He indicated the stockings. "I think we've had just about everyone light the tree now, so we might have to start cycling through again."

Colton wondered how they chose who did it, but it didn't seem like an appropriate time for questions.

"I just want to say how much I love our family," Graham said, and Colton's emotions tightened in his throat. He loved and missed his family too. "And we love all who come to belong to our family." He looked around, his gaze landing specifically on Annie, and Celia, and Patsy, Elise, and then Bree. And right next to Bree, Colton.

In that moment, Colton felt the sincerity of Graham's words, and he believed that the love and acceptance he felt from Graham came from God Himself.

Colton stilled, as it seemed like the rest of the family did too. Several long seconds passed, and then Graham said, "Patsy, would you light the tree this year?"

A smile like Colton had never seen shone from the woman's face, and she nodded as she got up from one of the chairs across the room. She went over to the wall with all the stockings, and put her hand on the bank of light switches there.

"Merry Christmas, everyone," she said.

"Merry Christmas," the room chorused back as the lights on the tree burst to life. *Oohs* and *ahhs* filled the room next, and Beau stood up too.

"The lights are all white this year," he said. "As you can see. It's a change, but really beautiful, right?"

Murmurs of ascent rose into the air, and even Colton found himself nodding. He thought about his family, and what traditions they had, and the only thing he could come up with was the envelope of money his father gave to every son every year. It was nothing like this. Nothing like a tree-lighting event where the person who literally took one second to push a switch was made to feel so special.

Graham hugged Patsy and said something to her as others started getting up and handing out the stockings. When Laney stepped in front of Colton and Bree and handed them each one, Colton's first instinct was to push it back into the woman's arms.

"I don't—" he started, but Laney just nodded.

"Yes," she said. "You're here, and that means you get something."

"It's best not to argue," Vi said. "Trust me." She held a child on each knee while her husband had all their stockings on the floor in front of them.

"All right, Mary," he said. "Remember how we're not going to grab everything?"

Colton watched them deal with their little children for another few moments, feeling absolutely at home in this place that was absolutely not his home.

He wanted to carry this feeling with him wherever he went, and he wanted to recreate it with his own family. All around him, mothers and fathers helped their kids, and Colton knew then that he wanted children too. Little children and teenaged children and adult children.

His eyes landed on Annie, and she raised hers to look at him. She didn't smile, though, and Colton lifted his stocking, still wondering if the magic of Christmas had somehow infected him.

She nodded, and Colton focused on the red plush object in his hand. He reached inside, feeling very much like a little boy on Christmas morning, long before he knew what the letters HMC stood for, or how much money he'd one day have in his bank account.

Back then, Christmas was made of magic and warm fireplaces. Hot scones for breakfast, and the scent of coffee in the air. Toys and plastic and new bicycles.

His stocking held a couple of things, and he pulled them out all at once. A giant chocolate bar sat in his hand, as well as a bracelet that had been made out of colored plastic.

"That's from Bailey and Averie," Bree said, nodding to the bracelet.

Colton looked from it to her, everything inside him cracking open. "This is great," he said, hardly recognizing his own voice.

Bree just smiled, because this was part of her normal life.

But for Colton, he felt like his life was just getting started—and he wanted it to be right here in Coral Canyon, where he could come to this lodge every Christmas.

He looked across the room to Annie, but she was focused on her daughters and then her own gifts. He couldn't wait to tell her he was going to move here.

He didn't know what he'd do here, as he'd need something good to fill his time. He didn't know where he'd live. He didn't know a lot of things.

None of them mattered. He knew he was supposed to be here, and he closed his eyes and thanked the Lord for showing him such a clear path to be here at this place, with these people, so he could make the changes in his life he needed to make.

CHAPTER 22

The festivities had just wrapped up in front of the Christmas tree, and Bree loaded the gifts she'd gotten from the Whittakers, Annie, Patsy, and Elise into the boxes she'd brought her presents in.

"Come on, Mister Muscles," she said to Colton. "Help me take this stuff out to the cabin."

Elise approached, a couple of boxes of her own in her hands. "Is Colton carrying for us?" She grinned at the cowboy who'd fallen fairly silent during the last twenty minutes while everyone opened gifts.

"That's right," Bree said, grinning as she loaded him up with as many boxes as possible.

"Now I know what I'm good for," he grumbled, but he wore a playful edge in his eyes that told Bree he didn't mind helping.

The three of them went out the back door, the silence of the countryside welcome after such a large family gathering.

They joked and laughed, and Bree let the warmth of having friends wash over her. Every now and then, the gravity of her situation crept into her mind, but days like today held enough power to push her negative thoughts and feelings back out.

"I just realized something," Colton said. "None of us are Whittakers, and yet we're all here. Where are your families?"

"I'm from Prince Edward Island," Elise said, and Bree hoped they'd make it back to the cabin before she had to say anything. In fact, she even increased her pace to do just that.

"It's just my mom, and she went to Vegas this year. My older brother got married this year, and he's with his wife's family," Elise said. "It's expensive to get there, and I opted not to go this year." She looked a bit haunted for a minute, and Bree understood completely. Elise brightened a moment later.

"What about you?"

"I'm headed back to Colorado as soon as the weather lets me," he said. "I have a meeting on the thirtieth that I have to be home for. After that...." He blew out his breath. "Anything is possible."

"Don't you have a job?" Elise asked.

"I do," Colton said. "But I think my cousins are going to take over the family company, and I'll quit."

"Wow," Bree said. "Can you get another job?"

"I guess," Colton said, and he didn't seem concerned about it at all. If Bree were about to lose her job, she'd be frantic, searching every job board within a hundred miles and texting anyone she knew with any sort of connection.

They passed the stables, and the cabin could only be another five minutes.

"What about your family, Bree?" Colton asked.

In that very moment, her phone rang, and relief unlike anything Bree had felt in a while sang through her. "Here." She thrust a third box at him despite his protests and pulled her phone from her pocket.

"Unknown caller. Probably a scam."

Colton bent and set the boxes on the ground, peering at her phone. "That's my brother." A massive smile overtook his face, but Bree's heart had started booming strangely in her chest.

"You're not going to answer?"

She didn't want to answer his questions or his brother's phone call, but out of the two, Bree chose the phone call.

"Hello?" she asked, spinning away from Colton and Elise.

"Oh, I don't get to overhear," he said. "I get it. Come on, Elise."

"Hello," a deep voice said on the other end of the line. "I think I got the right woman." A chuckle followed, and Bree didn't know why her heart felt like it had tripled in size and was now trying to choke her.

"We'll expect a full report when you get home," Colton called, but Bree didn't even turn around to acknowledge him.

Bree couldn't help feeling like she was indeed being scammed, but the man on the other end of the line seemed to be real. She closed her eyes and pictured the *handsome*, tall, dark-haired cowboy she'd seen standing next to Colton, both of them smiling as if they owned the world. Neither of them had been wearing cowboy hats in the picture, and in fact, Wes and Colton had been decked out in tuxedos.

"Are you still there?" Wes asked.

"Yeah," she said. "Yes, I'm here."

"I guess I owe you an explanation," he said.

"Okay." Bree felt like she'd lost the ability to think. Colton hadn't affected her like this. He felt like a brother from another mother, and her heart had stayed perfectly normal in her chest. But Wes....

Don't do this again, she counseled herself. Just because a man liked her didn't mean she had to fall head-over-heels in love with him.

"I guess I just liked talking to you the other day," Wes said. "You have a nice voice."

"Do I?" Bree had never been told she had a nice voice before. "I think you're going to have to work on your compliments." She giggled, and even Wes gave a light laugh.

"Well, you might have to send me a picture," he said. "Since I don't know anything about you but your voice, I figured it was safe to compliment."

"Oh, we're not to picture level yet, Mister," she said, surprised at how flirtatious she sounded. "Let's start with basics. You're Colton's brother."

"Yes," Wes said. "The oldest."

"I'm the oldest too," she said, and she couldn't believe she'd voluntarily brought up her family.

"Siblings?" he asked.

"Just one. Well." She ground her voice through her throat, so many doors about to fly open. Doors Bree had worked for years to close and keep closed.

The snow in front of her blinded her, and a shiver ran down her arms despite her warm coat. She blinked, and she could see Bronson's face.

"Well?" Wes asked. "I have four brothers, as I'm sure Colton's told you."

"He mentioned some brothers," Bree said, hoping they'd move on to something else.

"Yeah," Wes said. "I'm hoping to get everyone here for the New Year. My parents are getting older."

"They're not there?"

"Just me and my next youngest brother, Gray. Well, and his son. Colton's up there. Ames is doing something with some charity or something this year." Wes sighed as if working with a charity was just so taxing. "And Cy's in California, probably sleeping on the beach."

"Oh, wow," Bree said, glancing around at the frosty land-scape surrounding her. "I gotta be honest, Wes, I could go for a beach right now. It's freezing up here."

"Here too," he said. "Been snowing for a few hours."

"I think it's tapered off here," she said. "Colton should be able to get out of here on time."

"Good," Wes said. "Good."

The conversation lulled again, but Bree did not want to go

back to the cabin yet. "Tell me, Wes," she said. "What do you do?"

"Yeah, I think we'll save that for another day," he said. "I called to hear your voice."

"Oh, okay." Bree laughed, but she didn't really have anything to say to him. He was being cute though, and she did like that about him.

"So you tell me, Bree. What do you do? Tell me about the lodge. The Tetons. All of it."

"Have you ever been up here?" she asked, automatically turning toward the mountains.

"Maybe once, when I was a little boy," he said. "I don't remember it."

"Well, the mountains are amazing," she said. "Simply stunning. They have snow on them year-round, and if you've never been here, you should come, and we'll go on the Jenny Lake boat tour. It has the best views of the Grand Teton."

"Wow," he said, his voice lower and softer. "Keep going."

So Bree did, telling him about the amazing pine forests, the hiking trails, and the gondola they could ride to the top of the world. "I mean it's not really the top of the world," she said. "But it feels like it. It's incredible."

"Incredible," he repeated.

"And then, you can take me to dinner at Magic Moose. They have *the best* elk poutine in the entire universe."

Wes laughed, but Bree knew that elk poutine was no laughing matter. She sure did like the sound of his laugh, though and she determined that Wes Hammond put off a very good air.

"Magic Moose," he said. "It's a date."

"Yeah," Bree said, twirling right there on the sidewalk. "It's a date." The call ended a couple of seconds after that, and Bree stared down at her device.

"Did that just happen?" she wondered aloud. She started walking toward the cabin where she lived, her legs and feet a bit numb. She told herself it was because of the cold, but she knew it wasn't. No, her mind barely functioned and every appendage tingled, because Wes Hammond had called her.

Strange, she thought as the cabin came into view, and a steady stream of white smoke came out of the chimney. It would be toasty warm inside, and Bree needed the extra warmth.

She hadn't been able to get herself to swipe right on any of the men on Singles Spark, though four had swiped on her. But one conversation with Wes had her hormones twittering about taking another chance.

It made no sense. Bree didn't take chances. Not since she'd tried to skate across the frozen lake with Bronson, and he'd ended up in the icy water where she couldn't save him.

She slammed the door on that memory, steeling herself to enter her cabin, somewhere she'd always felt safe and protected. If Colton asked her about her family, she'd just say she didn't want to talk about it. She didn't have to tell him anything.

She opened the door and stepped inside.

"So?" Colton asked, bolting to his feet from the couch. "How was it? What did he say?"

"First of all," Bree said, pressing into the closed door behind her. "He's your brother, and I don't want you texting him stuff about me."

Colton looked like she'd said something scandalous. "I won't."

"Good." She held up two fingers. "Second, it was kind of weird. He just wanted to hear my voice?" She shook her head. "That wasn't a question. But I just told him about the mountains and Jenny Lake and stuff."

Horror struck her right between the ribs. She was so stupid. Why had she prattled on about such dumb things? Surely that wasn't what Wes had wanted to hear.

"He's a big outdoors guy," Colton said. "Though he hasn't done much for a while. Day job and all."

"Yeah, he wouldn't talk about being CEO." She cocked her

eyebrows at Colton. "Is that because of the family business transfer or whatever?"

"Probably," Colton said. "Wes...plays things close to the vest, you could say."

Bree pushed away from the door and walked further into the cabin. "As long as Wes is his real name, he can keep whatever else he wants right up against that vest." She paused and looked at Colton, only a couple of steps from him now. "Wes is his real name, right?"

She hadn't told anyone about Jay, and the real reason she'd broken up with him. Not even Elise. The last thing she needed was sympathy and everyone looking at her like, *Poor, poor Bree.*

"Wesley," Colton said. "But yeah."

"Good." She patted his chest, something sobering between them. "Thanks for bringing out my presents, Colton. Really."

"Thanks for answering my brother's phone call."

Bree thought Wes must be terribly lonely, and she'd always heard it was hard to be the boss. Hard to be at the top, because the only place to go was down. Her heart bled for Wes, and she found herself wanting to talk to him again.

She stepped into Colton and gave him a hug. "I'm glad you stumbled upon Whiskey Mountain Lodge," she said.

"Me too," he whispered.

"Knock, knock," someone said behind her, and Bree twisted in Colton's arms as Annie entered the cabin.

"Oh, hey." Bree cleared her throat and practically jumped away from the other woman's boyfriend. She started shrugging out of her coat. "What brings you out here?"

Annie didn't speak, and when Bree finally stopped fiddling with her coat for long enough to look at her, she plainly saw anger in Annie's features.

"Talk to you later, Bree," Colton said, heading for the door.

She wanted to call after him that nothing had happened. That she didn't like Colton as more than a friend. Annie should know that.

But he stepped past her, and Annie glared her into silence, and then they were both gone.

Bree finally took another breath, tired from all the ups and downs of the last twenty minutes.

Maybe she could call Wes again, as he alone seemed to be able to soothe her. *No,* she told herself. After all, she didn't want to come off as desperate.

CHAPTER 23

Annie closed her eyes and breathed in through her nose, trying to get the image of Bree standing in Colton's arms out of her head.

All the way out.

"Hey," Colton said, reaching for her hand. "Were you looking for me?"

"Yes." Her eyes flew open, and she pulled her hand away from his. "I texted you five times."

He held up his phone. "I just got them. Sorry, I was...dealing with something."

"Yeah, looked like it." Now that Annie was with Colton, she didn't want to be. But he'd disappeared for most of the morning, and she'd only seen him briefly during the tree lighting. Then he'd flitted away again. She'd had to ask around until she got to Vi, who said she'd seen him leave with Elise and Bree, laden with their boxes.

He was just being nice, she told herself again. She'd repeated the sentence during the ten-minute walk out to Bree's and Elise's cabin.

"It's not what you think," Colton said.

Annie brushed by him and went down the steps. The afternoon of puzzling and talking together fizzled in her mind. The family always had a beautiful Christmas Eve dinner, but Annie had considered skipping it to go to dinner with Colton. Leaving her daughters behind to go out with a man.

Stupidity flowed through her, all that existed in the world coming to Wyoming to fill her from top to bottom.

"Annie, come on," he said, coming after her.

"Tell me what it is then," she said, not slowing down at all.

"It was just loud in the lodge today," he said. "And I went out to Bree's, and we got talking. That's it."

"Talking." He must think her the world's biggest fool. "Didn't look like talking, Colton." She cut a glare at him. "It looked like hugging."

"Well, yeah," he said. "Because we're friends, and she'd just gotten off the phone with my brother, and—"

"Your brother?"

"Yeah," he said, smiling. Actually smiling. Annie's fury bubbled and boiled, and her fists clenched. "I kind of set them up."

"Who?"

"My brother and Bree."

Annie's step slowed. "You set up your brother and Bree."

"Yeah." Colton smiled. "See? Not what you think."

Annie wanted to believe him. Every cell in her body begged her to believe him. "If you wanted a quiet morning, why couldn't we have gone to breakfast?"

"I didn't see you when I came upstairs."

"So you run off with the first woman you see?"

"No. Come on." He sounded frustrated, and Annie hated that. She hated this barrier between them, and she knew what was at the root of it. Her jealousy.

"It was nothing," he said. "Her place is quiet. She feeds me eggs and coffee. And that's it."

Annie's chest stung, and she picked up the pace again. She had no idea what to say. She only knew she didn't want Colton to eat Bree's food or go out to her cabin. But Annie didn't have a quiet, out of the way cabin where they could escape for a little down time.

"Annie." He caught up to her again and took her hand in his. This time, she didn't pull away. "Don't be mad," he said. "Please. It's Christmas Eve, and I don't want you to be mad."

She didn't want to be mad either, and the closer to the lodge they got, the more her anger ebbed away. "I just...it feels like you're dating both of us."

"Absolutely not true," he said. "I haven't held her hand. I haven't kissed her. I haven't even *thought* about doing those things. I don't even want to. There's no spark with me and Bree. None."

"None?" Annie hated that she needed this reassurance. She didn't remember being so needy in her relationship with Ryan. She'd been much younger, and their romance had been a whirlwind, with her meeting him on a Thursday afternoon when he came into the restaurant where she worked, and him proposing exactly six weeks later, in the same restaurant. They'd gotten married another three months after that, and just like that, within five months Annie's whole life had changed.

"Absolutely none," Colton said. "Do you want to call my brother and ask him? He literally just talked to Bree. I think they're starting something."

"That doesn't really sound like Bree," Annie said.

"Which part?"

"The long-distance relationship part." Annie's throat closed, because such a relationship wasn't really something she wanted either. She knew things were up in the air with Colton, and she didn't want to try to get him to tether things down right now. Soon, but not right now.

"Yeah, those are hard," Colton said, his voice a touch cooler than before. Or maybe she was imagining things. With him, her imagination seemed to run on overdrive, conjuring up amazing fantasies, but also giving life to terrible fears too.

"I'm sorry," she said when they stepped onto the back patio. "I shouldn't have made assumptions."

"It's fine," he said, flashing her a smile. "Do you think we can get down the canyon for lunch?"

A glow filled her whole soul. "Yes," she said. "Let's go to lunch."

———

GETTING AWAY FROM THE LODGE WAS EXACTLY WHAT ANNIE NEEDED. She hadn't even realized how trapped she felt inside those walls, because the place was so big. But the moment she and Colton snuck away in his monster-sized SUV, the dark cloud that had been following her since that morning lifted.

The snow still stuck to the road, but Colton handled it like a pro. "You must be used to driving in the snow."

"A little," he said, glancing at her. "My parents live northwest of Denver, up in some hills. It's a little town called Ivory Peaks."

"Sounds quaint," she said, smiling. She ran her right hand through her hair, feeling silly, and sexy, and so free.

"It's quaint," he said. "That sounds about right. Has a cute little town square, the red-and-white barbershop pole, all of that."

"Did you spend much time in town?" she asked. "Here in Coral Canyon?"

"Not much," he said.

"The town is growing," she said. "But it still has a small-town feel." Annie loved Coral Canyon, and she knew every street. Once, she'd known every resident, but the town was simply too big for that now.

She chattered on about the town, and where her house was, and some of her clients. Colton seemed interested in anything and everything she said, and he held her hand on the way into the restaurant and on the way back out.

"I've never had bison before," he said. "And that was amazing."

"I'm glad you liked it." She waited for him to reach past her and open her door, the wind slipping down the collar of her coat. Colton did just that, and after she'd climbed into the truck, he crowded into the doorway.

"Thanks for coming to lunch with me." He leaned forward and touched his lips to hers, and Annie tried not to melt into him. She tried, and she failed. She turned to butter the moment he touched her, and she wondered if he knew it.

He kept the kiss sweet, and it didn't go on too long. When he backed up and closed her door, Annie finally opened her eyes. "Wow," she whispered to herself, feeling a bit detached from her body.

"The roads are better," he said as he climbed behind the wheel. "And hopefully we didn't miss too much at the lodge."

"We didn't miss anything," Annie said. "Unless you're dying to get that fairy garden finished before Christmas."

"I honestly haven't even thought about it," he said, and Annie laughed.

By the time they got back to the lodge, she felt like herself again, and she wore a big smile when she and Colton entered the lodge. She almost expected her girls to be standing there, tapping their toes and waiting for her to return. They weren't.

A couple of people loitered in the living room, and Rose and Vi and Lily had their kids playing on the floor near the Christmas tree.

"How was lunch?" Lily asked as Annie came into the living room.

"Really great."

"Where'd you go?" Vi asked. She reached down and took a wrapper from one of her girls.

"King Carver's," Annie said.

"Oh, nice," Lily said with a smile. She glanced at Colton. "You're really trying hard."

He blinked, his smile sliding onto his face a moment later, and Annie saw the marketing director shine through him. She knew, because she'd seen Andrew do the same thing whenever he had to talk to the press. Colton must have to do the same, because he wore a media mask right now as he looked at Lily.

"Am I?" he asked.

Lily blinked, and she cut a look at Annie. "I just meant it's an expensive place."

"Ah." Colton nodded and pressed his palms together. "Yeah, it was expensive, but the bison bolognaise was really good."

"I've had that," Rose said. "It is delicious."

"I'm not really a fan of the game meats," Lily said.

Colton went around the couch and sat down on the opposite end from Lily. "Do you three still sing?"

The sisters exchanged a glance, and Vi said, "We aren't recording right now. But we work on things from time to time."

"Yeah, chasing toddlers," Rose said, lunging for something one of her triplets tried to put in his mouth. "Not in your mouth, Collin." She sighed as she tucked the ballpoint pen behind her ear. "Not much music-making for me." She actually sounded sad about it.

"My mother loves your stuff," Colton said. "She'll die when I tell her I got to spend Christmas with the three of you." The smile he gave them now seemed genuine. He looked up at Annie and patted the sofa cushion next to him, a clear invitation for her to join him on the couch.

They hadn't made any plans to do anything that afternoon, and Annie figured visiting with the Everett sisters was as good of an idea as anything else they could do.

"Are your parents coming up tonight?" she asked.

"Not until morning," Rose said. "The beds here hurt my dad's back."

"I know what he feels like," Colton said.

"Your bed isn't comfortable?" Annie asked, settling next to him.

He took her hand in his and said, "It's okay. I'm kind of a diva when it comes to my mattress."

Vi giggled. "Mattress diva. Annie, you better make sure you explore that further before you two go any further."

"Yeah, like what else he's a diva about," Lily added.

Annie laughed with them and turned toward Colton. "I think she's right. I need a list."

He grinned at her, and Annie found him to be the most wonderful man she'd ever met. So handsome, and so easy-going, and so smart. The Human Genome Project. Executive marketing director. Colton Hammond could literally do anything.

"First, there's how my eggs are cooked," he said, his dark eyes sparkling with a tease. Annie loved it when he flirted with her, and he didn't even try to hide it from the other women in the room.

"Oh, boy," Lily said. "Beau's like that too."

"And you somehow tolerate it," Annie said.

"I do," Lily said, laughing.

"What else?" Rose asked, giggling with the others as she peered at Colton.

"Parking spots," he said. "I actually have one reserved for me at the building where I work." He looked from Rose to Lily to Vi and back to Annie. He gave a half-shrug and lifted one hand like, *What you gonna do?*

They all burst out laughing, Colton included, and Annie fell a little bit in love with him right then. He really could sit down with anyone and fit right in, and she marveled at that.

"She's in here," Eden said, and she came into the living room, followed by Emily.

"Hey," Annie said, accepting a quick kiss from her youngest daughter. "What's up?"

"We just wondered if you were back from lunch." She glanced at Colton. "Hey, Colton."

"Hi, Eden." He gave her a warm smile. "Any more chats with young Mitchell?"

"Maybe."

"Maybe?" Annie said, scoffing. "She was up half the night with that glow in her face, texting him."

Eden sat down on the floor with the two-and-three-year-olds. She picked up a crayon and started coloring on the same page as Daisy. "I like talking to him," she said without looking at Annie. "And he seems to like talking to me."

"I'm glad," Colton said.

Em pulled up a chair to sit by all of them, and she didn't say much.

"Where's Kelly?" Annie asked.

"He had to make a business call, so he went out to the car."

"On Christmas Eve?" Annie asked.

"I guess so." Emily sighed, and Colton raised his hand.

"We almost had a meeting today," he said. "Business never really sleeps. What does Kelly do?"

"He's a tech developer," Emily said.

"In Coral Canyon?" Colton asked, glancing at Annie. "I mean, you said the town was growing, but I didn't think…well, I guess technology is needed everywhere."

"He works remotely," Emily said. "So he's based here, and there's a small office downtown. But he's on a call with his team in Seattle."

"Oh, got it." Colton nodded. "We have some remote people too."

"What's your company?" Eden asked.

"It's called Hammond Manufacturing Company," he said. "My great-grandfather was a chemist, and he actually invented polyethylene plastic."

"You didn't tell me that," Annie said.

"Polyethylene plastic," Lily repeated. "I'm assuming that's an important plastic."

"It's the most widely used plastic in the world," Colton said. "And we own the formula and manufacture almost all of it in one of our ninety-four plants around the world."

"Oh, wow," Rose said, grinning. "You sound like a commercial." She laughed, and Colton chuckled with her.

"No wonder you can afford King Carver's," Lily said.

Colton once again shrugged as if he didn't have anything much to add to the conversation, a small smile playing with his lips.

"And so modest," Vi said as Daisy started to cry. "All right, girlies. It's time for a nap." She picked up the little girl and reached for Mary. "Come on, Mary. Let's go lie down."

That little girl started to fuss, because she didn't want to go lie down. The front door opened, and Annie looked that way to see Kelly coming back inside. He walked over to them, a smile on his face, and Annie did like him a lot. He and Emily were an amazing couple, and the look on his face as he bent down to give her a kiss on the forehead said he loved Em.

"I have to ask you something," Kelly said, straightening and putting his phone in his pocket. He glanced at Annie, and her hand tightened in Colton's.

"All right," Emily said, reaching for his hand so he could help her up. He did, and Annie thought they'd leave for a private conversation. Instead, Kelly kept Emily's hand in his as he dropped to one knee.

"Emily Pruitt," he said, and Annie sucked in a breath. Every woman in the room did, and Vi said, "We can take a nap in a minute."

Kelly gazed up at Emily, who'd covered her mouth with her free hand. Tears filled her eyes, but they didn't spill down her cheeks. Annie couldn't control her emotions either, and her eyes burned as she watched from the couch.

"I love you, and I want you to be mine forever. I want to be yours. Will you marry me?" He presented a ring that had somehow manifested itself in his fingers. Annie could see the Christmas lights glinting off the huge diamond, and she knew Emily would be well-taken care of with Kelly.

Emily still hadn't answered, and the entire lodge seemed to hold its breath.

"He's dying," Colton said in a stage whisper, which broke the tension in the room. And it broke Emily out of the shocked state she'd fallen into.

"Yes," she said, and Kelly grinned as he stood up. "Yes!" Emily threw herself into Kelly's arms, and they laughed together.

"Yeah," Colton said, clapping loudly. The others joined in, and Annie got up to hug them both and be the first to congratulate them. She wept as she held onto her daughter, and her heart warmed when Eden was the next one to step in and offer her congratulations.

And when Colton did? Annie thought she'd found the man of her dreams.

Now she just had to figure out how to keep him, with her—and in town.

CHAPTER 24

Colton loved the energy at Whiskey Mountain Lodge. He really did. He just needed a break from it sometimes. Everyone did; he saw people retreat to bedrooms or go outside in the afternoons, and Graham and Laney went the mile down the road to their farm, and sometimes various brothers or sisters-in-law or kids went with them.

Apparently, Eli had a pretty enormous house in town, and he took his family there for the afternoon on Christmas Eve, promising to be back in time for dinner.

Which, apparently, was a big deal. Everyone who scattered during the day would be back for Christmas Eve dinner.

After Emily had gotten engaged, Annie had run downstairs to retrieve her laptop, and she and her daughters sat with Kelly on the couch in the basement and started looking at the calendar, at venues, at wedding dresses. The seedlings of a plan took shape, and Colton finally leaned down and kissed Annie's forehead. "I'm going to go see if there's a pair of snowshoes available."

She barely looked up at him as she said, "Okay."

Colton retrieved his coat and gloves from his bedroom and went upstairs to the mudroom, where he'd been before he'd been interrupted a few days ago as he'd been preparing to go snowshoeing.

"Oh, hey," he said to Bree, who had just put something in the washing machine.

"If you wear something and spill all over it," she said crossly, "You should put it in the laundry, don't you think?"

"Definitely," he said, because he was smart enough to agree to whatever an annoyed woman said.

"And half of these gloves don't even have a pair." She tossed down several mismatched gloves in disgust and looked at him. "Are you going out?"

"I was hoping there'd be some snowshoes or something."

"Do you ride?"

"Like, a horse?"

"Yeah, cowboy." She reached up and tapped the brim of his cowboy hat. He tried to dodge her, but he didn't really grasp what she was doing until it was done. "A horse."

"I've been known to ride a horse," he said, though it had been a while. A long while. "My father has a couple of horses."

"Yeah, but do you ride them?"

"He does," Colton said. "I guess it's been a while for me. But how hard can it be? Isn't it like riding a bike?"

Bree's face split into a grin. "Oh, this is going to be fun. Come on." She grabbed his arm and towed him out of the mudroom and out the back door.

He stumbled after her, chuckling. He got his arm away from her on the patio, and they walked side-by-side toward the stable just over the rise in the lawn. "Have you talked to Wes again?"

"He called a few hours ago," she said, glancing at him.

"Was that just today?"

"Yes." Bree laughed. "It's been a long day, hasn't it?"

"It feels like it's been a year," Colton said, though he wasn't sure why. "In fact, I'm not sure time passes the same here as it does everywhere else. I feel like I've been here for months." He tried to do the math to figure out how long he'd actually been there. "Has it only been five days?"

Bree just giggled, and shook her head. "I know what you mean. The holidays can feel like a lifetime." She wrapped her arms around herself, and Colton heard something in her voice that caused him to peer closer at her.

"You okay?" he asked.

"Yeah." Her smile didn't agree with her words though. "I'm fine."

"You never did say why you spend your holidays here and not with your family."

"No," Bree said, her voice considerably cooler than he'd ever heard it. "I never did."

Colton got the hint, and he didn't press the issue. He had plenty of experience of being pushed into places he didn't want to be in, and he wouldn't do that to Bree.

"How many horses do you have here?" he asked instead.

"We used to have thirteen," she said. "They were kind of a hobby for the brothers. But they weren't great riding horses. A couple were, but." Bree shrugged one shoulder. "When the brothers decided it was silly for one family to live in a lodge so big and they wanted to start renting the rooms, they asked me to take over events full-time. I started with the horses. We sold the older ones to farms where they can graze out their days." She came alive talking about her job and the horses, and Colton smiled quietly to himself.

"And we bought new horses that were calm and gentle, good for children and older people, or anyone without experience with horses. So we have twenty-four now, and in the summer and fall, when most of our riding tours are, we have a few temporary workers come up to lead those groups."

"So you don't go out with them?"

"I train all the hands," she said. "So I know all the trails. I know all the landmarks. I know it all." She grinned at him, and Colton once again had the thought that she'd be perfect for Wes.

"You really are a know-it-all," he teased, and Bree laughed with him.

"I have to be right on top of the hands," she said. "They're mostly teenagers, and they really do try to get away with murder."

"I'll bet," Colton said, his mind automatically flying back to when he was a teenager. "You would've fired me and my brothers."

"Is that right?"

"Once, my father sent us next door to help the Wattsworth's with their haying. Or we were supposed to help with the haying. Really, the twins acted like they were sick, and they stayed in the air-conditioned house while Mrs. Wattsworth fed them peanut butter and jelly sandwiches. Me, Wes, and Gray did do a bit of work, but later, Mr. Wattsworth found us all asleep behind a beaver slide." He laughed at the memory. "Boy, was he mad. And he called my dad, and let me tell you, there's nothing quite as awful as disappointing my father." He realized why Wes hadn't told Dad that he didn't want to run for governor. He didn't want to ruin Dad's Christmas—but he didn't want to ruin his either. Or anyone else's.

Bree said nothing about her siblings or time as a teenager, and Colton's curiosity shot toward the sky.

He coached himself not to ask, reminding himself that it wasn't his business. She'd tell him when and if she wanted to.

"Here we are." She unlatched the door on the stable and went inside. "I take care of the horses in the winter too. Graham, Laney, Bailey, and Ronnie come to help. They have horses and cattle and goats and all of that too."

"Sounds like a good life," Colton said, and he meant it. He wondered if he'd been living the wrong life. The city life, behind walls of steel and glass, running around with thousands of other people, trying to find some sort of fulfillment.

He didn't want that life anymore. He'd known it the moment Priscilla had left him in his dressing room, and that was why he hadn't gone back to work. Hopefully, his absence hadn't damaged HMC too much, and he sent up a quick prayer that Laura, Jill, and Kent would be able to take Hammond Manufacturing into the next phase of its success.

Bree named the horses she passed, finally stopping outside a stall with a tall, black horse she called Bull Rider.

"You named a horse Bull Rider?" Colton couldn't believe it. Seemed strange to cross breeds and all that.

"We bought him," she said, gazing up at the horse fondly. "And it just fit."

"Does it?" Colton looked at the horse, instantly reaching for his mane and neck. He did have a calm spirit that invited a man to touch him, and Colton's soul sighed as the horse leaned into his touch.

"Yep, he's for you," Bree said. "I'll put him out here, and you can saddle him."

"Uh...can I?"

"Oh, my word," Bree said. "Fine, let me get out Fritz, and I'll get us ready to go."

"I can help," he said. "I just don't know if I can do it right. Tell me what to get."

"Grab the saddle you want from the far wall there." She nodded to her right. "There are child sizes, and let me tell you, with the amount of chocolate I've seen you eat, you won't fit in one of those."

"Oh, okay," he said as she walked away giggling. No way he could say anything about her weight, not that there was anything to say. He retrieved a nice, big saddle, a blanket, and a bit with reins.

Bree bustled around the stable while the horses stood stock still, letting her push and pull and get them ready to go. "They're excited," she said.

"They are?" He couldn't tell.

"They don't get out as much in the winter," she said.

"Are we tromping through snow?"

"A little," she said evasively, and Colton had the very real feeling that he would be wet and freezing cold by the time he returned.

"I just need time to get ready for dinner," he said. "I hear it's quite the to-do."

"That it is," Bree said. "Celia and Amanda work for days on it, and it is really special." She handed him a pair of reins and added, "Let's go, cowboy."

Colton followed her, almost out the double-wide doors at the opposite end of the stable from where they'd entered, when someone called his name.

He turned back and saw Annie walking toward him. "You're going riding?" she asked, stuffing her hands in her pockets.

"Yeah." He looked over his shoulder. Bree had continued with Fritz, and she didn't wait for him. Considering the episode from that morning, Colton couldn't blame her. He wanted to leave too.

"You'll be back in time for dinner, right?" She reached him, and Colton saw worry in her eyes.

He didn't understand it, and he didn't know how to erase it. "Bree's a pro," he said. "She said she trains teenagers and everything. I think she can handle me."

Annie searched his face, and Colton smiled at her. "Are you excited about Emily and Kelly's engagement?"

The negative emotion on her face broke, and she nodded. Colton leaned toward her, keeping the reins tightly held in one hand, and kissed her quickly. "I'm glad. We won't be long."

"Just you and Bree are going?" she asked.

"Yep." Colton kept on walking, because he was not getting into this discussion again. He'd already told Annie everything there was to tell about him and Bree. He was allowed to have friends.

He turned back to her. "Did you want to come?"

"No." She shook her head and squeezed her elbows to her

sides. "I'm not really an outdoorsy person, especially in the winter."

He kept the smile on his face, and it felt like the one he gave to reporters. He hated giving it to Annie, but he didn't know how else to reassure her. "All right. See you soon." He took the horse all the way outside and swung into the saddle, spotting Bree on the edge of the forest, waiting for him.

He got Bull Rider moving toward her, and he'd been right—riding a horse was like riding a bike, and he did remember how to do it.

"Everything okay?" Bree asked.

"Yep," Colton said, refusing to let Annie infect his thoughts too much. Still, a sliver of irritation squirreled through him while they clopped along a path under the trees that wasn't entirely covered in snow.

"Right up here," Bree said. "We're going to stop. Look up as soon as you can, and you'll see the beautiful Teton range on the horizon."

Colton kept moving, kept looking up. Only branches. Finally, the foliage thinned, and the sky spread above him, and right there, seemingly close enough for him to reach out and touch, were the towering Tetons.

"Wow," he said, his voice mostly air. Anything he'd been worried about simply dissipated, and Colton felt the power of God in his life as a presence not to be ignored. *Tell me what to do*, he thought. *And I'll do it.*

DINNER WAS A LIVELY EVENT AT THE LODGE, AND COLTON SAT NEXT to Annie and her daughters, ate way too much, and enjoyed singing Christmas carols with everyone else.

Finally, the parents of children in the group said, "Time for bed. If you don't go to bed, Santa Claus won't come."

Bedtime was easier that night than any other Colton had

witnessed, and he anticipated a relaxing evening, perhaps in front of the fireplace, his hand in Annie's as they shared stories of Christmases past. Maybe some midnight kissing....

That all evaporated when Beau and Lily started bringing out gifts. Some were already wrapped, and some weren't. The living room became almost like a factory, with scissors, and tape, and wrapping paper. Bows, and boxes, and bags.

Colton had no gifts to prepare for a small person, but he couldn't look away from the chaos in the living room.

Annie was helping Liam and Rose, as they had three two-year-olds to prepare for, and he wondered why they hadn't done it before Christmas Eve.

Someone stepped to his side, and he looked at Elise. "Is this what they do every year?"

"It's only been a couple," she said. "But yes. It's a tradition to put the kids to bed and then wrap the gifts and put everything under the tree."

"There's no way that's all fitting under the tree." It was big, but there was literally stuff everywhere.

"It kind of expands out," Elise admitted.

"I'll say." Colton had never seen anything like it. He'd grown up wealthy, but his parents had never spoiled their sons. They were expected to work, and yes, they got presents on their birthdays and for Christmas. Every one of them had gotten a car or truck for his sixteenth birthday, and Colton knew plenty of his friends growing up hadn't gotten that.

"Did you have big Christmases like this?" he asked Elise.

"No." She looked at him, pure nerves in her eyes. "I have to go."

"Oh-kay." Colton watched her bolt from the living room, and when he faced the fray again, Annie stood in front of him.

She was not happy. In fact, she planted both hands on her hips and glared at him.

CHAPTER 25

Annie felt like a mother hen, constantly chasing wolves away from her chicks. Of course, Colton was not her child, and she didn't need to chase Elise and Bree away from him.

She just felt like she did.

"What?" he asked, and Annie's annoyance soared. "Do you need help?"

"No," she said. "What were you and Elise talking about?"

"Christmas," he said, his eyebrows drawing down. His expression glittered dangerously, and Annie hated this darkness inside her.

She didn't know what to say next, and Colton gave her glare right back to her.

"Let me get something straight," he said. "You don't want me to talk to anyone but you, is that right?"

"Of course not," she said, an instant reaction to what he'd said. Because what he'd said sounded ridiculous. "You can talk to whoever you want."

"You just ran Elise from the room," he said, his voice low, almost a growl.

She glanced around, but there was no way anyone would overhear them among the taping, cutting, ripping, and talking.

"I'm going to bed," Colton said. "Good-night, Annie." He didn't touch her. Didn't lean down and kiss her. He simply side-stepped away from the fireplace, where he'd been standing and watching the Christmas Eve wrapping party, and slipped through the same doorway Elise had gone though. Was he going to talk to her again?

Stop it, Annie told herself. She wasn't sure why she didn't want Colton talking to anyone but her, just like she didn't under-stand the almost debilitating worry she'd experienced watching him mount that giant black horse and ride into the forest. Ryan hadn't gone horseback riding when he'd died. Hardly anyone died from walking through a forest very close to a lodge.

And yet, Annie hadn't been able to breathe properly until Colton and Bree had come stomping into the lodge again, laughing about something.

Then her worry had morphed to jealous annoyance, and Annie had been simmering there for hours now.

Sighing, she turned back to the wrapping party, knowing she should go back and help Rose finish wrapping the dolls she'd bought for her daughter.

She didn't. Instead, she went downstairs to the bedroom, hoping Emily and Kelly would stay up late helping with the gifts. The thought of planning a wedding was overwhelming for Annie right now.

Eden lay in her half of the bed, her phone only a few inches from her face. "Hey, Mom," she said when Annie entered.

"Hey, baby." Annie put a smile on her face, but it shook. Eden looked back at her phone, and Annie hoped she could climb beneath the covers and turn away from her daughter so she wouldn't see the turmoil in Annie's soul.

But in the next moment, Eden put her phone on the night-stand and sat up. "What's wrong?"

"Nothing." Annie turned her back to Eden and bent over her

suitcase. "I think I'm going to go down to the house tomorrow," she said, just now deciding. "See how it's fared in the storms. Make sure the furnace is working." It wasn't that odd of a thing. Sometimes, when furnaces had to work hard to keep the house warm, the pilot light would go out. Heck, the furnace here at the lodge had malfunctioned during a storm.

"Is it Colton?"

Annie straightened, her pajamas in her hand. She kept her back to Eden for another moment, trying to draw strength into her body when she breathed. That didn't really work, and she turned to her daughter.

"It's Colton," Eden said. "Come tell me what's going on."

Annie hated that their roles had been reversed, but she went and sat beside Eden. "I have this...jealousy inside me. And when he went riding today, all I could think about was the day your dad died." Her voice trailed into a whisper by the last word.

Eden didn't tell her it would be okay. That she had nothing to be jealous about. She just reached over and laced her fingers through Annie's.

"That was a bad day," Eden said. "I remember it too."

"Do you?" Annie asked. "What do you remember?"

Eden drew in a big breath and let it out slowly. "I went to school. Everything was fine. Then, sometime after lunch, I got called to the office to get checked out. And I never got checked out, and I was confused." She spoke in a monotone now, staring at the carpet at her feet. "I left my math homework, and I remember being so mad about it. That night. The next day. All through the funeral. All I could think about was that math homework, and how I wouldn't have it done when I finally went back to school."

Tears gathered in Annie's eyes, and she squeezed Eden's hand.

"I didn't even bring my backpack with me," Eden said. "Mrs. Daniels had this worried look on her face, and she hugged me when I left the room. I didn't get why. And then, you were in the office, and you were crying, and Grandma took me, and things were just a blur."

A *blur* summed up that day for Annie too. The next several days, even into weeks, created a haze in her mind too.

"I did the best I could," Annie said. "No one really knows how to react when they find out someone's died."

"Of course," Eden said, lifting her head to look at Annie. "Mom, I know that. I don't think you did anything wrong."

Annie nodded, trying to cage the emotions streaming through her. "Maybe I'm not meant to have another man in my life."

"Colton's a great guy, Mom," Eden said. "You just need to work through some things."

"I feel like I'm pressuring him to do something. Or to *not* do something."

"Maybe you are."

Annie leaned her head against Eden's. "I understand how you feel about Em now," she said. "The jealousy. It's horrible. I don't know how you've dealt with it all this time."

"I tell myself that just because Em is happy, or has a boyfriend, or another date, or whatever it was, doesn't mean there isn't enough for me."

"Yeah?"

"Yeah, like, just because Em is engaged doesn't mean I won't be able to find someone and get engaged too. There's not a cap on the number of people who can be engaged. You know?"

"Yeah," Annie said slowly. Just because Colton talked to Bree or Elise didn't mean he wouldn't want to talk to her too. He could have friends *and* a girlfriend.

Eden's phone lit up, and they both looked at it. "You talk to your guy," Annie said. "I feel much better. Thank you." She pressed a kiss to her daughter's forehead, and while Eden went back to texting Mitchell, Annie changed into her pajamas and got beneath the covers, like she wanted to.

She closed her eyes, prayers streaming through her mind so

quickly, she could hardly think the words before they were gone. She just needed help, and she had nowhere else to go to get it.

Finally, God allowed her to fall asleep, a merciful blessing for Annie.

———

THE NEXT MORNING, SHE NURSED A CUP OF COFFEE ON THE COUCH while everyone opened gifts. For how many people and children there were, the tearing off of paper actually happened in an orderly fashion, organized and controlled by Amanda Whittaker, the mother of the brothers that had all returned to Coral Canyon with their families.

Annie loved watching the joy light the faces of the children, and she felt the love of their parents floating on the air.

Colton had come into the room before the first present had been opened, but he didn't come to sit by her. She didn't have room on the couch anyway, but the fact that he didn't even glance her way stung.

He sipped coffee too, and laughed when Averie opened an Easy-Bake Oven and shrieked as if she'd just been given a box full of cash.

"Celia!" she said, balancing the box as she hurried over to the woman. "I can cook with you. I can cook with you!"

"That's right," Celia said, smiling. "You sure can."

Averie started crying, and everyone *ahh*'ed at her as she ran over to Eli and Meg, who accepted her right into their arms. They'd adopted Averie when she was two or three years old, and they'd adopted Isaiah as a baby. He simply watched with wide two-year-old eyes as his parents comforted Averie.

The present-opening went on, and finally, it was time for brunch. Annie got up and went into the kitchen with Celia, noting that Colton got out of the way real quick when she went his way.

She tried not to let it bother her that he didn't wait for her before he ate. Or that he sat next to Bree and Elise.

She felt all alone in this huge house, surrounded by literally thirty or forty people. She kept the smile on her face until brunch ended and both dishwashers hummed to get the dirty plates clean.

People started to disperse then, some going back into the living room to play with their new toys or take their presents back to their rooms. The Whittaker brothers, along with Todd and Liam, went out the back door, talking about something at the energy company they owned as they headed out to ride horses.

"I'm taking kids over six to my house," Laney announced. "We'll have crafts and snacks." That group left, and Annie hugged Emily as she came into the living room wearing her coat and carrying her purse.

"We're going down to Kelly's parents' for a while."

"Of course." Annie watched them go, a hint of sadness seeping through her. She'd have to share Emily with another family now, something she hadn't thought of.

The same jealousy that infected her when she thought of sharing Colton didn't come, and she wondered why she only saw green with him but felt a sad acceptance with her daughter.

She turned when more voices came into the room. Colton's voice. He didn't break stride when he saw her, and he seemed his normal, strong, sexy self as he came to stand in front of her.

"Hey," he said, a small smile gracing his mouth. He reached for her hand, and squeezed the tips of her fingers. "Merry Christmas."

"Merry Christmas to you too," she whispered, looking at Bree, who'd come into the room with Colton.

"We're going to a movie," he said. "Why don't you come with us?"

Her first instinct was to say no. She didn't want to intrude on them. But that didn't make sense. She was friends with Bree. She was Colton's girlfriend. They could all go to a movie together.

"Ready," Patsy said, joining the group. "Where's Elise?"

"She's taking her meds," Bree said. "She's coming."

"Colton's driving?" Patsy asked.

He still hadn't looked away from Annie, because she still hadn't said yes.

"What are you seeing?" she asked.

"I have no idea," he said. "But it gets us out of the lodge, and Bree mentioned something about extra butter on my popcorn." He grinned, and a flash of joy blipped through Annie because of it.

"All right," she said. "Let me go get my purse and see if Eden wants to come with us."

"You don't need your purse," he said. "I got you." He put his arm around her and faced the others. "Let's go load up. Someone's going to have to climb in the way back."

Eden entered the room, already wearing her coat. "Elise is right behind me." Sure enough, Elise entered the room too, and Annie looked around at the five women...and Colton.

"All right, cowboy," Bree said. "I hope you're ready for this."

"For what?"

"Driving five women to a romantic comedy." She patted him on the chest as she stepped past him to move toward the front door. "Buckle up."

Several others laughed, and Annie looked at Colton. He wore a horrified expression now, and Annie giggled at him. "Didn't think this through, did you?"

He blinked and looked at her. "Maybe I didn't." He sighed and drew her toward the door. "But I can't back out now."

Annie smiled all the way out to his SUV, because she felt like things between them were back to normal, despite her accusations and outbursts. She squeezed his hand, hoping he got the message of her gratitude for his forgiving heart.

He squeezed back, and Annie took that as an acknowledgement that he did.

CHAPTER 26

C olton sat on the end of the row, Annie right next to him. He figured that was the safest spot for him, and one that would put her mind at ease as well. He didn't like that he had to work so hard to make sure she was reassured, because he'd seen other relationships like that, and they rarely worked out.

What would happen if he couldn't reassure her one day?

Colton had plenty of his own worries, and he spent the movie holding Annie's hand thinking about her, then Wes and what he was dealing with in Ivory Peaks, and then the meeting on December thirtieth.

He was only a day's drive from Denver, and he hadn't planned on leaving until the twenty-eighth, but something in his gut told him to leave tomorrow. He could go to the farm and see his parents beforehand. Gray was there with his son, Hunter, and Wes would be at the farmhouse in Ivory Peaks until the twenty-ninth. They could have a few days together before the twins returned for the family New Year's Eve party Wes had texted about that morning.

And honestly, Colton needed some time to himself. He liked Annie a whole lot, and he wondered if maybe he could get a hotel and just get some space from everything at Whiskey

Mountain Lodge. Then he could ask Annie out on real dates and take her to breakfast or dinner. He wouldn't be expected to be around her for every meal, every event, every everything. He could have other relationships she didn't have her eyes on.

He went round and round, hardly watching a moment of the movie. When it ended, Annie sighed happily. "That was great, wasn't it?"

"Sure," he said, hoping she wouldn't ask any deep questions.

"You just came for the popcorn," she said as the lights came up slowly.

"It was great popcorn," he said. "And I had my doubts when we got here and all that smoke was pouring out of the machine." His heart had dropped to his cowboy boots, but he'd been reassured they'd get a new batch going, and it would be fine. And it had been.

The movie had been fine, and the best part was that it had killed a couple of hours. Colton left the theater first, followed by all the women, and he let them talk about the film all the way back to the lodge, their voices high and chirping in his SUV.

He went downstairs while they all went into the kitchen to get coffee, and Colton started going through his bag, pulling out the jeans and shirts he'd worn already and folding them to lay on the bed. He needed to repack, and he needed to decide if he was going to leave in the morning or that afternoon.

No matter what, he couldn't leave without talking to Annie. So he finished with his clothes and zipped his toiletries into his waterproof bag and sat down.

"What should I do?" he asked, tipping his head back. He felt somewhat removed from his body, almost like he could see himself sitting on the bed in a bedroom in the basement of a magnificent lodge in the wilds of Wyoming.

How had his life come to be this? Reduced to a bag of clothing and deodorant, miles from anyone he was related to, and wondering what to do with his life.

His mind flowed easily through the years of his life he could remember, and he'd been happiest working in the lab on the Human Genome Project. Science ran in the Hammond blood, and he'd gotten the most of it out of all the brothers.

So he was done with marketing. He could still work at the family company, as they had six full floors of laboratories, employing hundreds of scientists. His degree was in biology, and HMC did a lot of chemistry and technology, but he could probably do something.

"Or find another job," he said, suddenly remembering that Annie had mentioned the Whittaker brothers owning and running an energy company. Perhaps Colton should talk to Graham.

Satisfied with that plan, he went to find Annie so they could have a conversation about where they went from here. His heart pounded in his chest, because the last time he'd had a conversation like this, he'd ended up engaged. He hadn't wanted to break up with Priscilla, and while he hadn't shown up at her apartment to propose, that had been what had happened.

Colton wasn't going to do that again, but his boots still made ominous thunking noises as he went up the steps. Annie sat in the kitchen with the other ladies, and they all looked at him when he entered. He smiled around at them and sat down.

"I think I need to go home," he said.

"What?" Bree asked at the same time Elise did.

"I thought you weren't leaving until the twenty-eighth," Bree added.

"That's more than I knew," Annie said. "Isn't your meeting on the thirtieth?"

He felt bombarded with the questions, though they were easy. "Yes, it's on the thirtieth. I need a whole day to get there, and a couple of my brothers are at my parents'." He shrugged, not wanting to say he felt a little overwhelmed here at the lodge. "I feel like it's time for me to go."

Anxiety crossed Annie's face, but Colton couldn't address it in front of everyone.

"Then you should go," Elise said. "But you're not leaving this second, right? I have something for you in the cabin."

"You do?" he asked, smiling at her. "What is it?"

"I'm not going to ruin the surprise," she said. "Bree and I will go get it."

"It takes two women to get?" Colton asked, his eyebrows going right on up under the brim of his cowboy hat. "Wow, I can't wait to see what it is."

"I've seen it," Patsy said. "Don't get excited."

"Hey," Bree said, though she was smiling. "Come on, Elise. We'll be back in a few minutes. Don't leave without saying good-bye."

"I'm not leaving right away," he said as they stood up and took their coffee mugs into the kitchen. Patsy went with them, probably because Annie hadn't moved in at least a minute.

Colton reached over and took her hands in his. "I just need to tie up some loose ends in Denver," he said. "My plan is to come back here."

She looked at him. "It is?"

"Yeah," he said easily. "You said this town is growing, and maybe they need someone with a degree in biology." He gave her a smile he hoped would let her know *she* was one of the reasons he'd be coming back to Coral Canyon.

She stayed as nervous as ever, though. "All right," she said. "When are you going to go?"

"I think I can make it one more night," he said.

"If you're not happy here, you can leave whenever," she said. She pulled one hand away and brushed her hair off her forehead.

Colton frowned, trying to figure out what she meant. "Why wouldn't I be happy here?"

"I don't know." She got up and took her coffee cup into the kitchen too, turning back to him from clear across the massive space as she leaned into the sink behind her.

Colton felt like he'd stepped out onto thin ice. The loud,

sharp cracking noises filling the air was a testimony that he was about to go under, and he better dang well get back to safe ground.

"Are you mad at me?" he asked.

"No," she said, crossing her arms. Definitely mad. He'd seen Priscilla do that enough times to know.

"Just tell me what I did, and I'll try to fix it," he said. He'd told her that once before, and it had worked.

"I just thought we had more time."

"It's not over," he said.

"It's not?"

He got up, so confused now. "I just said I was coming back." His frustration grew with every second where Annie just stood there.

"Do you see us getting married?" she asked.

Colton froze, every emotion draining from his body. He blinked, the bow tie around his neck too tight. So tight. He actually reached up to his collar, but his fingers didn't touch a bow tie.

He wasn't in the dressing room at the Prince—the nicest hotel in Denver—about to get married.

Priscilla was gone.

A new version of Colton had been born that day. One that didn't think he'd ever get married again.

And now Annie wanted to know if they'd get married? He'd met her six days ago.

True, it did feel like six years, but there was no way Colton was ready to get married right now. Or even in the next year. He couldn't even fathom that.

"I guess that's the answer," Annie said, and at some point, she'd moved closer to him.

"I just...." He didn't know what to say. He'd told her about Priscilla. Hadn't he?

"We're back to that," Annie said softly. "You don't want to

get married. I've been alone for over a decade, and I do want a man I can share the rest of my life with."

"I didn't say I don't want to get married," he said. "I just feel like it's...a little fast for me."

"When you know—"

"Right now," he added over the top of what she said. "It's a little fast for me right now. Priscilla only left a few weeks ago."

"Seven weeks, I thought." Annie looked up at him, plenty of challenge in her gaze.

"Seven weeks is not very long," he said. He'd been with her for five years. He felt like Annie was trying to back him into a corner, get him to admit to something he hadn't done, or commit to something he wasn't ready to commit to.

"Are you over her?" she asked.

"Is that a joke?"

"No," she said calmly. "You seem to have a lot of women friends, and maybe she's one of them. You know, back in Denver."

Colton could not believe what he'd just heard. He stumbled backward a step, trying to get distance so he could find clarity. "What?" came out of his mouth. "*That's* what you think of me?"

Disgust roiled in his stomach. He needed to get on the road right now. He wouldn't arrive in Ivory Peaks until close to midnight, but he didn't care. He could find any number of seedy motels between here and Denver. He'd seen them as he'd driven north. They'd be there as he went south again.

"I don't think anything," Annie said with a sigh. "I just...I need to know you really think we have a shot."

Colton shook his head, because he was done. Done trying to convince her that he liked her. If she didn't know by now, he honestly had no idea what else to do—short of asking her to marry him right then. And he'd already decided he wasn't going to do that.

"You know what?" he asked, his voice more wounded than he liked. He'd heard himself sound like this before, and he'd hated it then. Just as he did now. "I've told you and told you and showed you how I feel about you. If that's not good enough, I'm sorry. I don't know how to do it another way."

"I didn't say it wasn't good enough."

"But it's not," he said. "If we didn't have a shot, Annie, I'd say good-bye right now and go on home. I told you I was coming back. I've told you I don't like Bree or Elise the way I like you. And I think it's really unfair of you to try to push me into a place I'm not ready to go yet." His chest hurt, and so much more to say coiled inside him. "Priscilla held me in a place I wanted to leave, for a long time. And I let her. I stayed with her, all the way up to the end, when she humiliated me in front of everyone I know, and a lot of people I don't know."

Breathing hurt, but somehow, Colton kept doing it. "And now you're trying to pull me out of the place I want to be in. I can't." He fell back another step. "I'm really sorry, but I can't."

"Can't what?"

"Most relationships evolve over time," he said. "Both people get to the same place eventually, like Emily and Kelly. Maybe she's been ready to get married for a while, and he hasn't. But she *waits* for him to come to where she is, and then they take the next step together." He gestured between the two of them. "I met you six days ago, and yes, I was instantly attracted to you. I think you're beautiful and kind and just great, but you're in a place I'm not in yet. I should get more than six days to get there too, so we can take the next step *together*. I'm so tired of not being *together* with the person I'm supposed to be together with." He shook his head and looked away, aware that Celia had come into the kitchen and had heard at least part of what he'd said.

Annie said nothing, and Colton had nothing more to say. "I'm sorry," he said. "I should go. I'll get my bag and go." He turned and headed for the hallway. He paused when she didn't call him back. He couldn't expect her to. He'd just told her she was trying to pull him to where she was, and he wasn't ready to go. She was actually smart not to call him back so they could continue this horrible conversation.

"Will you let Bree and Elise know I'm really sorry I couldn't stay to see what they have for me?"

"Colton," Annie said. "You can't just leave without saying good-bye to them."

"Why not?" He faced her again. "All it's going to do is make you jealous. I don't want to deal with that. I can't have that on my mind while I drive across Wyoming for the next eight hours."

She didn't contradict him and say his good-byes with Elise and Bree wouldn't make her jealous. He shook his head, barely able to stop himself from rolling his eyes. "I'll call you when I get to Ivory Peaks."

And with that, he went downstairs and collected his bag. When he went back upstairs, no one loitered in the kitchen, and the way to the front door was also clear. He tossed his bag in the backseat and got behind the wheel before pulling out his phone.

He dialed Bree, because Annie was right about one thing. He couldn't just leave her and Elise without saying good-bye. They were his friends, even if Annie didn't like it.

"Hey," she said, clearly breathing hard. "We're coming."

"Can you come to the parking lot?" he asked. "I decided to leave right now."

"Right now? Why?"

"Can you just come to the parking lot? Or I'll come down to your cabin. I just want to say good-bye."

"We're almost back. See you in a second."

Colton hung up and turned on the SUV so his seat would start warming up. Only a couple of minutes later, Bree and Elise rounded the corner of the lodge, carrying a huge, four-tiered chocolate cake between them.

"Oh, my word," he said, launching himself out of the warm car to go help them. Despite his foul mood, he laughed as he jogged across the parking lot to the two women who'd been so kind to him. So open and honest. So friendly.

"What is this?"

"It's a chocolate cake," Elise said. "We know how much you love chocolate."

"You must've been up all night making this." He took it from them and gazed at all the delicious chocolate frosting.

"That's what we do here at the lodge on Christmas Eve," Bree said, her breath coming in white puffs. "We stay up late getting gifts ready."

"Come on," he said. He took the cake over to the hood of his SUV and set it down. Then he gathered both Bree and Elise into his arms and held them in a three-way hug. "I know we just met a few days ago, but I feel like I've known you both my whole life."

"Same," Bree said, the word maybe a little choked.

"Me too," Elise said.

Colton stepped back, his emotions high. "So I'll call you both later, okay?"

"Why are you going now?" Bree said. "You said you weren't."

He didn't want to talk about it, and he gazed over her shoulder to the huge front door of the lodge. That door had once been a welcome sight for him, the yellow lights shining out of the windows, beckoning to him to come stay for the night, out of the snow.

"Because," he said. "I just have to. You know how you didn't want to tell me about your family?"

Bree pressed her lips together.

"This is like that," he said. "I don't want to talk about it right now."

"But you'll tell us later," Elise said.

"Maybe," he said. "Anyway, it's too cold to stand around out here. Hug me again, and I've got to go."

They did, and Colton got behind the wheel of his SUV again.

Neither woman retreated to the lodge, and he lifted one hand in a farewell wave as he backed out of the parking spot.

He took one last look at the lodge in his rear-view mirror from the mouth of the parking lot, and then he pulled onto the street and headed down the canyon.

"That's that," he muttered to himself, the future he'd imagined for himself here in Coral Canyon only an hour ago disappearing into dust.

———

A SINGLE LIGHT SHONE OUT OF THE FRONT WINDOW OF THE HOUSE on the outskirts of Ivory Peaks, and Colton looked at the front door, almost expecting Wes to walk through it.

He'd called his brother as he'd left Coral Canyon, and Wes had said he'd make sure Colton didn't have to come tripping into the house in the dark.

He watched the farmhouse for a moment before he got out of the SUV, taking his bag with him in one hand and balancing the giant chocolate cake in the other. It was just as cold here as Wyoming, but the chill didn't bite the same. Colton was used to it anyway. He went up the steps and the doorknob twisted easily under his grip.

Inside, the formal living room glowed under the bright bulbs Wes had left on, but further into the house, Colton couldn't see anything at all. He'd snuck into and out of this house plenty of times, and he knew how to tiptoe down the hallway to his old bedroom without getting caught or making a single sound.

Tonight, though, he flipped off the light in the front living room and walked down the short hall to the back of the house. He set the cake on the counter, and it looked like it had survived the trip quite well. His fingers knew right where the switches were, and he flipped one to fill the kitchen with light.

A groan sounded to his right, and he turned to find Wes sitting up, one hand covering his eyes as he continued to moan.

"Why are you out here?"

"I was waiting up for you," Wes said, rubbing his eyes. He squinted toward Colton. "What time is it?"

"Twelve-thirty," Colton said. A weariness ran through his bones, straight to his heart. "I thought I'd see if Mom has any of that guava lemonade, and then I'm going to bed."

"She does," Wes said, standing. He wore a navy T-shirt and a pair of basketball shorts. "You drove straight through?"

"I stopped and got dinner somewhere," he said. "Ate it in the car." He hated eating in the car, because Colton liked enjoying his food. And driving while he held a burger in his hand wasn't enjoyable. He continued toward the fridge and opened it to find his lemonade.

Bottles and bottles of it sat on the top shelf, and he searched through peach, strawberry, and raspberry before he found the guava he liked. The lid popped off with a satisfying squelch, and he took a long drink while Wes studied him.

"What?" he finally asked.

"Something happen between you and Annie?"

"Why would you think that?"

"I might have called Bree."

Colton rolled his eyes. He hadn't told Bree anything, but she'd obviously spoken to Annie. He wondered what Annie had said, but he dismissed the thought. He didn't care. She could say what she wanted to say. He knew he'd been true to her and said nothing, not even one thing, and that was what mattered.

"I thought you liked her."

"I did," Colton said. "I do. She's just...in a different place than I am."

"Bree said you said some really smart things."

"She wasn't even there," Colton said. "And I hate that you talked to her about this. It's none of your business. Hers either." Colton glared at his oldest brother, though he didn't want to fight with him too. "I'm a big boy, and I can handle my life." He took his half-empty bottle of lemonade with him as he went to get his bag. "I'm in my old room?"

"Yep." Wes watched him start down the hall.

"Thanks for waiting up for me," Colton said over his shoulder. That got Wes to follow him, and while Colton didn't want to talk about Annie, he wouldn't mind talking about HMC and how Wes felt about passing the torch to the cousins.

He went through the second door on the right, glad when Wes followed him and leaned into the doorway. "I guess you want to know what I'm going to do," Colton said.

"I think I already know."

"I think I'm done there," Colton said. "At least as the marketing director. I wouldn't mind looking at what openings we have in the labs."

"As a scientist?"

"Yeah." Colton dropped his bag on the bed and sat beside it. "As a scientist."

"HMC would be lucky to have you in any lab," Wes said.

"Thanks." Colton gave his brother a smile. "So at the meeting on Wednesday, I think I'll agree to whatever we all think is fair. And I'll ask about a job in one of the labs."

"So you and Annie really are...." Wes held up both hands as Colton glared at him. "Forget I said anything. Okay."

"What about you talking to Bree like that might go somewhere?" he challenged his brother.

"That *might* go somewhere," Wes said. "For real."

"You really think so?"

"Sure," Wes said. "Why not? People meet on dating apps all the time."

"A phone call is not a dating app," Colton said.

"Yeah, it's better," Wes said. "More personal."

"For the record," Colton said. "I told her you'd be perfect for her."

"You did?" Wes looked horrified. "Why would you do that?"

"Because it's true," Colton said. "So finish up here, and keep talking to her, and go settle down already. Someone needs to before Mom disowns us all." He gave Wes a smile, and they chuckled together.

"She is relentless sometimes," Wes said. "She even asked Gray if he was looking for a new wife."

"Oh, brother," Colton said. "I bet I know how that ended."

"With him telling her to stay out of his business, and he'd do what he wanted?" Wes shook his head, still laughing softly. "Yeah, about like that. Then he came back a couple of hours later and apologized, though he was adamant that she not ask him about his—and I quote, 'love life'—in front of Hunter. I guess it's a sore subject or something."

"Why would it be a sore subject?" Colton kicked off his boots and unzipped his bag, ready to be out of his clothes, at least these restricting ones. "Oh, I know."

"Maddie," they said together.

"Yeah," Wes said. "I guess that was a real bad situation—worse than even we knew about—with her and Hunter. So Gray is real careful now."

"Fair enough," Colton said. "It's his life, and his son, and he's the only one who knows what to do." Colton sure didn't know what to do with his own life, and he wouldn't want Gray trying to advise him.

"I'm trying to be *less* careful," Wes said.

Colton looked at him, his eyes widening. "Really? You?" He laughed, his thoughts zeroing in on Bree as he did. She didn't need someone being less than careful with her feelings, and Colton would feel like a complete jerk if it was his brother who caused her to cry the way the last guy had.

"I know, right?" Wes asked, folding his arms as he grinned. He had plenty of silver hair too, and even Gray's had started going, well, gray. Hammond genes at work again. *Plus*, Colton thought. *We handle a lot of stress.*

His father had been emphasizing the importance of taking care of their money since each boy turned thirteen. That was when Dad sat them each down and had a talk about what would happen when they turned twenty-one. A tiny part of Colton felt like he'd missed out on some of the fun times of being a teenager, because he didn't want to disappoint his father, and he wanted to make sure he didn't squander the opportunities provided for him.

Ames and Cy didn't seem to have the same drive and motivation as the older three, and they'd bought cars and motorcycles when they'd turned twenty-one. Colton couldn't even remember the first big-ticket item he'd bought. Probably his house in Virginia, where he'd lived while he worked on the Human Genome Project.

"Anyway, I'm having fun getting to know Bree," Wes said. "I figure I might as well. I might have to buckle down and be serious again soon enough."

"Okay," Colton said. "Just...don't hurt her, okay?"

Wes's smile faded. "You think I'm going to hurt her?"

"I think you're incredibly charming and very good-looking, and yes, when you start talking to a woman and then stop, that could hurt her."

Wes made a noise halfway between a scoff and a snort. It must've hurt his throat and the back of his nose, right up in his sinuses, but he didn't act like. "Charming and good-looking?"

"Yes, and I showed her a picture of us. She was definitely interested in you."

"Why wasn't she interested in you?" Wes asked. "You seem to know her really well."

"Yeah, I guess." Colton stripped off his shirt and reached for a T to wear to bed. "We became friends pretty fast. There was no spark between us." He looked over his shoulder and pulled on his shirt. "So don't worry about that."

"It hadn't even crossed my mind," Wes said.

Colton wished it hadn't even crossed Annie's mind. She seemed to look for ways to find Colton being interested in people he wasn't. "All right," he said. "Get out. Go to bed. Call

Bree. Whatever. But I'm exhausted, and I have to deal with Mom and Dad tomorrow."

"Yeah, you're going to need it," Wes said, actually coming into the room, not leaving it. "Mom seems to have all kinds of uncomfortable questions to ask right now."

"She always does." Colton turned toward Wes, and they embraced. He held on for an extra moment, and then two. Something brotherly and powerful passed between them, and Colton appreciated his brother more than he ever had.

"And we'll strategize for the meeting with Gray too," Wes said, stepping back. "It's good to have you back, Colt." He meant more than just back physically, and Colton knew it.

Wes left the room, pulling the door closed behind him, and Colton sank back onto the bed, his jeans still on. He reached for his phone, determined to make good on what he'd said he'd do.

He'd said he'd call Annie and Bree, but it was too late for that. So he sent them each a text. *Made it to Ivory Peaks.*

He wanted to add more to Annie's, *like, I miss you.* Or *Please don't be mad at me. I hate it when you're mad at me.* Or *Will you go out with me when I return to Coral Canyon?*

But, at this point in time, Colton didn't even know if he'd be returning to Coral Canyon. So he left the texts as they were, made sure his phone was silenced, plugged it in, and got out of those annoying jeans.

CHAPTER 27

G ray Hammond woke up before the sun, which wasn't all that unusual. He rolled over, a twinge of pain shooting down through his hip, reminding him that he'd run ten miles yesterday, and he better take it slow today.

Most people probably took Christmas Day off from their workout schedule, but Gray had a marathon coming up in April, and three months could pass in the blink of an eye for a man like Gray.

He sat up and took a few minutes to stretch his back, his arms, his legs. Hunter snoozed several feet away, on an air mattress Gray had brought with him.

His mother would've set up a bed for her only grandson, but Gray didn't like creating extra work for her. She and Dad could barely keep up with the farm, and now that Dad had it in his mind to have Wes run for governor, he'd been spending more and more time in his office.

Gray dressed quickly and moved over to his ten-year-old. "Hunter," he said softly. "Get up, son. We're goin' out to the farm this morning."

Hunter's eyes opened, a frown pulling down his eyebrows.

He didn't groan or complain though, and a few seconds later, he sat up too. "Can I feed the pigs?"

"Yep." Gray wasn't going to argue with whatever Hunter wanted to do. He was glad to have his son with him for the holidays, and while he hated waking his son before dawn, they both loved working on the farm.

"I'm going to go make coffee." Gray eased out of the room and went down the hall to the kitchen. He'd beaten his mom and dad to the coffeemaker, which was probably for the best. How they'd survived for so many years drinking bad coffee, he didn't know.

He got the coffee dripping, and he stepped to the back door to put on his boots. He took his cowboy hat from the hook beside the door and settled it on his head too, hearing his son coming down the hall.

"You want chocolate milk?" he asked Hunter.

"Yes, please." Hunter went to the back door and got his hat and boots too, without Gray even having to ask him. An outpouring of love for his son filled him, and Gray pulled out a gallon of chocolate milk and poured some for his son.

"Do you want a bite now, or do you think you can work for a couple of hours?" Gray had arrived on Christmas Eve, just after lunch, and he hadn't realized the state of the ranch until after they'd opened Christmas presents and eaten breakfast. But he'd like to get the animals taken care of early, then go out in the afternoon too. With the cold Rocky Mountain weather, the animals needed fresh water a few times a day, because it could freeze easily in temperatures such as the ones that existed right now.

"I'll have a granola bar," Hunter said, his voice a bit rusty this early in the morning. He came into the kitchen and opened the pantry to get his mini-breakfast. As soon as Gray had a cup of coffee in a Styrofoam cup with a lid, he said, "Let's go."

They coated up and put on gloves and stepped into the chilly morning. Hunter walked right next to Gray, and they'd always gotten along real nice. Gray loved his son with every fiber of his being, and he'd fought Sheila for full custody, because she'd wanted to take their son to Florida.

Florida, a state she'd never been to. She didn't know anyone there, and she didn't have a job lined up. When Gray—one of the best corporate lawyers in the state of Colorado—had brought up all of this evidence, he'd claimed that he thought Sheila was trying to keep Hunter from Gray, and that she could possibly flee the country from Florida.

At that point, Hunter had been five years old, and Gray couldn't believe his life had come to that courtroom. Sheila had cried, and she'd said she couldn't believe Gray could think that about her. But she wasn't the same person Gray had fallen in love with, he knew that. And he also knew how to divorce himself from his feelings so he could make legal decisions without a clouded mind.

And he'd won full custody. Sheila had gone to Florida, and Gray hadn't heard from her for years. Four long years.

At first, Hunter had been too young to realize his mother wasn't around. But Gray made it a point to talk to him about Sheila, especially as he entered school and started hearing about other boys' mothers, and having to deal with events like Moms and Muffins.

Sheila had started calling about a year ago, and it had become apparent very quickly that she wanted Hunter in her life, basically as a trophy. So she could show her parents what a great grandson they had. So she could show her multiple boyfriends what an amazing son she had.

Gray had gritted his teeth and allowed her to see her own son. He couldn't keep Hunter from her, and he'd done the best he could to talk to Hunter about everything. Absolutely everything, from sex to girls to swearing to drugs to rated-R movies. They talked about math and science too, both things Hunter was exceptionally gifted at. They talked about dogs and horses, and Gray hadn't thought there was another human alive that loved fishing as much as he did. Then he'd had Hunter, and the boy seemed to truly enjoy their weekends in the mountain rivers, catching fish for dinner.

Gray reached over and put his arm around Hunter's shoulders. "Did you have a good Christmas, Hunter?"

"Yeah," the boy said. "Real nice. Thanks for the baseball stuff, Dad. Can we play today?"

"Sure," Gray said. "Uncle Wes says he knows how to use that tractor to clear the yard, but I'll do it." He chuckled. "I don't trust Wes. He can barely drive a car."

Hunter smiled too, and everything inside Gray aligned. Yes, he was lonely sometimes. He wished he had more help than he did almost all the time. But luckily, he worked at the family company and could set his hearings and meetings around his son's school schedule.

All that's about to change, he thought, but he pushed the worries from his mind. He didn't need to work at all. He had plenty of money in the bank, and he'd stay on at HMC for at least the next twelve months, as their legal advisory. After that, Jill, Laura, and Kent could hire a different lawyer for their needs, and Gray would move on.

He'd never minded moving on. He possessed a gypsy soul, and even now, he itched to do something different. He'd always liked to cook, and maybe he'd go to culinary school—if they had one in the Denver area.

He didn't want to take Hunter from his support system of friends and family, that was for sure.

"Pigs right there," Gray said, dropping his arm. "You pull out all the leftover food, okay? We don't want them eating rotten food."

"Yes, sir," Hunter said. "And de-ice the trough and put in more water."

"All the way to the top," Gray said. "Takes longer to freeze."

"Okay." Hunter hesitated and looked further down the dirt road where they were walking. "Where are you gonna be?"

"I'm going to start with the horses," Gray said. "And move over to the chickens. If you get there before me, go ahead and start with them, all right?"

"Yes, sir." Hunter moved toward the pig pens now, his step sure. Gray watched him a moment, then bent his head into the wind and kept going toward the stables.

A couple of hours later, Gray couldn't feel his fingers, and Hunter looked a couple of breaths away from passing out. "Let's go eat, bud." He reached for his son, and Hunter came to his side. "I bet Uncle Wes or Grandma has something cooking by now."

"I hope so," Hunter said. "Do you think Grandma made ebelskivers?"

"I bet she would if you asked her to." Gray smiled at him. "Grandma makes whatever you want, doesn't she?"

Hunter grinned too. "Yeah, I guess she does."

"So you be real polite, and you ask her."

"Okay."

They walked back to the sprawling farmhouse in silence. Hunter could've had his own bedroom in the unused wing of the house, but he didn't like being separated from everyone else. He would one day, Gray knew, but for now, he was glad Hunter would rather sleep on an air mattress at the foot of his bed than off by himself in another room.

One step inside the house, and relief coursed through Gray. First, the heat made his muscles sigh. Second, it was Colton at the stove, not Wes or Mom.

"Colton," Gray said, surprise and happiness in his voice. "When did you get here?"

"Late last night," he said, turning with a spatula in his hand. "Get over here, Hunter." He wore a huge grin, and he scooped Hunter up into a hug as if the boy was still five years old.

He was twice that now, but he still laughed and hugged his uncle as if he were a little boy.

"Look at you," Colton said. "I think you've grown a foot since I saw you last."

"It's only been a month," Gray said, shrugging out of his coat. He took Hunter's too, and added, "We're starving. What're you cookin'?"

"Fried eggs," Colton said. "You want some?"

"I don't like the runny yolk," Hunter said.

"That's insane," Colton said. "But okay."

"He wants ebelskivers."

"Oh, you're going to have to ask Grandma for those," Colton said. "She just went out to the porch to get the newspaper." He grinned over Hunter's head to Gray. "The *newspaper*. I asked her if they still printed those, and she threw an oven mitt at me." He laughed, and Gray thought he looked real good for what he'd been through.

Colton hadn't made it to the I-do the way Gray had, and after his divorce was final, he'd disappeared for a few months. Maybe half a year.

But Hunter had pulled him back to reality. His son needed him, and no one else was going to register the boy for kindergarten. Gray had to do it. Gray had to do everything.

A perfect sense of failure pulled through him. Some days, he felt like he got so much done. Dishes. Laundry. Papers signed. Meetings and presentations done. Parent-teacher conferences attended.

No matter what he did in any given day, no matter how many tasks he accomplished, there was always something he didn't do. Didn't accomplish. Didn't excel at. He failed every single day, and he was *so tired*.

It was never enough. *He* was never enough.

The front door closed with a bang, and Gray nudged Hunter toward the hall leading to it. "Go ask her."

"Grandma," Hunter said without hesitation as he walked toward her. "After you read your paper, can you make ebelskivers for breakfast? I'll help with the butter and sugar."

"Of course, baby," Gray's mother said, and Gray ducked his head as he smiled. He loved his parents. They were good people, and they'd survived raising five boys, and Gray had learned to love to work from both his mother and his father.

"Morning, Mom," he said, stepping over to give her a kiss. "All the animals are fed and watered for now."

"Oh, you're such a good boy, Gray," she said, beaming up at him. "Can you go help Gramma up? She'll want some ebelskivers too."

"Sure thing." Gray went down the hall while his mother and Hunter took Colton's place in the kitchen. His grandmother was ninety-six-years-old, and Gray thought she'd pass any day now.

Mom said she spent the mornings in bed, and the afternoons in the recliner in the living room. She or Dad had to help Gramma move anywhere she went, which made taking care of her needs—like bathing and using the bathroom—hard for all of them. It wasn't like his mom and dad were spring chickens.

Gray knocked on the door to the small bedroom and then turned the doorknob. "Gramma?" He entered the room, noticing the scent of something old. Mothballs or something that had been sitting for a very long time. "You awake?"

"Yes, boy," she said, and Gray smiled at her.

"I'm here to help you into the living room," he said. "Mom's making ebelskivers, and you love those."

"Help me up." She reached one weathered, veiny hand toward him, and Gray moved right to the side of the bed and gripped her hand firmly. She wore a long nightgown with purple flowers on it, and he stayed right beside her as she shuffled out of the room.

"Bathroom?" he asked.

"Yes." She detoured into the bathroom, and Gray went with her. She transferred her hand to the counter for her support, and Gray stepped out.

"Ready," she called a few minutes later, and he went in and helped her out into the living room and kitchen area.

"Gramma," Colton said, bolting to his feet. "It's so good to see you."

"Colt," she said, as Gramma never said more than she needed to. Said it took too much energy, and she needed all she had to keep living. "You're back."

"Just gone for a few days, yes," he said. He took Gramma the rest of the way to her chair. "I'll bring you some breakfast as soon as it's ready."

"Coffee," she said, and Colton hopped to getting that for her. Gray watched him, because there was definitely something different about him. What it was, though, Gray wasn't sure.

He kept his questions to himself through saying good morning to his dad and Wes, who came into the kitchen together. He didn't ask anything during breakfast. He held his tongue while he helped Wes and Hunter clean up the kitchen.

"You wanna get on the computer?" he asked Hunter.

"Yes, sir."

"Get ten minutes of typing before you play a game," he said, and Hunter skipped down the hall to the bedroom they shared.

Gray turned to Wes and Colton. "So," he said. "Do we need to talk about the upcoming meeting?"

"I'd like to," Colton said. "I feel out of the loop." He looked at Wes and back to Gray. "Did he tell you?"

"Tell me what?"

"I didn't tell him," Wes said.

"Tell me what?" Gray asked, his mind sharp and moving through multiple scenarios at once.

"I'm thinking maybe I'd like to work in one of the labs."

Surprise lifted Gray's eyebrows. "Is that so?"

"I thought you were going to tell him about Annie," Wes said.

"Who's Annie?" Gray refused to remove his eyes from Colton, who shot a dark look at Wes.

"No one," Colton said, lifting his chin. And Gray had seen that tell before. He'd known Colton his whole life, and he'd been trained to see tiny things other people might overlook. "You met someone up in Coral Canyon?"

"Yes," Wes said. "He did."

"No," Colton said, but he was clearly lying.

Gray chuckled and shook his head. "Okay, whatever." But he suddenly knew what was different about Colton. He didn't seem like the shell of a man he'd been when he'd left. After Priscilla had left him only minutes before their wedding was set to happen, Colton had shrunk and shrunk into a person Gray hardly recognized.

Now, looking at his brother, he could see Colton had returned.

"Let's use Dad's office," Wes said, heading in that direction. Gray and Colton followed, and Gray snuck another look at his brother.

"Is she nice?" he asked.

"Yes," Colton said, an admission of his new relationship and his lie.

Wes's phone rang as he entered the office, and he said, "Oh, I have to take this."

"Is it Bree?" Colton asked.

"Who's Bree?" Gray asked. He felt like the one out of the loop, and he didn't like it.

"This woman Wes is talking to," Colton said, his voice a bit too gleeful.

Wes turned around, irritation flashing in his eyes.

"What?" Colton asked. "You told him about Annie."

Wes looked at his phone, which continued to ring.

"Take it," Gray said, and Wes swiped the call on.

"Hey," he said, his voice this flirty, gentle sound Gray had *never* heard come out of his mouth. He stared in disbelief as a smile crossed Wes's face and he went out the front door, sans coat.

"He likes her," Gray said, a bit of awe in the words.

"Oh, yeah," Colton said. "And here's the thing. He's never met her. Doesn't even know what she looks like."

"Are you kidding? How'd he meet her then?"

"*I* met her," Colton said. "Up at Coral Canyon. We became fast friends, and I handed her the phone once when I was talking to Wes, and she talked to him for a couple of minutes. Next thing I know, he's asking me for her number, and they're talking."

"Wow," Gray said, the shock moving through his system slowly. "And you and this Annie woman? Did you become fast friends with her too?"

"Oh, yeah," Colton said, sitting down in a chair across from their father's desk. "Instant spark there."

"But...." Gray sat beside him, hearing all kinds of things Colton wasn't saying.

"But nothing. She lives there. I live here. I've only known her a few days."

"Are you going to call her the way Wes talks to Bree?"

Colton shifted in his seat, and Gray saw it. Felt it down in the tips of his boots. "You broke up with her."

"Kind of?" Colton said, sighing. He didn't say anything else, and Gray wasn't one to push—at least not when he wasn't in court.

"So I guess Coral Canyon turned out to be a good place to go after all," he said.

"For Wes," Colton said. "I'm staying right here."

"Hmm." Gray had always thought he'd stay right where he was too, but with two of his brothers suddenly in relationships, Gray couldn't help wondering if he should book a visit to Coral Canyon too.

CHAPTER 28

Wes didn't want to go back to the city. He hadn't realized how stifled he felt there until he'd been on the farm for the past several days. With Colton, Gray, and Hunter there too, Wes had truly been able to relax.

He'd spoken with Bree every day too, and he sure did like her more and more with every minute he talked to her.

He'd enjoyed full breakfasts that were served hot, not just coffee on the way to the office. He liked going outside in the afternoon, when the weak winter sunlight shone down on all the snow Mother Nature had left behind last week. He'd laughed while he played baseball with Gray and Hunter, then Colton, Ames, and Cy, all of them getting soaking wet despite the fact that Gray had cleared the snow off the front lawn.

He felt more grounded, more down to earth, as he worked to keep the stables clean and the horses fed. He'd been reminded of simpler times, and he wanted that simplicity back in his life.

He liked talking to his brothers, and they'd been over the agenda for this morning's meeting at least a dozen times in the past four days. None of them were going to fight anything. Wes didn't want to be CEO anymore. He was ready for something new. Colton wanted to get back to his scientific work in the lab, and Gray would stay on for twelve months in a legal advisory period.

Wes had no idea what he'd do.

He'd thought about traveling, perhaps visiting every state in the country, something he'd put on his bucket list as a teenager.

In fact, working through his bucket list seemed like something Wes should do. It made him feel old, though, and like he was getting close to death. He was nearing fifty, but that wasn't that old. He'd heard people say fifty was the new thirty, and he wanted to *do something* more with his life. What that "more" was, he didn't know. Wes didn't like feeling lost, he knew that. He needed to find a tether, and fast, or he could be blowing in the wind before he knew it.

He knotted his tie around his neck and stepped into his perfectly polished shoes. He never attended a meeting without every piece of himself exactly in place, and today would be no different, even if everyone in attendance was a family member.

He'd have to take their proposal to the executive board after the New Year, and they needed to hammer out all the details today so Gray could prepare the documents for that meeting.

He arrived in the kitchen first, unsurprised to see Gray had been up and made coffee already. He and Hunter had been out on the farm by dawn since Christmas, and Wes felt a rush of affection for his next youngest brother.

They came inside together, and Wes turned to face them. "Ready?" he asked Gray. Gray had always been the most country out of all the brothers, and he wore his cowboy hat to the office most of the time.

"I need to shower and change," Gray said. "But otherwise, I'm ready."

"Haven't seen Colton yet," Wes said. "But we do need to leave in about a half an hour."

"I'll be ready." Gray went down the hall to the bathroom, and Wes helped Hunter get down a bowl and a box of cereal.

"What are you going to do today?" he asked the ten-year-old.

"Grandpa is taking me out to the firing range." The boy seemed happy enough, and Wes nodded.

Colton entered the kitchen wearing a suit and tie, his hair properly combed, his shoes just as shiny as Wes's. "Ready for today?" he asked as he poured his coffee.

"Yeah." Wes drew in a deep breath and let it out. "For the meeting anyway." He cut a glance toward the hall where all the bedrooms were. "Not for telling Dad about the transfer."

"He'll be fine," Colton said, but he often thought things would be fine when they wouldn't. Or at least he had no plan for how to make them fine if they didn't turn out that way. He was a perpetual optimist, and while Wes normally liked that about him, today it only sparked his irritation.

"You should drop the governor bomb on him today too. Then he won't know which way to go." Colton grinned as if Wes's life were a game.

"Nope," Wes said. He'd tie everything up at HMC first, then he'd talk to his father about the governorship. He'd endured days of talk of it already, and a brick settled in his gut at the thought of that conversation.

He sipped his coffee, the minutes ticking by impossibly slow. Finally, Gray returned, also in a suit and tie, but he wore cowboy boots and that hat as he grabbed his keys.

"I'll drive."

"You'll have to stay after," Colton said. "We should take two cars."

"I'm not staying after," Gray said. "They can wait for whatever they need after we talk. It's the holidays." He shook his keys. "Let's go."

They piled into his pickup truck together, Colton between Wes and Gray. Wes wasn't sure he could endure more conversation about the meeting; they'd been over everything to death.

So he asked, "Colton, what are you going to do about Annie?"

A sigh leaked from his mouth. "I don't know. You know

what? I thought I'd have heard from her by now. But nothing. Not even a response to the text I sent that I'd arrived here safely." He sounded absolutely miserable, and Wes had no idea how to help him. Other than pray, which he'd already done a multitude of times. Surely the Lord was tired of hearing from Wes Hammond, especially about his business and his brothers.

But to Wes, that was all he'd ever had. The company and his family.

He wanted more.

He wanted his own family. A good woman to spend time with. Children.

Bree's name ran through his mind, because he didn't have a picture of her to focus on. He couldn't even imagine what she looked like, and he'd refused when Colton said he had a picture of her. Wes didn't want to see it. He rather liked that she existed in his mind, and that his relationship with her wasn't built on anything physical.

"Have you tried calling her?" Gray asked.

"No," Colton said. "The ball is in her court. I can't just snatch it back."

"Do you like her?" Gray asked.

"Yeah." Again, Colton sounded like liking Annie was an absolutely terrible thing to have to suffer with.

"Maybe give it a few more days," Wes said. "After the New Year. Then call her. Maybe she'll have cooled off or whatever." Colton had never really said what had happened between him and Annie, just that they'd "kind of" broken up.

"I don't want either of you to breathe a word of this to Ames or Cy," Colton said, the fire back in his voice now. He shot Wes a particularly nasty glare. "I don't need the whole family giving me unsolicited advice."

"Hey, I don't do that," Gray said.

"Only because you want to get paid to give advice," Colton said dryly.

Wes burst out laughing, because that was true. Gray kept his mouth shut—until there was money on the table.

"I can agree not to say anything," Wes said. "But that's a two-way street. The last thing I need is Ames running some background check on Bree 'just to make sure' she's not a criminal." He rolled his eyes. "He's kind of crazy about that stuff."

"Yeah, well, you would be too if literally every woman you dated had been a fraud," Gray said. And he had some experience with that, so Wes didn't argue.

"But background checks?" Colton asked. "It's a little much."

"He's a cop," Gray said. "Everything he does is a little much."

"When are they arriving?" Colton asked.

"Ames should be here tonight," Wes said. He'd called everyone and arranged a New Year's Eve party for the following night. "Cy said tomorrow morning. I think he's staying in Green Canyon tonight."

Colton nodded, as did Gray. Wes couldn't wait to have all of his brothers home again. And at the farm too, not the downtown penthouse where they'd last gathered for their father's birthday in the spring.

"So we have a deal?" Colton asked. "We just say everything is great, no women troubles, no talking to women, nothing." He looked at Wes and then Gray.

"Deal," Gray said. "Not that I have any of the above."

Wes looked past Colton, sensing something in Gray's voice. "You could," he said. "Put yourself out there. You could get a date in seconds, Gray."

"Yeah, because I'm rich." He rolled his eyes. "No, thank you. I have Hunter to consider."

"You're smart," Colton said. "And you know, good-looking."

Gray looked at Colton, a long second passing before he laughed. "Thanks, Colton. I mean, I do try."

"You run more than any human should," Wes said. "You're definitely a catch."

"Don't want to be caught," Gray said.

Wes had thought he didn't want to be caught either. Now, he wasn't so sure. Now, all he seemed to think about was his freedom from HMC and when he could talk to Bree again.

The rest of the drive happened quickly, and Gray parked in the garage beneath the company building. They rode the elevator to the top floor, and Wes noted how cold the rooms were. He nudged up the temperature on the thermostat in the conference room, and not ten minutes later, the door opened again.

Laura entered first, and she had the traditional dark, Hammond hair. Her eyes were dark too, and she wore a pantsuit that she'd probably had tailored to fit her body precisely. She reminded Wes so much of himself, and a sense of peace about transferring the company to her filled him.

She'll do a great job, he thought. And she would. She was as invested in Hammond Manufacturing Company's future as any Hammond had ever been, Wes included.

"Morning," she said, reaching out to shake his hand. Jill followed her, and she was a couple shades lighter than Laura in all regards.

Wes liked her the least, as she tended to have a forked tongue that didn't know when to stop talking. Nothing he said to her could be kept in confidence, he knew that. So he'd learned not to tell Jill anything he didn't want the whole world to know. Which was nothing, so he literally never spoke to her.

He shook her hand too, though, and looked to Kent. The youngest of the Hammond children in his uncle's line, Kent had definitely gotten the Hammond nose—long and sloped. He looked powerful, but he didn't act it. Wes knew that from experience too.

"Morning," he said to them all. "I'd offer you water or coffee, but my assistant is out for the holidays."

"No matter," Laura said.

"Sit," Wes said, falling into his CEO role easily. "Let's sit and go ahead and tell us what you're thinking."

He already knew what they were thinking, because they'd gone to Gray first. They'd had to, because he did all the paperwork for HMC, and that included anything to do with the transfer of power.

It took several seconds for everyone to find a seat and sit down, and then Wes looked at Laura expectantly.

"We're looking for a straight-across trade," she said. "I'll be CEO. Jill will take over as executive marketing director. Kent will slide into the role of acquisitions."

"I don't do acquisitions," Gray said. "That's not a straight-across transfer."

"You'll still be here for a while," Laura said without missing a beat. She didn't fiddle with her hair or adjust in her seat either. She had plenty of experience in leadership roles too. "And during that year you're still with us, we'll find someone to replace you."

"Not that you're replaceable," Jill said smoothly. "We know you're excellent at what you do, Gray."

"You all are," Laura said. "But we sense that you're...tired. And we're ready to take HMC into the next phase of its life." She looked and sounded absolutely confident about that.

"Great," Colton said. "I think we're ready for you to do just that." He looked at Gray and Wes. "Right?"

"I am," Wes said, surprised at how easily he could open his fingers and let his role at HMC go. He knew it would be hard to clean out of his office. Move off the top floor. All of that.

"So I've drawn up some papers," Gray said, inserting himself smoothly into the meeting. "That provides our standard severance package for CEOs, for all three of us." He pulled a folder out of his briefcase. "As Wes has reached a decade as CEO, he'll get a ten-percent bonus in the package. Colton brings a special skill set to HMC, and I believe he'd like to be considered for a scientific position. If you're not aware, he holds a master's degree in biology and biological research from Yale University. Since he is stepping down from this senior role, his severance will be the same, and he's also been at a high level for over a decade. His ten-percent is in the package. I've been the corporate lawyer for my entire career." He paused, and Wes watched him. He'd never known Gray to be overly emotional. Even when his marriage had dissolved and he'd taken his ex-wife to court to make sure she didn't take Hunter somewhere Gray would never see him again, Wes had never seen him get emotional. Never shed a tear. Nothing.

But he swallowed and took a long second before he continued. "As is custom, I'll stay on for twelve months, ending my tenure here on December thirty-first of next year. I'll help hire a new lawyer for the company, whether from within the family or without, and I'll receive a severance package at that time, at our usual rate, as well as a retirement package."

"I'm sure it's all in order," Laura said, picking up the folder Gray had put in front of her. The others did the same, and Wes felt some of the weight he'd been carrying for fourteen years lift off his shoulders. He could almost hear the Lord Himself telling him what a great opportunity he had in front of him.

"I see nothing to object to," Laura said, closing the folder though she couldn't have read everything in it so fast.

"Barring any opposition from the board—which we don't expect," Wes said. "We'll vote in our meeting on the sixth. And Colt and I will have thirty days to be out of your way. HMC would be in your hands by February seventh."

Laura didn't even blink, and Wes saw the professionalism in her. She'd do great in meetings with big fuel moguls who always wanted more than Wes wanted to give them.

"The transition can begin as soon as the board approves," Gray said, waving at Kent to keep the folder. "You can arrange to shadow Colton and Wes to get a feel for what they do, meet their staff, all of that."

'The staff stays," Colton said, glancing at Gray. "Is that right?"

"Absolutely," Gray said. "They get twelve months, same as me. After that, if Laura wants someone new, she can hire and fire at her discretion."

Wes thought of his assistant and his secretary. They'd been with him for years and years, and he felt like he owed it to them to give them a heads-up about his departure before they heard it from someone else.

So right after this meeting adjourned, he'd call Bree. Then he'd call Matthew and Myra.

Then...Wes didn't even know what he'd do after that. And it felt great.

More talk. More handshakes. The cousins left, and Wes stood there, almost numb. Colton and Gray seemed to have fallen into the same pit he had, and it wasn't until Gray zipped his briefcase and said, "All right. Let's go. And I want to stop at Joe Dog's on the way out of town. We've all earned a foot long," that Wes's eyes even focused.

"That went well," he said.

"Really well," Gray agreed. "I suspected it would. They're family. They don't want to rock the boat, and they don't think we did a bad job."

"It's just time to pass the baton," Colton said. "And I want the Pirate's Chest at Joe Dog's." He grinned, and Wes's step landed lighter than it had in years. Over a decade. Fourteen years.

He followed his brothers out of the conference room, taking a moment to bump down the thermostat. He was the last one on the elevator, and he gazed down the hall as the doors slid closed, everything around him feeling just a little surreal.

He let Colt and Gray chatter down to the truck and over to Joe Dog's. He just wanted the Plain Jane, and he did enjoy his all-beef hot dog with ketchup, brown mustard, and bacon-and-onion jam.

Before he knew it, Gray had driven the hour out of the city and turned onto the lane where the farmhouse sat.

"Someone's here," he said, after making the last turn and driving through the tree line that blocked the view of the farm and house from the dirt road.

Wes peered at the black sedan that looked like it had driven through a mud storm. "No one I know," he said.

"Me either," Colton said.

"Could it be Laura or one of them?" Gray asked, eyeing the car like it was a cobra. Wes could admit he was doing the same. "We should've told them we hadn't spoken to Dad yet."

"If Dad had found out, he'd have called me," Wes said. He checked his phone. No missed calls. Not even a text. Even as he looked at his phone, a message came in.

Bree's name filled the screen, her note popping up a moment later. *Is it over? How did it go? I've been on pins and needles all day, thinking about you. Call me!*

Thinking about you. Wes couldn't keep the smile from his face. It had been a long time since a woman had been thinking about him—at least in a good way.

"Holy—that's Eden." Colton's level of panic reached Wes, erasing the smile and pulling his attention from his phone. He looked first at his brother, who had wide eyes and his mouth hanging open, and then to the black sedan, where a tall, curvy woman with brown hair now stood at the hood of the car, watching Gray drive past.

"Who's Eden?" Wes asked at the same time Gray said, "She's real pretty. Too young for you, but pretty."

Colton wrenched his head around to keep his eyes on her, whispering, "It's Annie's daughter. I have to get out." He nudged Wes. "Let me out, Wes."

"Gray needs to stop the truck first," Wes said. He'd jumped from moving vehicles before, but he wasn't keen to do it now, thirty years older than the last time he'd done it.

Gray finally stopped, and Wes got out as quickly as he could, thinking Colton would crawl over him if he didn't move.

Colton strode away, back toward the black sedan and the woman who stood there. He obviously wasn't over Annie, and Gray murmured, "Good luck, Colton. Get past whatever you need to get past, because it sure seems like you want Annie in your life."

CHAPTER 29

Annie lifted her head from the pillow she'd put on the couch. She'd left the lodge on the twenty-sixth. She didn't have to stay there, and the glances and questions had become too much before dinner was served on Christmas Day.

Everyone wanted to know where Colton was, why he'd left, and when he'd be back. He'd seemed to get inside everyone's heart in the six days he'd been in town, and Annie couldn't blame them.

He'd definitely crawled right inside hers. She'd made up some excuse about checking the house, and she'd packed and left. She'd only communicated with three people in the past few days since then, and in her opinion, that was three people too many.

But she couldn't ignore her daughters, and she knew their texts came from a place of concern for her. Celia's did too, and Annie hadn't been able to simply read her texts and ignore them.

Thankfully, no one had followed her down the canyon, and she'd checked the house. All fine. She'd made crepes for dinner. Delicious. She'd eaten out for every meal one day, something she'd always wanted to do.

She'd stayed in her pajamas the next day, watching movies

and eating ice cream straight from the carton. All the things she'd always wanted to do when Ryan had died, she did.

Back then, she couldn't skip showering for days on end, because she had two daughters who needed her. Back then, she couldn't afford cable TV, and forget about the streaming services. Back then, she made meals with all the food groups in them, and ice cream was never on the menu.

She had not cried, because Annie had no one to blame for Colton's departure from her life—except herself.

Anger simmered in her veins, and though she'd tried to deflect it onto him, the lodge, all the other women up there, she knew it always came back to her. She was to blame, and everything Colton had said to her had been true.

One hundred percent true.

Her teeth pressed together, and she had to work to get her jaw to loosen. She wondered how long the furious stage of grief lasted, because she'd like to move past it. If only she knew *how* to do that.

She'd tried journaling. She'd tried sweets. She'd even taken walks in the freezing cold, trying to clear her head. Nothing worked. She simply wanted Colton back.

He'd texted very late on Christmas night—or very early in the morning the day after Christmas, depending on how she looked at it—to say he'd arrived in Ivory Peaks.

She hadn't responded. She didn't know what to say. *Please come back*, sounded desperate.

His meeting was scheduled for tomorrow, and Annie told herself he'd be gone by now anyway. He'd just moved up the departure date a little bit, and really, it had been merciful. She'd had a few days to wallow while she didn't have to work. Next week, she'd have to get up and go to work whether she had a broken heart in her chest or not.

She had no idea what time it was when the kitchen door opened. It even took her a moment to realize it had, and that both Eden and Emily had entered the house.

"Hey," she said, trying to make her voice as cheerful as possible. She glanced around, seeing the evidence of her non-cheerfulness all around her. Wrappers, dishes, water bottles. They sat on every available surface, as if she'd dropped them and left them to sit wherever they'd landed. Because she had.

"You're sleeping on the couch," Eden said, glancing at Emily.

"What are you girls doing here?"

"Oh, Mom." Emily came around Eden and waited for Annie to sit up. "What are you doing?"

"Watching TV," she said, though she had no idea what flickered on the screen in front of her.

"You slept out here?"

Annie shrugged. "Seemed like a long walk into the bedroom."

Emily put her arm around Annie, and she leaned into her daughter. "Mom, I think we all know what this means."

"We do?"

"The last time you slept on the couch was when Dad died."

Annie's heartbeat jumped as if she'd been hooked up to a jolt of electricity. "I'm sure that's not true."

"It is," Eden said, coming to sit next to Emily. "And it means you're in love with Colton."

Annie shook her head. "Even if I am, which I'm not admitting to, it doesn't matter. He's right. I was trying to pull him to where I am, and he's not ready."

"Then wait for him to be ready," Emily said. "Just call him and tell him that you're willing to wait until *he's* ready."

Annie looked at both of her daughters, each of them wearing pure concern in their eyes. "Okay," she said. "It sounds easy, right?"

"It *is* easy, Mom," Emily said.

"Maybe for you," Eden said, glancing at Emily. "Mom." She focused on her again. "I know how hard it is to wait for someone to fall in love with you when you're already in love with them. Okay? I *know* what that feels like."

Tears gathered in Annie's eyes then, and everything burned.

"But I really think he could get where you are, and quickly too."

"You say that," Annie said. "But you don't *know* it." She shook her head. "What if he's never ready?"

She'd just vocalized her greatest fear. Yes, she'd fallen for Colton in the several days he'd been at the lodge. She already felt stupid enough for allowing that to happen. And if he could *never* be ready to marry her?

What's the point? She'd been asking herself that question for four days now, and she still had no answers.

"Let's go to Ivory Peaks," Eden said, standing up.

All of Annie's muscles tightened. "No. I'm not going there. I don't even know where it is."

"I'll drive you," Eden said. "I have a map on my phone."

"Go get in the shower," Emily said. "I'll get a bag packed for you with that sexy red dress you wear for weddings."

"No," Annie said more forcefully this time. "I'm not wearing that dress in the winter. It's ridiculous. I'm not going anywhere."

"I've already called him," Eden said.

The breath left Annie's body, and she couldn't even demand to know what her youngest meant by that. "And he's expecting us, and if you don't go, then he'll think you don't want to be with him."

A franticness Annie had only felt one other time in her life filled her bloodstream. She suddenly had so much to do and not enough time to do it. Somehow, she managed to get to her feet, casting one more look at Eden and then Emily before she went down the hall to her bedroom and bathroom.

Before she got in the shower, she looked at herself in the mirror. "Tell the truth," she told herself. "Start at the beginning." She held up one finger. "I love God." Another finger. "I love my girls, both of them, just how they are." A third finger. "I love myself. I'm smart and capable of anything." Her chest started to vibrate, because she didn't want to keep going. But another finger went up, and Annie looked at it and then into her eyes again.

"I love Colton, and I want to get him back."

Five fingers. "I'm willing to wait where I am until he's ready to move forward. Together."

And one more. "I don't want to be alone anymore."

Her truths spoken, she showered and got ready, taking her time. She went down the hall with her purse, finding the girls in the kitchen, eating a pizza they'd had delivered.

"Let's go," Eden said, picking up a suitcase Annie hadn't packed.

"That red dress better not be in there," Annie said.

"It's not," Emily said. "I packed sensible winter clothes." She grinned at Annie and left her half-eaten slice on her plate as she stood up. "But I'd wear the sweater with the white stripes. You look great in that."

"I'm wearing this," she said, gesturing to the black slacks and yellow blouse she wore.

"Mom, it's mid-afternoon," Eden said. "We won't see him until tomorrow morning."

"He has a meeting tomorrow morning."

"Great," Eden said without missing a beat. "Then we'll see him after that. Come on, it's time to go."

Annie took Emily into her arms and hugged her tight, squeezing her eyes closed as her daughter said, "Be brave, Mom."

She followed Eden outside, hugging her in the driveway before they got in the car and buckled their seatbelts.

"All right," Eden said brightly. "To Ivory Peaks."

———

HOURS LATER, AFTER THE SUN HAD SET, AND THEY'D BEEN DRIVING for a long time, Eden pulled up to a hotel with shining lights in the front windows.

She handled the bags, which was good, because Annie felt like she could barely handle her limbs. Eden checked in, got the room key, and led them down the hall to the assigned space.

They brushed their teeth and changed into their pajamas. Annie sat on the edge of her bed and said, "Thank you, Eden. I'm not sure why I just...I didn't fall apart like this when your dad died."

"I know that, Mom." Eden switched off her lamp. "You're the strongest woman I know. You literally do everything, for everyone. It's okay to need help sometimes."

"How did your date with Mitchell go?"

Eden grinned, and Annie felt some of her old self start to regrow. "Great," she said. "We're going out tomorrow night too."

"Will we be back in time?"

"I will be," Eden said, somewhat evasively.

"I don't have a car here," Annie said.

"Colton can bring you back," Eden said.

"You're presuming he's going to forgive me and take me back."

"He will." Eden grinned up at her. "He really likes you too, Mom."

Annie sighed, the thought of being stranded in Colorado without a car causing a zing of anxiety to sing through her. A bit of excitement too, if Annie were being honest with herself.

She got in bed and snapped off her lamp too. "Guess I better start working on my speech," she said into the darkness. "Or did you write one of those for me too?"

"Nope," Eden said. "But don't worry about it. He'll be surprised just to see you."

"He will? Isn't he expecting us?"

Eden didn't respond, and Annie's blood turned cold.

"Eden?"

"Mom, don't be mad."

"You always say that when I have a good reason to be mad."

She reached for her lamp again, fumbling until she clicked on the light. "What's going on?"

"I didn't call him," Eden blurted out. "I'm sorry for lying. But I didn't call him, and he doesn't know we're coming, and I said that to get you to come."

"You're kidding," left Annie's mouth.

Eden said nothing, and she didn't roll over, no matter how hard Annie glared at the back of her head.

"Well, I can't just march up to his house and talk to him," Annie said. She couldn't.

Again, Eden said nothing.

Annie laid back down and eventually reached up and turned off the light. She wished she could turn her mind off as easily. It went round and round, and Annie tried to seize onto what she needed to do—what Emily had said to do.

Be brave, Mom.

She didn't know how, and the fear of what might happen in the morning kept her silent and still. That was when she turned to the Lord and started praying, pouring out her whole soul to God and begging Him to help her.

Please, please help me.

CHAPTER 30

C olton coached himself not to run toward Eden, but he really wanted to. He checked the car, but there was no sign of Annie anywhere.

"Eden," he finally said when he got close enough. "What's going on?" He had so many more questions—*where's your mom? Is she okay? Why didn't she come?*—but he kept them contained in his chest for now.

"I was just waiting for you," she said with a smile, as if she dropped by his parents' farm every day about this time. "Now that you're here, I can go. And not a moment too soon. I have a date tonight, and I'm hoping for a New Year's kiss." She got behind the wheel, started the car, and backed away before Colton could comprehend what had just happened.

"What?" he said to the retreating sedan. Then again to just the air. He turned around and caught the backs of his brothers as they went in the farmhouse, and Colton felt utterly lost.

He turned around again, intending to call to Eden, but she was already gone. He didn't have her phone number, but he patted his pockets anyway. He didn't even know where his phone was at the moment.

"Colton."

He spun around, his heart beating faster and faster as his eyes caught up to the sound of Annie's voice.

She stood there, right at the corner of Gray's truck, as if she'd been dropped in this spot straight from heaven.

One thing he did know, God had led him to her. So maybe the Good Lord *had* dropped her off right here in Ivory Peaks, straight from heaven.

He started toward her, intending to sweep her into his arms and hold her close. Whispers of apology tickled the back of his tongue as he broke into a jog.

"Annie," he said, right before reaching her. He drew her to his chest and held her, so many things aligning in his life. He didn't embrace her for long, though, his questions taking over.

"What are you doing here? What's going on?"

"I came to talk to you," she said. She reached up and nervously tucked her hair behind her ear. "I think everything you said at the lodge is absolutely right. I am in a different place than you. I was trying to pull you to me when you weren't ready to come."

Colton searched her face, not quite lining up all the dots yet. "Okay," he said, expecting more.

She opened her mouth, but words didn't come out. She took in another lungful of air and pushed it out. She tried again, adding, "I'm willing to wait until you're in the same place as me, so we can move forward together."

Colton's hands stung from the cold, and they started to shake. He couldn't think.

"That's all," she said. "That's all I have to give you. Time. If, in the future, you just can't get to the place where I am, and we can't take the next step together, so be it. But I'd like to see if we can try, and I'm hoping you'd like that too."

Colton absolutely did want that. He found himself nodding, his voice suddenly on vacation.

"Yes?" Annie asked. "You want that too?"

"Yes," he said, his voice almost a croak. "Yes, I want that

too." He stepped into her again, easily slipping his arms around her waist. "I'm sorry I said so many hurtful things to you."

She closed her eyes and laid her forehead against his chest. "You didn't."

"I've felt bad for days, and you didn't text, and I thought I'd messed everything up."

"I'm the one who did that," Annie said. "And I've been so mad at myself, and so embarrassed, and I didn't know what to do."

"So you had Eden drive you here and drop you off?" Colton actually looked over his shoulder. "Did she really leave?"

"She really did." Annie lifted her head and looked back at him. "So I kind of need a ride home." She smiled, the gesture starting out small and timid and growing over the next few seconds.

"I think I can give you one," he said, grinning back at her. "But we're having a family party for New Year's, so I hope you don't need to be home for a few days. I think Wes will kill me if I miss it."

"I'm in no hurry," she said coolly. "In fact, that's my new motto."

Colton blinked and then started laughing, relieved when she giggled with him. "I've missed you," he said, sighing as he brought her flush against him again.

"Will you come to Coral Canyon?" she asked.

"Yes," he said, his mind working again, thank goodness. "I have things here I have to do with HMC. But as of February seventh, I'm unemployed, with nothing to do."

"I can put you to work," she teased, and Colton chuckled.

"I'm looking forward to some time off," he said.

"Yeah, right," Annie said, pulling back and gazing up at him again. "I seem to remember someone telling me that a man has to have something good to fill his time with."

"Really?" Colton asked. "Whoever said that must be really smart."

Annie laughed, tipping her head back and lighting Colton's soul with joy. He slid his hand along her neck, and she quieted instantly.

"Your hands are cold," she murmured.

"I need you to warm me up." He leaned down to kiss her, and hallelujah, she met him halfway. Colton could kiss Annie forever, and he'd never been happier for a pop-in visit than he was right now.

He pulled away after several seconds, and said, "So, do you want to meet my family?"

"Oh, I've met some of them," she said, and Colton's heart stopped again.

"You did?"

"I went to the door," she said. "Your SUV is here."

"Oh, right," he said. "How long have you been here?"

"About fifteen minutes. I saw two brothers go in as I came out, so I haven't really met them. But I met your mom and dad, your grandmother, and a brother named Ames. They all seem very nice. Lovely."

Colton scoffed, wishing he'd been able to introduce Annie to his parents. "Ames is going to be thrilled when I tell him you said he was lovely."

"He was nice," Annie said, giggling.

"Was he wearing the leather jacket?"

"Yes."

Colton rolled his eyes. "He never takes it off. Thinks he's some kind of motorcycle cowboy."

"He did have a cowboy hat on too," Annie said, stepping with him as he led her toward the house.

"Wait until you meet Cy," he said, going up the stairs.

"When will he be here?"

"Tomorrow," Colton said. "So you have some time to acclimate to everyone. Although, you came from the Whittakers, and there are a million of them. There will be eight of us total. You make nine."

"Nine is nothing."

"Keep telling yourself that," he said as he opened the front door.

"I did almost leave when Ames asked me to submit to a background check."

Colton froze. "You're lying. Please tell me he didn't say that."

"He did." Annie looked into the house. "Is that normal?"

"For Ames, yes. For normal humans, no." Colton would have words with his younger brother later, that was for sure. "Sorry about that. I hope you said no."

"Oh, your grandmother swooped in and said, 'don't ask her that. She's not a criminal.'"

"Thank goodness for Gramma," Colton said, his nerves vibrating through him. "Here we go."

He took her down the hall, and all conversation stalled mid-sentence. "Guys," he said, pulling his courage close. "This is my girlfriend, Annie Pruitt. Annie, this is my family. I think you've met my mom and dad, Chris and Beverly."

"Bev," Annie said. "She told me to call her Bev."

Colton watched his mother practically melt, and he had to look away from her before he started laughing. "You've met my grandmother, Opal. And one of the very obnoxious twins, Ames. I think you passed my oldest brother, Wes." Wes raised his hand, thank goodness. "And the next oldest, right above me, Gray."

"And Gray is Hunter's father," Annie said with a smile. Everyone beamed back at her, and Colton experienced a rush of love and gratitude for his family.

"So are you two all good?" his mother asked.

"Yes," Colton said, squeezing Annie's hand. "We're good."

"Good," his mom said. "Now come sit by me, Annie, and tell me everything about yourself."

She laughed, but she did go sit next to his mother on the couch. Colton shot a look at Ames, who didn't even flinch. He went into the kitchen and got out a couple of water bottles.

"She's great," Wes said.

"You haven't even said two words to her," Colton said.

"She has a good air about her," Wes said. Colton paused and watched Annie with his mother, and he couldn't argue with that.

He felt like the luckiest man on the planet in that moment, and he realized what a blessing he'd been given when Priscilla had left him without marrying him.

"HOW MANY DIFFERENT KINDS OF M&MS DO YOU HAVE?" ANNIE asked, surveying the long row of bowls on the kitchen counter. She looked at Colton with wonder in her eyes. "I've never even seen this many M&Ms."

"My dad loves them," Colton said with a smile. "You know how they've been doing all those different flavors? He gets a bunch of them every time they come out with a new one and saves them for New Year's Eve." He went down the counter until he got to the coconut ones. "These are my favorite." He picked up a handful of them and took her several.

She ate them without complaint, but she almost immediately puckered up her lips and shook her head. "No. Those are a no."

Colton laughed, beyond glad to have her here in Ivory Peaks with him. They'd had a great afternoon together, and she'd even done well with the twins. They currently sat at the kitchen table with cards in their hands, eyeing each other. They liked to dress tough, and Ames currently wore a pair of sunglasses backward on his head, though the sun had set five hours ago. Cy had walked in wearing full leather, with spurs on his motorcycle riding boots. *Spurs.* Colton had teased him until he'd taken them off, replacing them with real cowboy boots.

Then he'd gone out on the farm with Gray and Hunter to do the afternoon chores, while Wes disappeared down the hall with Dad, and Colton and Annie had visited with Gramma Opal and his mother.

Gramma Opal had gone to bed thirty minutes ago, and they

still had ninety minutes until the New Year. Colton wanted his kiss, and he wasn't going to bed without it.

"We're getting out the sherbet," Wes said, coming into the kitchen. "And then we'll put on the concert before the count-down." He opened the freezer and started pulling out cartons of sherbet.

"I want lemon," his mother said, joining them. "Do you like sherbet, Annie?"

"Sure," she said, watching Wes put more and more cartons on the counter. "Do you have every flavor of that too?"

"Yes," Colton said. "We don't know when to stop in the Hammond family." He picked up the closest container. "This one's raspberry."

"Lime," Wes said. "Lemon. Orange. Raspberry. Pineapple. Piña colada." He tapped the top of each one as he said it. "Peach and blood orange." He looked at Annie and Colton. "And you can make a float with it by pouring Sprite over the top." He turned and pulled out a couple of two-liter bottles of the soda.

"This is incredible," Annie said. She moved down and picked up the pineapple sherbet. "I love pineapple sherbet. So does my father. This reminds me so much of home." She beamed at Colton, Wes, and their mother, and said, "I want a float."

"A float you shall have," Wes said, getting out cups and spoons and dishing up the pineapple sherbet for Annie and pouring soda over it.

"I want lemon," Mom said again. "No soda."

"I'll take raspberry and lemon," Colton said.

"Oh, mixing it up," Annie said. "I like that."

Colton scooped his own sherbet while Wes served their mother. "Okay," Wes said. "Let's put the concert on."

They all retreated to the living room, and Colton sure did like how close Annie sat to him.

"This is ridiculous," Cy said a few minutes later, plenty of disgust in his voice. "I'm done."

Colton caught him tossing his cards on the table and getting up. He filled a massive bowl with at least six scoops of variously flavored sherbets and practically stomped into the living room. "Did he win?" Colton asked.

"He always wins," Cy said darkly.

Ames took his time at the table, putting the cards back together. He left the sherbet on the counter and came into the room too. He sat by Mom and smiled at her. "Hey, baby," Mom said, and Ames played right into that, snuggling into her side and smiling at her.

Colton rolled his eyes. He loved the twins, because they were family, but he didn't understand them. They seemed determined to make sure everyone knew they were present—and different. Colton wondered when they'd outgrow that, as they were thirty-eight-years-old now, and didn't need to jockey for positions in the family anymore.

Ames was a good cop, though, and he worked with drug dogs and kept the highways coming in and out of the city clean. He had to look like the bad cop, he claimed, or he didn't inspire the right kind of fear in the criminals he was trying to catch. Colton got that; he did. He just didn't understand why his brother couldn't wear a pair of jeans and a T-shirt to the family New Year's Eve party.

Cy loved motorcycles—both twins did—and he'd taken his inheritance and founded a custom bike shop that provided new motorcycles to veterans returning home from time in the service. They also built custom motorcycles for people who'd lost everything they owned in natural disasters, and he'd started a foundation that granted bucket list items for people suffering from terminal illnesses.

He just liked to look like the big, bad boss. Underneath, his roar was more like a meow.

The concert played on, and Colton kept one eye on Wes as he texted, and texted, and texted. "He must be getting along with Bree," he murmured to Annie, who looked at him with questions in her eyes.

"He's got a thing with Bree." Colton nodded toward his brother.

"Oh, you did say you set them up."

"Well, kind of. I know it's still new." And Colton hoped it would lead somewhere, as Wes hadn't had a real relationship in a while.

Finally, the countdown began, and Colton squeezed Annie's hand. He counted backward with everyone else, and when they got to zero, he shouted, "Happy New Year!" with his parents and brothers before turning to Annie.

"I'm so glad you're here," he said, grinning at her. He kissed her, hoping and praying this year would hold something amazing for him and Annie. As she broke the kiss with a laugh, a warmth Colton hadn't felt too often in his life covered his shoulders like a comfy blanket.

And he knew his prayer would be answered.

CHAPTER 31

B ree sat on the couch in her cabin, her fingers actually starting to hurt with how much she'd texted Wes that night. He'd called earlier to detail the meeting, and he said everything had gone really well. He expected the board to agree to the transfer, and he should be out of the role of CEO sometime in February.

A pleasant warmth filled the cabin from the roaring fire nearby, but Bree didn't have the TV playing, and she was all alone. Elise had stayed at the lodge for the countdown, and Bree had walked back to their house by herself. She'd been there for hours, talking with Wes and texting Wes. If there ever was a lull, she entertained herself with a game on her phone, or the Singles Spark app.

She still hadn't swiped right on anyone, but she got several swipes each day on her own profile.

Wish you were here, Wes said. *It's almost midnight. You don't have anyone there to kiss, do you?*

Bree scoffed, her fingers already flying across the screen. For him being someone she hadn't met face-to-face yet, she sure was attracted to him. Her smile came instantly when his name popped up on the screen, and her heart beat fast at the thought of kissing him.

"You're doing it again," she muttered to herself as she sent him a reassurance that no, she didn't have anyone here to kiss. *All the cowboys I know are married*, she sent as an added explanation for why she was alone tonight.

Are you only interested in cowboys?

Bree paused at the question, because she hadn't really thought about it before. She knew what she liked in a man, sure. And a cowboy hat and a strong moral ethic was definitely part of that. *Not only*, she said. *You aren't a cowboy? Your brother wears the biggest, brightest cowboy hat I've ever seen.*

I'm maybe halfway, Wes said. *I own a hat, and maybe now that I won't be in the office every day, I can actually wear it.*

She'd spoken to him on the phone several times now, and Bree knew he spoke with more polish than the men in Coral Canyon. She knew he was a CEO. She should've been able to put the two together and come up with a businessman, not a cowboy. But maybe he could be both....

Bree liked the idea of that, and she smiled to herself again. *Anyone nearby for you to kiss?* she asked.

Just Annie and my mom, he said. *No danger here.*

Who's the last woman you went out with? Bree studied the question, giving herself a minute to think about sending it. In the end, she did, because she wanted to know. Wes could choose not to answer.

Oh, wow, he said. *Let's see....* He didn't put a name on the screen, or say how long it had been. Bree waited and waited, and she hadn't anticipated the question being so difficult.

Moment of Truth, he said, and Bree grinned at the game they'd created between them. Her neck hurt from looking down so much, and she leaned back into the couch and held her phone above her face so she wouldn't miss a moment of this conversation.

I haven't been out with anyone in a while.

You haven't? Why not?

Not interested.

You aren't interested in dating? Or you haven't met anyone you were interested in?

MoT:

Bree pulled in a breath and held it.

Both.

She let her phone drop to her lap, the four letters burning her eyes. "Both," she repeated, her voice so loud in the quiet cabin. So Wes hadn't met anyone he was interested in, and he wasn't interested in dating.

Then what were they doing?

Her phone buzzed against her leg, but she didn't lift it to look at the messages. She suddenly felt so tired, and she wanted to go to bed whether she'd welcomed in the New Year or not. Until those texts, she'd anticipated a New Year full of possibilities. Full of excitement for the unknown, for what might happen with Wes.

And now she knew he wasn't really interested.

Her phone vibrated, and an alarm started to ring. Bree flipped over her phone and silenced the alarm, saying, "Happy New Year," to herself and the empty cabin surrounding her.

Wes had texted four more times, and Bree couldn't help reading the short messages.

So no one for a while.

I'm hoping this upcoming year is different.

5 – 4 – 3 – 2 – 1…

Happy New Year, Bree!

A wave of foolishness rolled over her, and she disliked that she'd jumped to the worst conclusion possible. But her dating history had taught her to do just that, and she needed to learn to slow down a little bit.

Happy New Year, Wes, she sent to him.

Her phone rang, and Bree swiped to answer his call. "Hey," she said.

"Definitely doesn't sound like a party there," he said.

"I told you I was in my house by myself."

Cheering sounded behind him, and Bree smiled. "I wish I was by myself," Wes said, almost under his breath. "Give me a sec." He moved, the noise coming through the line getting louder and then quieter. "Okay, I'm headed to my room."

"How long will you be at your parents'?"

"Oh, I don't know." He exhaled. "I'll probably go back to the city tomorrow night. Maybe the day after that."

Bree nodded, not sure what else to say.

"Bree?" Wes asked, and she liked the way he said her name. She wasn't sure why, only that no one had said it with quite so much care in such a long time.

"Yeah?" She pulled in a breath and held it.

Wes didn't say anything, and Bree wasn't sure what to think.

"Happy New Year," he finally said, and Bree had the distinct impression that wasn't what he really wanted to say. "I'll call you later, okay?"

"Okay."

The call ended, and Bree sighed as she leaned back and closed her eyes. She only had a couple more days before the Whittaker family would leave the lodge and the guests would come back. She was determined to sleep in until the fifth, and she padded down the hall to her bedroom, her phone on silent but her mind still moving.

She couldn't get one question out of her mind—what were she and Wes doing?

———

THE HOLIDAYS ENDED; THE WHITTAKERS LEFT THE LODGE; THE guests returned.

Bree got back to work, posting the daily activities on the

whiteboard outside the kitchen and sending out the group texts guests could opt into. She got the horses out of the stables and back to work, and Bree liked her routine. She thrived on it, actually, and she liked that she didn't have a whole lot of time to text and talk with Wes.

Sure, she laid in bed at night, thinking about him, and she gave herself ten minutes each night to glance through Singles Spark. Several men caught her eye, but she still hadn't done anything yet.

One man kept coming up in her notifications, as he swiped on her every single day. Four days, five days, and then six days.

Bree finally tapped over to Alex Jenkins, and Bree's first impression of him was that he had a great smile. Happiness exuded from his eyes, and Bree pulled in a breath...and swiped right.

The next morning, she'd just finished sweeping out the barn when her phone made a noise she'd never heard before. She pulled it out of her pocket, a measure of confusion clouding her mind for a moment. Then she saw the orange spark in her notifications bar, and she pulled down to tap on the icon.

Alex had messaged her.

The wind picked up, and Bree couldn't stand out in the cold, dumbfounded. She stepped back into the barn, which certainly wasn't warm, but it at least protected her from the wind.

You finally swiped on me, Alex had said. *I swear I'm not a stalker. You just have a great face, and I was hoping we could chat a little and get to know each other.*

Bree had never had anyone tell her she had a great face. Wes didn't even know what she looked like. A slow smile filled her face, and she quickly tapped out, *You have a great smile. You're the first person I've swiped on — because of that smile.*

Aw, thanks. He sent her a cartoon fox with a big smile on his foxy face. *What do you do, Breeann?*

I go by Bree, she said. *And I'm an event coordinator for a luxury lodge.*

Sounds fancy, Alex said.

What do you do?

I drive a tour bus.

Ah, so we're both in the hospitality industry. For some reason, Bree liked that. She looked at Alex's face again, feeling a good vibe from him. *I hate to run, but I have horses to feed before our first ride.*

Go, Alex said. *We'll talk later.*

Annie slipped her phone back in her pocket, feeling warmer and warmer by the minute, despite the fact that she stepped out into the winter wind. But it couldn't touch her as she thought about her new conversation with Alex.

A week passed, and Bree's guilt sat in her stomach twenty-four-seven. She was still talking to Wes, but her conversations with Alex had picked up too. She hadn't defined a relationship with either one of them, but she felt like she should.

She stood at the sink, the warm water rinsing away the suds off the mug she'd been washing. She had no idea how long she'd been standing there, but all the soap was gone. She had to make a choice.

Wes or Alex?

She liked talking to them both, and since she hadn't met either one, she simply didn't know how things would go in person.

"Alex lives in town," she murmured. But she couldn't imagine calling Wes and telling him…telling him what, exactly?

"I don't want to talk to you anymore?" she guessed.

"Talking to yourself?" Elise asked as she came into the kitchen.

Bree flinched and turned off the water. "Just a little bit." She cleared her throat, put the mug in the dish drainer, and turned around. "I'm headed out to get all of the painting supplies for this afternoon's class."

"All right," Elise said, clearly not realizing Bree's inner turmoil.

Bree put on her coat and went out onto the porch. She got her phone out and tapped to pull up her text string with Wes. She hadn't spoken to him on the phone in two or three days, and she knew he was busy. Could she just text him?

No, she thought, and she tapped to get the line ringing. Her heart started to sprint in her chest, and with every ring, she thought she might get to avoid this difficult conversation. The call went to voicemail, and Bree had serious second thoughts when his voice sounded in her ear.

And then she opened her mouth and words just came out. "Hey, Wes. It's Bree. I'm...I'm so sorry, but I've met someone else up here, and I think I'm just going to...I don't think we should talk anymore. I sure did like getting to know you—and I'm sorry." She had no idea what she'd said, and her thoughts felt so tangled. "Okay, bye."

She sighed as she lowered her phone and ended the call. "Was that the right thing to do?" she asked, tipping her head toward the heavens. She took a moment to listen, but she couldn't hear anything.

She never had been able to hear the Lord very well. Since Bronson's death, she'd been stumbling through life, going to church and praying and doing her best to be who she thought she wanted to be. But she simply felt removed from everyone, including God.

Her phone chimed, and she knew it would be Alex. A flame started in her soul, and she glanced at the message.

Wondering if you'd like to go to dinner with me.

She sucked in a breath. He'd asked her out. He wanted to meet her. The smile on her face appeared instantly, and she couldn't type fast enough to say, *Yes, I think dinner with you sounds amazing.*

Before Alex could reply, Bree's phone rang. Wes's name sat on the screen, and Bree almost dropped her device. She didn't want to answer. She'd left a message. Couldn't things just be left at that?

Maybe he hadn't listened to the message, and she'd be forced to say it all again.

"You can do this," she told herself, and she swiped to answer the call, hoping Wes had felt the distance between them too, and that they could walk away before either of them got hurt.

CHAPTER 32

Annie finished her cleaning for the day and went back to the home office she shared with her daughters. Colton had driven her home, but he'd had to go back to Colorado to finish all of his business meetings.

She expected to hear from him that night, as the board was meeting that day to approve or disapprove the transfer of titles within his family company. Annie had been praying for relief from her nerves, because she couldn't control what the board did. She didn't even know what a board looked like in a business as big as the one Colton's family owned.

She'd enjoyed the New Year holiday at his parents' farm in Ivory Peaks immensely, but her life and business were here. Colton knew that; they'd talked about it for a long time. He'd reassured her over and over that once he was free from HMC, he'd be joining her in Coral Canyon.

Annie looked around her small house. It had always served her and Ryan and the girls well. But she had not invited Colton in when he'd dropped her off last week. Her whole house could fit in the living area of his parents' farmhouse, and she knew he was used to much more opulent living.

She hated that she had these insecurities about herself, her life, her house. *It shouldn't matter*, she'd told herself a few times now. Colton had never given her any indication that he cared where she lived, or how much money she had or didn't have. But Annie knew they needed to talk about money before anything major happened.

As she put a pot of water on the stove to get it boiling, she reminded herself that she and Colton weren't going to get married immediately. He wasn't in the same place as her, and that was okay.

Halfway through her dinner for one, as Emily was out with her fiancé, doing some sort of shopping, and Eden had a date with Mitchell, Annie's phone rang. She picked it up and connected the call to Colton with the word, "Well?"

"It's done," he said, laughing afterward. "It's going to be us, Annie. In Coral Canyon. Real soon."

Relief flooded her, and Annie sighed even as gratitude enveloped her. "Are you happy?"

"Insanely," Colton said. "I've been tired here for a long time."

"You've said that."

"So I'm headed your way this weekend, and then I have to start working with my cousin. I might not be back until the end of the month."

"That's okay," Annie said. "You take care of what you need to take care of." For a few days there, she'd simply thought that she'd never see Colton again. She'd believed they had a good thing going, even if they'd only met several days earlier. But she also knew that sometimes good things fell apart, through no fault of anyone's.

She thought of his older brother, who'd been calling and talking to Bree. She'd started dating someone else, and she'd ended the phone calls with Wes, and Colton claimed his brother was really broken up about that.

So yes, sometimes good things fell apart. Annie was determined, though, not to be the reason she and Colton fell apart. She could be patient. She was in no hurry. There were crucial conversations still to be had, and Annie wanted to know every-thing about their future together, from children to grandchildren to finances. She wouldn't be going into a second marriage blindly, and she'd fallen just as fast for Ryan the first time. They hadn't talked about anything, and they'd had some trying times as they learned how to be married and how to raise a family with their different beliefs.

Not that they'd been that different. But she didn't want the girls to eat snacks after dinner, and Ryan hadn't cared about that. He didn't mind if they didn't have baths before school, but Annie couldn't stand the thought of sending them off dirty.

"When I get there this weekend, will you go to dinner with me?" Colton asked, and Annie warmed from the inside out. She loved that he asked her out, and she could admit that she liked being courted.

"Sure," she said.

"Pick somewhere good," he said.

"There's a new place I've been wanting to try. It's Indian food."

"I like Indian food," he said.

"Good." Annie went on to ask him about his mother, and how Wes was doing. They talked for a while, and then she said, "Colton, I know you need to go. You have a busy day tomorrow, and my girls will be home in a few minutes. But I wanted to talk to you about children."

He didn't say anything for a moment, and Annie's heart played leapfrog with itself. "All right," he said.

"Just be thinking about it," she said. "For this weekend. We can talk when you get here."

"Okay." Something crashed on his end of the line, and he said, "Annie, I have to go."

"Go,"

"Bye," he said.

Before she could say good-bye, the line went dead, with Colton saying, "Are you kidding me?"

Annie laughed, because she knew he'd agreed to cat-sit for a neighbor in his building, and she was sure the feline had just done something naughty. Sure enough, about twenty minutes later, just as she heard the garage door opening, she got a text from Colton.

Look at this cat. He knocked over my coffee. A picture came through a moment later, and there were spilled coffee grounds, a tipped container, and a very innocent-looking black and gray cat. Annie giggled at the cat's wide eyes, imagining Colton's displeasure.

You'll have to drive through somewhere in the morning, she texted him.

I need that for tonight!

Annie burst out laughing, because she believed Colton. The man burned the wick at both ends, especially now that he had to finish things up at HMC.

"Oh, she's right here," Eden said. "Flirting with her boyfriend." She wore a massive smile on her face, and Annie didn't deny that she was flirting with Colton, who *was* her boyfriend.

The thought felt strange for only a moment, and then acceptance flowed through her. "Hey, girls. How were your dates?"

"Great," Eden said, taking off her coat and draping it over the back of the recliner. She circled it and sat down while Emily launched into all of the things she'd done that night with Kelly.

Annie had a brief moment where she wished she could go to bed at a decent hour, but she knew it wouldn't be that night. And she didn't want it to be. She wanted to sit up with her daughter as she showed her shoes and ribbons and pictures of delicious chocolate cake.

"This was the steak dinner," Emily said, turning her phone. "It was amazing, Mom. But it's so expensive, and I don't know." She looked down at her device, her sigh right there on her lips. Annie wanted to give her everything. The world, and the steak dinner for her wedding too. She'd always wanted to do that for her girls, but she'd hardly ever been able to. It was hard to be a mom and a dad and a business owner. She'd done the best she could.

"You should try Fizzles," Eden said. "They're just starting up, and they're looking for clients. I bet they could cater your wedding dinner for way cheaper than Nuptials."

Emily looked at her sister. "I've never heard of Fizzles."

"It's new," Eden said, swiping on her phone. "Mitchell showed it to me."

"He did?" Annie asked. "Are you guys talking about marriage already?"

"Mom, come on." Eden barely looked at her. "I'm not you."

"Hey," Annie said, only slightly offended. She couldn't help it if she knew who she liked, or that she fell fast. Plus, she was certain the Lord had put Colton in the vicinity of Whiskey Mountain Lodge at precisely the moment it had started to snow too hard to keep driving.

"His aunt owns it," Eden said, handing her phone to Emily. "They've been in Jackson for years, and they're just now expanding. Coral Canyon is the fastest growing town out here, and she just opened a small storefront."

"Awesome," Emily said, swiping on the phone. "This looks amazing. I'm going to call them tomorrow." She beamed at Eden. "Thanks, Eden."

"Yeah, of course." She yawned and stood up. "Okay, I'm going to bed. I have to be at the Pherson's at seven-thirty."

"Don't forget to do that basement bathroom this time," Annie called after her youngest daughter. Love filled her, especially because Eden had stayed for all the wedding talk. Emily didn't even realize just how much she talked about her wedding, and Annie was probably overly sensitive about it on Eden's behalf. But she'd stayed.

"I'm going to bed too," Annie said, picking up her phone and standing up. "Love you, sweetie."

"Love you too, Mom."

Down the hall, with her teeth brushed and in her pajamas, Annie closed her eyes, her last thought of Colton before she drifted into a happy sleep.

————

THAT WEEKEND, COLTON RANG HER DOORBELL FIVE MINUTES AFTER he'd texted to say he'd made it to town. Annie slicked her hands down the front of her apron and left the kitchen to answer the door.

The most handsome cowboy on the planet stood on her front porch, wearing that white cowboy hat, that ridiculously puffy coat, jeans, and a smile. "Hey," he drawled. "Don't you look amazing?"

She looked down at her dirty apron. "You're just saying that because you see chocolate on this thing." She laughed as she stepped back and let him into her house. "Come in."

He did, pausing in her personal space to slip his arm around her waist. "Mm, it's good to see you, Annie," he murmured before continuing into the house. She closed the door behind him, more nervous than she should be.

"My place is small," she said. "But the cupcakes are done, and they're delicious." She led him into the kitchen, which seemed to be ragged from floor to ceiling.

"How long have you lived here?" he asked, shrugging out of his coat and hanging it on the back of a kitchen chair. His eyes roamed everywhere, as if making an assessment on her house right that minute.

"Twenty-five years," she said, pointing him in the direction of the double fudge cupcakes, as if he couldn't see them for himself.

"Are you committed to staying here?" He picked up a cupcake and started peeling off the decorative wrapper.

She watched him all the way until he'd taken that first big

bite. She wanted to kiss the chocolate frosting from his lips, and she looked away as heat filled her. "I don't know."

"I think it would be amazing if we got our own place," he said. "Here in town somewhere. You said they're building a lot of houses." He looked at her, deadly serious. "A fresh start, for both of us." He took another bite of his cupcake, his eyes never leaving hers.

"The girls live here with me," she said.

"They can live with us," he said.

"You're talking like we're going to get married and move in together next week." Annie put a smile on her face. "And we both know that's not going to happen." In fact, as Emily was already engaged, she'd likely get married before Annie and Colton did.

"I guess I should've warned you that I wanted to talk about the living arrangements this weekend." His eyes sparkled as he polished off his first cupcake. Annie knew it wouldn't be his last.

"I don't need to be warned," Annie said. "Though I'm a little surprised it's been on your mind."

"You're always on my mind, Annie," he said.

She smiled at him, glad when he took her into his arms and kissed her properly. He tasted like chocolate, and he was downright delicious in every way.

"So kids?" he asked, swaying with her right there in the kitchen.

"What do you think?" she asked. "I'm forty-six years old, Colton. I don't know if you want biological children, and that might be a huge issue for you."

"I can't imagine you want to have another baby," he said.

"No," Annie said. "I don't. Not really. But if *you* wanted a baby, Colton, I would...I would do it. If I could. If I *can*. I would." She hated how rambly she sounded, and she was glad she had Colton to hang onto.

"Let me give it some more thought," he said, stepping back.

"So the house?" He picked up another cupcake and went over to the kitchen table. "Come sit by me."

"Coffee?"

"Yes, please."

Annie brought over mugs, sugar, and cream before she filled two coffee cups and sat at the table with him. "I'd sell this house," she said. "And move to a new place with you." She had a lot of memories in this house, but she'd learned that she took her memories with her. They existed inside her own mind. She didn't have to be physically in this house to remember the good times she'd had with Ryan. Or the victories she'd won with the girls. Or the birthday parties, the Christmases, the muddy paw prints.

Colton grinned at her. "Well, that's my list. What else have you got?"

"What else have I got? What do you mean?"

"To talk about before we get engaged."

The breath left Annie's lungs. "What?"

Colton simply took another bite of his cupcake, chewed, swallowed, and reached for his coffee cup.

"Money," she blurted out. "I think we should talk about money."

"What about it?" He put two spoonfuls of sugar in his coffee and stirred.

"Are we going to share? Stay separate? Do I need to sign one of those prenuptial agreements? What are you thinking?"

"I guess I better talk to Gray," Colton said. "I'm sure he'll advise me to have you sign a prenuptial agreement, yes. But Annie, I'm not worried about it. I'll buy the house. What's mine is yours." He sipped his coffee as if life really worked out this easily.

Annie couldn't quite keep up with the conversation, and her thoughts kept deviating back to the word *engaged*. He'd spoken it. Was he going to ask her today? This weekend? *When?*

She needed to know when.

She didn't want to be wearing a chocolate-smeared apron when he got down on one knee.

"All right?" he asked.

Annie could only nod.

"Okay." He got up and cleared his throat. He rummaged around in his coat pocket for a moment, pulling out a little black box.

"Colton," she said, her voice made of air. "This doesn't have to happen this weekend."

"Yes," he said. "It does."

Annie wasn't sure if her eyes grew hot from tears of joy or tears of desperation. She hadn't wanted to push him into anything he didn't want to do. He'd literally said that to her just under two weeks ago.

"It does," Colton said, dropping to both knees right there in front of her, in her dirty, old kitchen, while she wore that chocolate-covered apron. "Because I'm in love with you, Annie Pruitt. And I don't need more time."

He cracked the lid on the box to reveal the most beautiful diamond Annie had ever seen. She gasped from the size of it, and looked back into Colton's eyes.

He was in love with her.

He'd said it, and she could see that love shining in his pretty, dark eyes.

"Will you marry me?" he asked, his words catching a little bit on his scratchy throat. He didn't clear it again though, and Annie found her mind had gone blank.

She wasn't sure how long she stood there, or when her daughters had come into the kitchen.

"You say yes, Mom," Eden said, and Annie's eyes flew to her daughter's.

"Y-e-s," Emily said, spelling it out as she swiped at her eyes.

Annie's tears fell then, and she focused back on Colton. He was absolutely everything she wanted in her life, and she felt sure she'd fallen into a dream the day she'd met him. She could hardly wait to come home to him after a day of cleaning, and go to bed with him, and share her life with him.

"I'm old, sweetheart," he said, reaching for the chair. He got off his knees and sat back in the chair beside her. "I thought this would be an easy question for you."

"It is," Annie said, still crying. "It's yes, Colton. Absolutely yes."

He grinned, slipped the ring on her finger, and kissed her while her daughters clapped. "I love you," he said against her lips, and Annie said it back to him too, realizing in that moment that her birthday wish had come true.

She'd gotten her cowboy billionaire.

And she couldn't wait to start the next chapter of her life with him.

He pulled away, his smile still in place. "Now, let's talk about the *really* important stuff." He stepped over to the counter and picked up another cupcake. "I would like to have these at our wedding. Doable?"

Annie tipped her head back and laughed, embracing her daughters as they came over to hug and congratulate her and Colton.

"Yes," she said when the excitement had died down. "We can have those cupcakes at our wedding."

"Perfect," Colton said, starting on his third one.

Annie thought that word summed him up about right, and she smiled while silently thanking the Lord for His creation of cupcakes…and Colton.

Read on for a sneak peek of **HER COWBOY BILLIONAIRE BUTLER** featuring Wes Hammond and Bree Richards. **You can read it in paperback right now!**

SNEAK PEEK! HER COWBOY BILLIONAIRE BUTLER CHAPTER ONE

Wesley Hammond refused to be a former CEO who walked out of his corner office, with two walls of floor-to-ceiling windows, carrying a brown box with his belongings in it. He'd already carted out the sad plants, the family pictures, the toiletries he kept in his desk drawers, his clothes, and all the menus of the downtown Denver establishments that delivered until midnight.

He'd done that by taking a few things every day over the course of the past few weeks, after the board had approved the transfer of power from Wes to Laura. She'd been in his office every day too, six days a week, and Wes found himself getting along well with her. Better than he ever had before.

Laura had the passion for HMC that Wes had started with, and he knew in his heart that this transition was good for him, and good for the company. It didn't make leaving for the last time any easier, though.

His heart beat down two paths, and he could hardly determine which one to go with. Excitement that tomorrow, he didn't have to get up, shower, shave, and put on a suit. He didn't have a schedule to stick to. He didn't have a call at six a.m. to accommodate the branch manager in London. He'd have to be in charge of his own schedule now, and he'd sorely miss Myra, who kept him looking knowledgeable, and Matthew, who always made sure Wes arrived in the appropriate place on time.

Or trepidation that he had no schedule to stick to. No phone calls to make. No one in charge of him, except for him.

"Are you ready?"

He turned at the voice he'd worked with for so long to find Myra standing in his office doorway. "Yes," he said, picking up his briefcase. "Is Matthew done?" His secretary had been on the phone with a regional manager out of Pittsburgh fifteen minutes ago, talking fast and trying to get something taken care of before the weekend started.

"He just hung up," Myra said. She entered the office fully now, walking toward him with a smile on her face. "What are you going to do tomorrow?"

Wes took a deep breath, smiled, and blew it out. "Well, tomorrow's Saturday, and I'd love to sleep in and then find somewhere to play golf."

Myra gestured to the windows behind him. "You've looked outside, right?"

Wes turned and looked, though he'd seen the snow falling earlier. It hadn't stopped all day, and it had a certain magic about it. "Yeah," he said. "No golf. Maybe I'll go skiing."

"I didn't know you skied."

"I don't." He faced her again. "Never had the time, but I will now."

Myra laughed lightly with him, and she turned to go back out the door. "I'm going to miss you, Wes. You're the best boss I've ever had."

"That's because I'm not your boss," he said.

"You always acted that way," she said, nodding. "And I appreciated that."

"Laura's good," Wes said. He'd told Myra this many times. "You can leave anytime too. It's only her that can't fire you for the first twelve months."

"No, Laura is great," Myra said. "I'm hoping things will just continue on as they are, and that if we work well together, that I can stay. I've loved working for a family company."

"Our benefits are excellent," Wes joked as they left the office. He didn't stop and look back. He'd never go inside again, loosening his tie after a stressful meeting and asking Matthew to screen all his calls.

"Even if I left now," Myra said. "I have an excellent retirement, because you allow employees to invest in the company too."

"What do you own?" Wes asked.

"I'm almost to two percent," she said.

"That's amazing," Wes said, truly surprised. "You cash those out, that's what? Two million?"

"Three and a half," she said. "At the employee rate."

"Good for you, Myra," he said, stopping at Matthew's desk while the man scurried around, putting files away. He never left for the day until his desk sat clean and pristine. He claimed that then, when he got in the next day, he knew right where everything was.

Wes looked at Myra, with her honey-colored hair and dark brown eyes. She'd been an excellent assistant—and a good friend. "How's Janey doing?" he asked.

A smile lit Myra's face at the mention of her daughter. "Great," she said. "She sent me a picture of the palm trees this morning, just to rub it in."

Wes chuckled, wishing he were in Florida, on the beach along the Gulf of Mexico. He'd even go back to school to do it, as Janey was. The fact was, Wes could go to the beach now. Any beach. Anywhere. Any time. He had plenty of money. The truth was, the cold had never bothered Wes, and sometimes he actually craved it. So he wouldn't go to the beach.

His mind moved automatically to Wyoming, and the woman he hadn't spoken to in five weeks now. His last conversation with Bree Richards hadn't ended well for him, and every time he tried to hear her voice again, he couldn't.

That particular aspect of Bree had fled his memory, and he hated that. He hated that she'd broken up with him too, though he could admit that they hadn't actually been dating. A better way to say it was that she'd cut off their conversation. He'd asked her if she was sure she didn't even want to talk to him anymore.

She'd said she'd met someone else—up there in Coral Canyon. Up where Wes didn't live. He couldn't tell her then that he'd been planning to come meet her in person come February seventh—which was tomorrow. He'd erased her voicemail, and she'd apologized a bunch of times.

Wes had too, because he was sorry things between them hadn't really been able to take off. He felt completely stalled, stuck on the ground, reaching for the stars that seemed so far above him that he'd never touch them.

He stifled the sigh threatening to come out of his mouth and looked at Matthew when he said, "Ready. And I'm buying tonight, so pick your poison." He grinned, and Wes had the sudden urge to grab the man in a hug.

So he did, ignoring the grunt of surprise that came from Matthew. Wes clapped him on the back a couple of times, stepped back, and gave Myra a quick hug too. "You guys have been amazing," he said, his emotion stuck way down deep in his stomach. That was one thing this job had taught him—how to contain emotions until he was alone and could deal with them.

"Thanks for putting up with my moods, and my wild changes, and well, my everything." He nodded, glad to have that out of the way. "And I want to go to Rothburg's, so you better bring the platinum card."

Matthew grinned and held it up. "Right here, Wes." He glanced at Myra. "And you've literally been the best boss—and friend—I've ever had."

"Same," Myra said.

Wes looked at them, the bond between them fourteen years in the making. "All right, then. I wish you guys could come with me."

"Where are you going?" Matthew asked, picking up his own briefcase. The three of them started toward the elevator.

"I'm going to take a little cross-country trip," Wes said, deciding on the spot. "I think I'm going to fly to Maine, rent a truck, and visit every state in the country." And if he started back east, he wouldn't get to Wyoming any time soon.

He couldn't believe he even wanted to go to Wyoming. He wouldn't even recognize Bree if he saw her, as he'd never seen a picture of her. Colton had gone back to Coral Canyon several times over the past five weeks, as his fiancée lived there. His brother was preparing to make the move permanent in the next couple of days, and Wes would've volunteered to help had Colton not hired a moving company.

"Sounds amazing," Myra said. "I can't wait to see your pictures."

"Yeah," Wes said, stepping onto the elevator. "Because I only post on social media when I travel." The three of them laughed, because that was true, and Wes knew it. He wished he knew what to do with his life now, and all he could do was trust that God would lead him where he was supposed to be, when he was supposed to be there.

Maybe something would come up in Vermont. Or Georgia. Or South Dakota. The possibilities were wide open, and Wes's excitement finally outweighed his fear of the unknown.

———

THE MONTHS PASSED, AND WES DECIDED HE'D NEED TO GO BACK TO New England when it wasn't winter time. That had been a mistake. He'd hit Florida during baseball season's spring training, and that had been fun. He'd watched the cherry orchards bloom in Michigan, and he'd dug his toes into the white sand along those beaches bordering the Gulf of Mexico.

He experienced the spring thunderstorms in Texas, where the thunder could roll through the sky for a full minute before it clapped. Where the rain could douse a man in under ten seconds. Where he finally found all those cowboy roots he'd come from.

His great-great-grandfather had owned a ranch in Texas, and Wes had visited it and met the people who ran it now. The Stokes were great people—a big family like the Hammonds. Lots of boys, all of whom still worked the ranch where they lived.

He'd experienced summer arriving in the Rocky Mountains, and as he crossed the border from his home state of Colorado to Wyoming, his throat only hitched a little bit.

The past six months had taken him to thirty-nine states, and Wyoming was number forty. He only had ten to go, and plenty of time and money to get to them. He'd heard Alaska was beautiful in August, and his plans included hiking in the Tetons in Wyoming, visiting Yellowstone National Park in Montana, hitting something in the Idaho panhandle—maybe the quaint town of Coeur d'Alene—as he headed toward Seattle.

He then planned to get on a ship that would take him to Alaska, where he wanted to see as much wildlife as he could, hike any trails he was fit for, and simply be outside, where he felt closer to God than he did anywhere else.

The trip had been good for Wes's soul, that was for certain. He spoke to his parents often, as well as all of his brothers. The family party at New Year's had been good for them, bringing them closer as a family unit. Ames and Cy had started to stray, and if Wes were being honest, so had he.

He sent them pictures of his day and told them the random museums he'd visited. Cy had told everyone that he'd met a woman in San Luis Obispo, and he wanted to bring her home to meet everyone. The plans for that were still being made, and Wes figured he could fly to Denver from almost any city in the world. If his quest to visit all fifty states got interrupted for a few days, he wouldn't die.

He hadn't had any revelations about what he should do once he'd visited the last ten states on his list. He didn't have to do anything, he'd told himself a thousand times. He could go out to the family farm and help his parents with it. Ames and Gray had both been doing that more and more, and it was actually good for them to have that purpose in their lives.

Wes simply wanted a purpose too.

He didn't set his GPS specifically for Coral Canyon, though he certainly knew the town's name. He drove into the beautiful mountain town just before the Fourth of July, and he admired their Main Street that had red, white, and blue flags, banners, and streamers everywhere.

People seemed to be everywhere, and he decided to find somewhere to park and then something to eat. It wasn't nearly as hot here as it had been in Denver, and he sure did like the higher elevations. The magnificent Teton Mountain Range sat in the distance, towering up and piercing the cloudless blue sky.

A measure of joy and peace filtered through him, and Wes had the distinct impression that he'd like to live in a town like this. He pushed the thought away, because it sounded crazy. He couldn't live here, though his brain immediately started questioning him. *Why not?*

Colton lived in Coral Canyon, and Wes had always been close to his brother. He pulled out his phone and called Colton, always preferring to call over text. He supposed he was old-school that way.

"Hey," Colton said. "Are you in town?"

"Just finding somewhere to park," he said.

"Downtown?"

"Yep."

"It's crazy downtown right now," Colton said. "You should've come here. We can take the ATV's over."

"You ride an ATV around town?"

"Everyone does," Colton said, and Wes reminded himself he wasn't in the big city anymore. He hadn't been for a while. He did love a big city, but he'd also fallen in love with all the remote towns that existed along the highways in this country, and he loved the ones where the roads had no lines on them, no sidewalks bordering them, and kids riding bicycles down the middle of them.

He'd grown up in Ivory Peaks, which was exactly like that, and Wes suddenly wanted a town like that where he could settle and stay. Maybe meet a woman and have a family. He was nearing fifty, though, and in order to have a family, he'd need to find a woman several years younger than him.

People do it, he told himself. He had to, because he didn't want his legacy to be the fourteen years he'd spent running HMC, or the fourteen before that going to school, learning the ropes of the manufacturing business, and investigating politics.

Thankfully, his cross-country trip had put the idea of him running for governor to rest, and his father hadn't brought it up again.

"We'll meet you at Stagg's," Colton said. "It's a great place, and you can't miss it. Has tons of big antlers on the outside."

"Fifteen minutes?" Wes asked.

"Fifteen minutes," Colton said. "Just me and Annie."

"Great. See you then." Wes hung up as he spotted a parking lot up ahead with a troop of Boy Scouts standing at the entrance. "And it's just me," he muttered to himself. Always just him.

He pulled up to the boys in uniform and handed them a ten-dollar bill so he could park. With his wallet in his back pocket and his phone in his hand, he got out, taking a nice, deep breath of the mountain air he loved so much.

Oh, yes, Wes needed to find a town like this to live in. He loved the busyness of it, knowing that all of these people would soon retreat back to their lives, homes, and jobs, and then Coral Canyon would go back to being the small town with big charm.

He smiled at the hanging flower pots outside of the bakery,

and the window display in the pet palace. If he'd owned a dog, he'd definitely have gone inside to see what clothes or toys he could get for his barker.

Colton was right; Wes couldn't miss Stagg's. And not just because of the antlers, but because it was very popular, and several people milled around outside on the sidewalk. He stepped through them to the hostess station, and asked, "How long for a party of three?"

The woman standing there scanned her list. "Twenty minutes."

"My name's Wes," he said.

"Three?"

"Yes, ma'am."

She looked up at him, and Wes grinned at her as he tipped his cowboy hat in her direction. A warm smile spread across her face too, and Wes's spirits lifted. Perhaps if he found somewhere permanent to stay, he *could* meet a woman and make a real life for himself.

He turned away from the hostess station and found a patch of empty cement to wait for Colton and Annie. He listened to the others around him talking, barely paying attention to what they were saying.

Wes had been trying to focus on how he felt, and he absolutely felt comfortable here in Coral Canyon.

Maybe this is your final destination, he thought. He automatically resisted the idea, but it wouldn't go far.

Then he heard a voice that flipped a switch inside him, and he instinctively turned toward it. "All I'm saying is I'm not doing that dating app again," the woman said.

Wes searched for her in the people waiting beside him, his heart banging against his ribcage now. *Bang, bang, bang.* His pulse moved into his ears, and he couldn't hear whoever Bree was with. He couldn't see her either.

Somehow, Bree's voice cut through the other noise, the

hammering of his heartbeat, all of it. "And I'm not calling *him*," she said. "So don't even suggest it."

He found her sitting at one of the tables-for-two on the other side of a black railing. She shook her hair, dark curls falling over her shoulders and down her back. She looked at the woman across from her, who held up both hands as if surrendering. Wes had to get a better look, and he wasn't sure who he touched or pressed through to get closer. He just knew that he now stood a couple of feet behind Bree's friend, his view of her clear and focused.

She was absolutely gorgeous, and Wes felt like someone had stunned him. He gripped the railing with one hand as her friend said, "So, what are you going to do, Bree? Stop trying?"

"Yes," Bree said, the word almost a shout. "I'm going to stop trying. I don't need a man in my life. All they do is break my heart."

Wes wanted to shout that he wouldn't. That he hadn't. That *she'd* been the one to cool things between them, before they'd even had a chance to see if they'd get hot.

She looked at her friend with dark, soulful eyes, and Wes knew he could get lost in them. She wore makeup, but not too much, and when she reached up and tucked her hair behind her ear, he caught sight of dark purple fingernails.

He'd once told her that he'd dated a woman with bright red nails, and that he'd hated them. *What color would you choose?* she'd asked.

Purple, he's said. *A nice, dark, deep purple.*

Just like what she had on her fingers.

It means nothing, he told himself. She hadn't remembered that conversation. Even if she did, she'd just told her friend she wasn't going to call him. At least he hoped he was the *him* she'd referenced.

His phone rang, startling him away from the railing. The last thing he wanted was for Bree to see him. But she did look over to him, as he literally stood maybe eight feet from her. Her eyes swept over him, past him, maybe not even seeing him.

He ducked his head anyway, never more grateful for a cowboy hat than he was in that moment. Colton's name sat on the screen, and Wes swiped on the call, his heart beating at him to get out of there. Now.

"Hey," he said. "Stagg's is super busy." He walked away from Bree, part of him begging him to stay. Telling him to go back and pull up a chair and say, *Hey Bree. You might not remember me, but I haven't stopped thinking about you in six months. I'm Wes Hammond.*

Stick out his hand. See if she'd shake it.

"Can we go somewhere else?" Wes asked, desperate now. If Colton didn't agree, Wes would simply march back to his truck and find something else to eat in the next town he came to.

And I'm not calling him.

"Sure," Colton said. "Oh, I see you. We'll make a plan."

"Great." Wes hung up, still striding away from Stagg's—and the most beautiful woman he'd ever laid eyes on.

SNEAK PEEK! HER COWBOY BILLIONAIRE BUTLER CHAPTER TWO

B reeann Richards sighed as she opened her desk drawer and put her purse inside.

"Rough day?" Willie asked from the next desk over.

"When the Fourth is over," Bree said. "Life will be normal again." She collapsed onto her desk chair, knowing that her exhaustion came from more than just working two jobs. It came from the additional debt she'd incurred over the five months she and Alex had dated. The man said he drove a tour bus, but he never seemed to have any money to do anything. And he wanted to do expensive things, like go river rafting and eat at expensive restaurants.

Because of him, Bree had another gash on her heart, thousands of dollars in credit card debt, and this second job working for the employment office, helping other people find jobs.

"At least the restaurants won't be so crowded," Willie agreed. She went back to her computer, and Bree should too. Her phone rang, though, and a small blip in her heartbeat told her she hadn't gotten over Wes yet. Sure, she'd just told Elise she wasn't going to call him—and she wasn't.

Didn't mean she couldn't fantasize about making that call and hearing that voice.

But this call had Graham's name on it, and Bree swiped it open. "Hey, Graham," she said.

"Heya, Bree," he said. "We've decided to go ahead and hire a butler."

Bree couldn't help smiling. "I think it's so odd to call them that," she said. "But all right."

"It's better than bellhop," Graham said. "And besides, he'll have to help with more than just taking bags to rooms."

"What else?" Bree said, jiggling her mouse to get the computer to wake. "I'm assuming you called me, so I can make a job listing for you?"

"That's right," Graham said. "We want him to have experience with horses."

"You're only looking for males?" Bree asked.

"No, anyone," Graham said. "But they have to be able to carry heavy baggage up and down stairs."

"I'll put sixty pounds," Bree said, typing information into an intake form for new listings. "Horse care required. What else?"

"Cooking a plus. Customer service," Graham said. "Current driver's license, with no accidents in the past three years. He'll be a valet too."

"Valet," Bree said.

"Patsy would love someone who can be part of the admin team," Graham said. "So a business background maybe."

Bree's eyebrows went up as she keyed in the info. "How much are you paying this person?" She wondered if she could lift sixty pounds, as she had all of these other qualifications.

"It's a full-time position," Graham said. "Though we don't have room at the lodge for them, so they'll have to come up the canyon every day. I don't know. Beau said seventy-five."

"Thousand?" Bree couldn't keep the surprise out of her voice.

"Yeah," Graham said. "If we can get someone who does all these miscellaneous things, but really has a business mind...the lodge needs that. Patsy does a great job of running things day-to-day. You all do." Graham exhaled heavily. "We think we just might need someone with more of a, I don't know, some type of background that can help the lodge stay current. Maybe even expand. Thrive."

"Yeah," Bree said. "I know what you mean." Whiskey Mountain Lodge was a stunning mountain villa, with views of the Tetons that were unmatched. All the rooms were fully booked almost all the time, especially in the summer. They did fine. But they weren't growing. Even Bree felt stagnant in her position there, and she wouldn't mind some help with the horses, and some new blood to offer new ideas for events.

"Okay," she said. "Let me read this back to you." She did, outlining the requirements for the job, the salary, and then she asked, "When do you want it to close?"

"Can we leave that open?" Graham said. "Open until filled."

"Sure," Bree said. "I'll get this processed, and it'll be on the website by tomorrow morning."

"Great," Graham said. "I'll tell Andrew, and he'll get the word out."

"Perfect." The call ended, and Bree finished up with her end of posting the listing. It would take a few hours for the system to generate the listing, and she clicked the final approval box and got the process going.

She met with a couple of people as they came in to look at the job board. She took two more listings, noticing a man hanging around outside the workforce office. That wasn't entirely uncommon, as sometimes people had to work up the courage to come in and admit they needed help finding a job.

Coral Canyon was booming right now, though, and there were more jobs than people to take them. She was still considering applying for the butler position at the lodge herself.

By the time the office closed, and Willie and Bree could go home, the loitering cowboy had left. Thank goodness. Bree didn't need any more experience with handsome cowboys. No, sirree. She was done with them, thank you very much.

Still, in the back of her mind, and in the tiniest corner of her heart, she still wanted one—a good one. There had to be a good man out there somewhere, didn't there? One who didn't lie about his name, and one who didn't lie about his job, and one who wouldn't bleed her dry financially and emotionally. Right?

She closed her eyes and asked the Lord, *right?*

He didn't answer, of course, and Bree was starting to wonder if He ever would. She banished that poisonous thought though, because all she had to do was go outside and look at the mountains to know God existed.

And if He existed, He wouldn't abandon His children here on earth. Bree simply had a harder time communicating with Him than other people did. *Seemingly everyone,* she thought, but she put that out of her mind too.

Pastor Clemens had said the Lord spoke to different people in different ways, and Bree couldn't carry the burden of comparing herself to anyone else when it came to the Lord too. Heaven knew she was already doing it in every other aspect of her life.

Willie exited the building first, and Bree turned to lock the door behind them. They had the next two days off, and Bree couldn't wait for her four-day weekend. When she turned, Willie gave her a hug, and they walked toward their cars.

Willie's phone rang, and she said, "It's Connor," with a laugh in her voice. "See you Monday, Bree."

"Yeah, bye." Bree didn't wait around to hear Willie chirp hello to her boyfriend. She pressed against the rising jealousy in her stomach, telling herself that she didn't need another low-life cowboy loser in her life. She didn't.

"Ma'am," someone said, and Bree looked up. Adrenaline spiked in her body, sending her pulse flying though her feet froze.

The cowboy who'd been loitering near the windows had taken up camp near her car. He actually sat on the tailgate of his truck, his long legs dangling toward the ground. He certainly looked the part of a Wyoming cowboy, but he hadn't sounded like one. He carried more of a Texas twang in that *ma'am*, and Bree couldn't help taking in his strong jaw, that long, sloped nose, and his dark gray eyes.

Her pulse picked up for an entirely different reason now, and she tried to put the brakes on it. Unsuccessfully. She'd broken up with Alex five weeks ago.

"Did you need a job?" she asked. "I saw you outside earlier."

He shook his head, changing it to a nod only a moment later.

"Is that a yes or a no?" she asked.

He nodded, and she wondered why he wasn't speaking.

"We have a website," she said, reaching into her purse and pulling out a card with all the information he'd need on it. She thought he could definitely lift sixty pounds—probably a hundred—right up over his head. But if he couldn't talk, he couldn't get the job at Whiskey Mountain Lodge.

Customer service was a requirement. She stepped toward him and handed him the card, her fingers coming dangerously close to his. "If you look there, you can see all the openings. We have a ton of stuff right now."

He looked at the card and then her, and Bree had a severe sense of déjà vu. Did she know him? Where had she seen his face before?

She knew a lot of people around Coral Canyon, as she'd moved here the moment she'd graduated from college. She'd left home the day after getting her high school diploma, and she hadn't been back in nineteen years now.

A pang of missing hit her, and she supposed she should at least call her parents that weekend. See how patriotic things were in Mountain Dale. But Bree knew there'd be red, white, and blue everywhere, same as here, though the two towns existed in two totally different states.

"If you need additional help," Bree said. "There's always a couple of people here to go over things with you." She put a kind smile on her face, though her energy for the day was nearly gone. "My name's Bree, and I work every day. Well, we're closed tomorrow and Friday for the holiday, but first thing Monday morning. I only work until noon, usually. Today was just weird."

She commanded herself to stop talking, wondering why she was still babbling on in the first place. She didn't want to admit that she felt something magnetic pouring from the handsome cowboy on the tailgate, and he was holding her in place.

Adjusting her purse, she stepped toward her car. "Okay, bye." She wanted to kick herself in the teeth. He didn't need to know her work schedule, or that she had another job up the canyon that she worked—usually—from one until whenever everything was done.

At least she wouldn't have to come down to the workforce office for the next four days. She'd just opened her door when the cowboy said, "Thank you, Bree."

She froze again, her heart pittering, and then pattering, and then pouncing. It seemed to take a very long time for her eyes to lift from where she'd been searching for her keys in her purse to the man who'd just spoken.

She knew that voice.

She knew this man.

How?

While she stared at him, he cleared his throat and jumped down from the tailgate. He kept his cowboy hat dipped down, keeping that gorgeous face from her sight, and walked toward the driver's door.

"Wait," she said—more of a blurt really. "Do I know you?" She went halfway around the front of her car, keeping some distance between them. He hadn't parked immediately next to her either, and two spaces separated them.

"No," he said, pulling open his door. "Thanks." He lifted the card and got in his truck. The engine started and he pulled away before Bree could even move.

Confusion riddled her mind, and her eyebrows pulled down. She *did* know him—or at least that voice. She'd heard that voice say her name before.

A wild, terrible thought entered her mind, and she spun to watch the black truck disappear around the corner.

It couldn't be…. Why wouldn't Wes just say who he was?

Her throat had never been drier, and yet, Bree couldn't move. When she finally thawed, she couldn't get her phone out of her purse fast enough. She still had Wes's number in her phone. She'd just call him and ask him if he was in town and had happened to talk to someone about a job today.

"But you gave your name," she said. "So if it was him, he'd know it was you." She looked down the road again, half-expecting the truck to come back. Bring Wes back to her. Could that really happen? Could she and Wes have a second chance at…whatever they'd started the first time?

She got behind the wheel of her car and started the engine so the air conditioning would start to blow. Then she dialed Wes, clenching her teeth while she squeezed her eyes shut, a constant prayer streaming through her mind.

Three rings. Then four. Five.

His voicemail kicked on, and it was so impersonal and a recording, so she couldn't really identify if he was the same man who'd literally said six words to her. Frustrated, and not wanting to leave a message, she hung up.

He'd see she called. Then he'd either call her back or ignore her. "Please let him call me back," she said as she pulled out of the parking lot and went the same direction as the black truck had. She thought of no one and nothing else for the long drive back to her cabin up the canyon from town.

Time for her second job to begin.

————

Wes did not call back. The patriotic parade on the Fourth of July found Bree waving a miniature American flag with one child in her lap and two more on the blanket beside her. Rose and Liam always needed help, and Bree loved their triplets.

She worked around the lodge on Friday, prepping everything for the next couple of weeks so she wouldn't have to work so late into the evening. Saturday, she did the same, putting on a children's craft class, taking a group horseback riding, and coordinating a fishing expedition for the guests at the lodge that holiday weekend.

She found some solace and comfort at church on Sunday, but her question of *who was that cowboy?* had yet to be answered by anyone, man or divine being.

Monday, she woke early and made sure Patsy had everything she needed for that morning's mountain yoga class, and she checked in with Lionel, the oldest teenager who worked in the stables with her to make sure they had what they needed for their rides that day.

"And don't let Simon give you any trouble," she told Lionel. "If he does, tell him I'll dismiss him when I see him next."

Lionel nodded and looked at the clipboard. "Yes, ma'am."

Then she drove down the canyon to the office. She scanned the parking lot, her heartbeat ricocheting around inside her chest.

The black truck wasn't there. The gorgeous cowboy didn't come in. Bree wasn't sure why she felt so defeated and disappointed. She should've known someone like her wouldn't be able to attract the gaze of a man like that. Still, she'd been dreaming of Wes, and she'd almost texted Colton to ask him to send her that picture he'd shown her once, months and months ago.

But she didn't want him to know she'd never truly let go of his brother. She'd told him at least a dozen times that she'd made the right decision when she'd called Wes and ended their phone calls. Even after she'd broken up with Alex—and Colton had been the first to know—Bree had denied him concerning Wes.

"All right," he'd said. "But he's not dating anyone right now...."

Bree just needed a break. She drove back to her cabin and

hurried to eat lunch before heading over to the lodge to make sure the afternoon check-ins went well. She liked to have brochures and schedules of their upcoming weekly activities on the counter, and she always worked check-in to help with the traffic and to answer any questions about events.

Bree loved working at Whiskey Mountain Lodge, and she truly felt like part of the Whittaker family. She loved Elise, Patsy, and Sophia, and she wasn't surprised to enter the office and find she was the last to arrive.

"Afternoon," she said to the others, reaching up to secure her ponytail a little tighter. She'd grown her hair out of the last six months, and she liked how feminine the longer locks made her look.

"There you are," Patsy said. "We have the Kings coming today, and I need to be here for them. But Graham hired a new— butler, I guess?—and he started this morning. Could you help him this afternoon?"

"He hired someone already?" Bree asked, stowing her phone in the back pocket of her shorts.

"Yes," Patsy said. "He's pretty great too. Smart, articulate, strong." She smiled and picked up a piece of paper. "He did great this morning with check-out, and I think he earned fifty bucks in tips."

Bree's eyebrows went up. On top of the seventy-five-thou- sand-dollar salary, the guy probably didn't need the fifty bucks in cash. Or maybe he did. Bree had learned a long time ago that she didn't know the intimate details of anyone's life. Not really. She could never know what really went on behind closed doors, and she'd learned that at a very early age.

Patsy handed her the paper. "It's Colton's brother."

Bree's heart positively stopped, and her eyes dropped to the paper while her mind raced. Colton had four brothers; it could be any of them.

But *Wesley Hammond* sat at the top of the paper, and Bree's fingers lost their capability to hold a single sheet of paper. It fluttered to the ground.

Then Patsy said, "Ah, here he is. Wes, come in. I have some VIP clients this afternoon, so Bree is going to be your trainer for check-in." Patsy was smiling for all she was worth, and Bree knew why.

She knew a little bit about Wes Hammond, and he could charm the socks off of anyone. Patsy touched Bree's arm, and that thawed her enough to turn around.

She came face-to-face with the man she'd given the job card to last week. The devilishly handsome cowboy sitting on the tailgate.

He still wore that delicious hat, his in a shade of charcoal instead of the white one Colton wore all the time. Those dark eyes drank her right up, and Bree could scarcely breathe. He wore a T-shirt with an outline of Wyoming on it, with a pair of jeans and cowboy boots. He was tall and tan and lean and luscious in every way.

"Bree," he said, and oh, how wonderful it was to hear her name in that deep, rich-as-gold voice. "I'm Wes. Nice to meet you." He put out his hand, and Bree simply stared at him, her heartbeat crashing like cymbals in her ears.

———

Read HER COWBOY BILLIONAIRE BUTLER to find out if Bree and Wes can make a relationship work the second time around. **It's now available in paperback!**

Keep scrolling to view series starters from three of my other series!

CORAL CANYON COWBOYS ROMANCE SERIES

Visit stunning Wyoming for another family of cowboys... The Youngs! The series includes second chance romance, friends to lovers, family saga, Christian values, clean and sweet romance, single dads, equine therapy themes, police dog training, brotherly relationships, return to hometown, fish out of water, and country music stars!

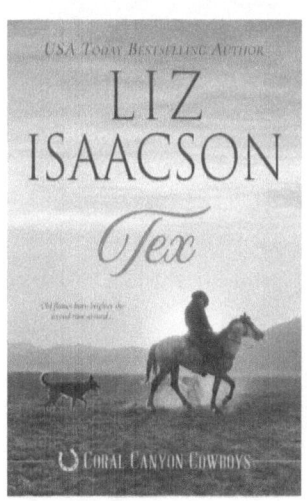

Tex (Book 1): He's back in town after a successful country music career. She owns a bordering farm to the family land he wants to buy...and she outbids him at the auction. **Can Tex and Abigail rekindle their old flame, or will the issue of land ownership come between them?**

GRAPE SEED FALLS ROMANCE SERIES

Journey to the beautiful Texas Hill Country for heartwarming, clean cowboy romance with that hint of faith you'll love. This series includes an Army cowboy, a cowboy billionaire, seasoned romance between older characters, Christmas romance, and three brothers looking for a ranch and a the woman of their dreams!

Choosing the Cowboy (Book 1): With financial trouble and personal issues around every corner, can Maggie Duffin and Chase Carver rely on their faith to find their happily-ever-after?

This is an introductory novelette to the Grape Seed Falls Romance series, with full-length books starting with **CRAVING THE COWBOY**.

A spinoff from the #1 bestselling Three Rivers Ranch Romance novels, also by USA Today bestselling author Liz Isaacson.

THREE RIVERS RANCH ROMANCE SERIES

Escape to Three Rivers, Texas for small-town charm, sweet and sexy cowboys, and faith and family centered romance. You'll get second chance romance, friends to lovers. older brother's best friend, military romance, secret babies, and more! The Three Rivers cowboys and the women who rope their hearts are waiting for you, so start reading today!

Second Chance Ranch (Book 1): After his deployment, injured and discharged Major Squire Ackerman returns to Three Rivers Ranch, wanting to forgive Kelly for ignoring him a decade ago. He'd like to provide the stable life she needs, but with old wounds opening and a ranch on the brink of financial collapse, it will take patience and faith to make their second chance possible.

ABOUT LIZ

Liz Isaacson writes inspirational romance, usually set in Texas, or Wyoming, or anywhere else horses and cowboys exist. She lives in Utah, where she writes full-time, takes her two dogs to the park everyday, and eats a lot of veggies while writing. Find her on her website, along with all of her pen names, at feelgood-fictionbooks.com